TWISTED CLAY

To Kim,

Entering this book
is like driving, at speed,
without a seatbelt.

lots of love,

Johnny

GW00566878

TWISTED CLAY

Frank Walford

TWISTED CLAY

FRANK WALFORD

REMAINS

CROMER

PUBLISHED BY REMAINS BOOKS
An imprint of Salt Publishing Ltd
12 Norwich Road, Cromer, Norfolk NR27 0AX United Kingdom

This paperback edition first published by Remains Books, 2014

Printed and bound in the United Kingdom by Lightning Source UK Ltd

Typeset in Paperback 9.5 / 13

ISBN 978 1 84471 716 3 paperback
ISBN 978 1 84471 756 9 electronic

1 3 5 7 9 8 6 4 2

"*Twisted Clay* is a gruesome study of progressive insanity, but the study is obviously subordinate to a desire to excite and horrify."

— H.M. GREEN

CONTENTS

RE-TWISTING
THE CLAY

JOHNNY MAINS

I'M GOING TO keep this short and sweet.

My first introduction to the work of Frank Walford was in the mid 90s and the book in question was *The Ghost and Albert and Other Stories*, first published by T. Werner Laurie [1945]. I picked up a second-hand copy at a car boot for 50p. I didn't know anything about the author, certainly didn't know anything about his infamous novel and took it back to the place I was staying and read it over two or three days. I thought it was a cracking read; the stand-out for me was 'The Coming of Flamea' – a story about a fictional character coming to life.

I went to the library to see if there was anything else by Mr Walford, and was told that there would have to be an inter-library request put in, and did I have the required 50p to do such a task? I did not, went home, and promptly forgot about him.

A few years later I was hitchhiking in Ireland, and was picked up by a lovely couple and they invited me back to their house to camp on their lawn – the weather was pretty miserable, and the promise of some hot soup and a couple of cans of Guinness swayed me pretty easily. Their house was massive. I think he was a newspaper reporter, and they had one of the most impressive private libraries I had ever seen. I've yet to see better, and I think *my* library is rather magnificent. I was scanning through the books and a name popped out at me. Frank Walford. The book was called *Twisted Clay*, there was no dustjacket, and the boards were a dirty mustard colour. I didn't think it was right to ask my hosts if I could take the book to the tent to read it, so made a note of the book down in my diary and had some lovely potato and leek soup.

Years passed. I could never find a copy of the book, and in the early days of Ebay I was more interested in collecting *Dawn of the Dead* memorabilia, which was very cheap to pick up back then. It wasn't until May 7, 2009 at 12:36 pm on a website I occasionally post on called *Vault of Evil*, a member called James Doig posted:

An entertaining read in a similar vein is Frank Walford's *Twisted Clay*, first published in 1933 and banned here in Australia for 30 years. It was reprinted by Horowitz a few times in the 1960s. It's about a precocious 15 year old lesbian who murders her father when she learns he wants to take her to Europe to undergo experimental hormone treatment to help her. She suffers bouts of insanity during which she is compelled by the ghost of her father to dig him up and plug the hole in the back of his head (he complains his brains are falling out, you see). When she's caught digging him up for the second time she's committed to an asylum. When she escapes she takes to prostitution and acquires a taste for murdering her clients Jill-the Ripper style. After that it gets silly.

This was *Twisted Clay*? It sounded mental! I had to read it. I again tried to find a copy of the book, but any available copies were fetching hundreds. Today, there is a copy on Abe Books, selling for $2,000. I asked James Doig if he would help get me a copy of *Twisted Clay* scanned in to make my wish of owning the book a reality. James sent me the pdf file to read and I wasn't let down in the slightest. It's strange, *The Ghost and Albert and Other Stories* is completely different tonally and is such a minor work compared to this triumph.

I have also commissioned two essays by noted Walford scholars Jim Smith and James Doig. These give extra depth and a detailed background to this astounding book and its author. I wonder how Frank felt having the book banned for 30 years in his native country; on one hand, rather thrilling, it would have afforded him plenty of notoriety, but on the other, completely awful as his book wasn't bringing in the money it should have.

THE ARTWORK IS from the Claude Kendall hardback, and has been tightened and freshened up by Richy Sampson. I toyed with the idea of commissioning new artwork for it, but I'm sure you'll agree that this cover cannot be bettered!

As to the format of the book, I don't want to be responsible in creating another hard to own book when there are several editions of this work which are beyond the price range of the casual reader. So, I've taken the plunge to launch the Remains classics line – so it should remain a constant price in both e-book and print on demand. And this book will forever be in print, so if you spill your cup of coffee on it, or loan it to a friend and it never returns – order another one in.

It's been 52 years since *Twisted Clay* was last reprinted. I am honoured to have brought this very strange and criminally neglected classic back to life. To have the backing of Frank Walford's family to publish this book as the very first title in the Remains list thrills me to the bone. Ladies and Gentlemen, get your shovels ready, we've got some digging to do . . .

FRANK WALFORD AND THE 'BLUE MOUNTAINEERS'

Jim Smith

KATOOMBA IN THE early 1930s would seem to have been an unlikely place to produce a remarkable output of creative writing. This small town, with a population of a little over 10,000, 100 km west of Sydney and 1000 m above sea level, was better known for being the centre of the Blue Mountains tourism industry. This was based on the opportunities to do vigorous walks in the mountain air and contemplate the awesome surrounding valleys from the cliff tops. Katoomba's small literary 'salon' of that time included the following writers: Frank Walford (1882–1969), Eric Lowe (1889–1963), Eric's wife Nina (1884–1971), Eric and Nina's daughter Barbara (1913–2000), Osmar White (1909–1991), Eric Dark (1889–1987) and Eleanor Dark (1901–1985). Of these, only Eleanor Dark is today regarded as a significant literary figure. Hopefully, this republication of Walford's first novel *Twisted Clay* will bring about recognition of his literary achievement.

All the writers who were later to call themselves the 'Blue Mountaineers' were born outside the Blue Mountains and came independently to Katoomba between 1919 and 1923. Frank Walford was the first to arrive.

The Life of Frank Walford 1882–1924.

Frank Walford was born in Balmain in 1882.[1] After matriculating from Fort Street Boys High School in 1898, he spent the next ten or so years in restless travels, alternating between office jobs and adventures in Northern Australia. His more conventional employment included clerical work in banks, the customs department, a shipping office and the carrying business 'Walford & Walford' in Sydney. In tropical Australia, Walford claimed to have worked as a timber getter, mule packer, prospector, drover, "alligator" hunter, buffalo shooter, kangaroo hunter, orchid collector, and pearler. During this period he owned his own boat, the *Spindrift*, which he sailed from Sydney, through the Barrier Reef, and as far as Broome. Walford's unpublished manuscripts and his 'autobiographical novel' *A Fools Odyssey* refer to some illegal activities such as "Chow running" (now referred to as people smuggling), drug smuggling and the maiming and killing of various people.[2] It is likely that some of these are fictional accounts. In the somewhat lawless frontier conditions of Northern Australia, Walford had to learn to defend himself and became a good boxer. He described himself as a "good shot with rifle, dead shot with revolver, excellent hand with knife".[3]

By 1910 he settled down in the Parramatta district. He joined the Labor party, engaged in various political controversies, and was active in community organisations. In 1912 he married Madge Owen. Walford's long career in

professional journalism began in 1913 when he was a reporter
and columnist for the *Cumberland Times*. During his Parramatta years he ran a duck farm, became a respected
amateur boxer and published his first booklet *The Jumbly
History of Parramatta*, a long satirical poem on local affairs.[4]
He ran for the State seat twice as the Labor candidate, being
narrowly defeated in 1913 and 1916.[5] While supporting Australian involvement in World War One, he was a prominent
anti-conscriptionist. He started his own Parramatta based
newspaper *Walford's Weekly* which ran for five months. After
it closed, he moved to Katoomba and began working for the
Blue Mountain Echo in February 1919. Four months later he
became editor of an insert into locally distributed copies of
Sir James Joynton Smith's Sydney paper, *Smith's Weekly*.[6]
Walford and Smith began the Katoomba Chamber of Commerce in 1922.[7] During his years in Katoomba, Walford
energetically explored the local bushland and set up a cave
north of Medlow Bath as a base camp.[8] He wrote poetry
from his teenage years and published many poems in a self-
published anthology in 1919 and in the local press.[9]

In 1920 Madge gave birth to twins, Owen ('Bill') and
Hilda.[10] In 1921 the local *Smith's Weekly* supplement became
the *Katoomba Daily*. On the *Daily's* press Walford printed
The Eternal Ego, a philosophical work, which appears to have
been partly inspired by the exultation and self-confidence he
felt during his early years of exploring the Blue Mountains.
However the naïve neo-Nietzschean style and language of
the booklet make it embarrassing to read today. Walford
campaigned during his years at the *Katoomba Daily* for
ways to boost local tourism. He put particular emphasis
on the need to open new 'sights', renovate and mark old
overgrown walking tracks and attract winter visitors to the
area.[11]

The Writers Group Forms.

The Lowes came to Katoomba in 1921 from a grazing property in far western New South Wales. They had both been writing short stories since 1912. Osmar White, who had been born in New Zealand, arrived in Katoomba in the early 1920s after the breakup of his parents' marriage. Dr Eric Dark came with his wife Eleanor to take up a local medical practice in January 1923. The Lowes, Darks, Walfords and Whites were near neighbours. Walford met Dr Eric Dark when the latter joined the Katoomba Chamber of Commerce in 1925. Dr Dark became close friends with Eric Lowe, who wrote in Dark's surgery after hours. Eleanor Dark befriended the Lowes' daughters. Osmar White first met Dr Dark as a patient when he was treated for an injured hand. These writers shared a common enthusiasm for bushwalking and rock climbing in the local area, discussing literature and politics and listening to music together. During the period 1923–26 the published literary output of these 'Blue Mountaineers' was confined to short stories and poetry. Eleanor and Nina were working on the manuscripts of novels.

During the 1920s Walford wrote a vast number of words for the *Blue Mountain Echo*, with his various campaigns for local advancement, weekly columns and general local reportage. These seem to have been happy years for him, during which he wrote many exuberant articles about the joys of living in the Blue Mountains and lyrical descriptions of its scenery. He established a close relationship with Eric Dark, working with him on campaigns to promote local tourism. Walford published *Paths of Dew*, another anthology of his poems in 1927 as well as a guide to local bushwalks off the beaten track.[12]

Members of the Katoomba writers group had begun to

disperse in November 1926, when the Lowes went to Ade-
laide. Osmar White travelled around the state working as a
journalist and freelance writer. The *Echo* ceased publication
at the end of 1928 and Walford moved to Parramatta where
he started up the *Parramatta City News*. After a few years this
paper folded and Walford and Eric Lowe published *Eggs*,
a newspaper for poultry farmers financed by Dr Dark. In
January 1930, the Walfords' daughter Valmai was born.

In mid-1930, with the return of Osmar White and Eric
Lowe's family to Katoomba, the 'Blue Mountaineers' began
to reunite. Walford, while working at Parramatta, commuted
back to Katoomba to continue his bushwalking trips and ran a
local gravel quarry.[13] By August 1932 he was back in Katoomba
full-time and operating with Lowe another venture financed
by Dr Dark, the Blue Mountaineers Guide Service.[14]

The early to mid-1930s saw the beginning of a remarkable period of creative writing and literary success by
members of the 'Blue Mountaineers'. In 1932 Eleanor
Dark's first published novel *Slow Dawning* appeared as did
Dr Dark's pioneering work on physiotherapy, *Diathermy in
General Practice*. In 1933, Osmar White published his first
novel, *Beyond Ceram*, and Walford's *Twisted Clay* was published in England and the following year in America.[15] In
1934 Eleanor Dark's *Prelude to Christopher* appeared and
Eric Lowe signed the contract for the novel, later partly
serialized in *The Bulletin* from 1936, that was published by
Collins in London in 1938 as *Salute to Freedom*.

Eleanor Dark's novels have received an enormous
amount of literary analysis. However, no one has previously drawn attention to a remarkable similarity in the
plots of three of the novels written in Katoomba in the early
1930s. Jean Deslines of *Twisted Clay*, Myrna Stewart of *Salute*

to Freedom and Linda Hendon of *Prelude to Christopher* are all highly sexualised, independent and unconventional women who eventually succumb to insanity. *Twisted Clay* and *Prelude to Christopher* both conclude with the suicides of their highly strung female protagonists.

After making contact with Bill Walford and his wife Dulcie in the early 1980s, I was allowed to examine the papers of Frank Walford. Bill died soon after, but I continued to visit Dulcie who told me much about Frank Walford's life. One day she told me that Walford had said to her that Eleanor Dark had "stolen the idea" for *Prelude to Christopher* from him. Eleanor Dark's body of work, both before and after the publication of *Prelude to Christopher*, demonstrates that she had more than enough literary imagination and psychological insight to conjure up her own plots. It is likely that Walford gained as much inspiration from Dark as she did from him. What Walford's remark illustrates is that the members of the *Blue Mountaineers* writers' group were engaged in debates based on their reading of books on psychology and, in particular, books dealing with psychopathology and sexuality.

Jean Deslines, in *Twisted Clay*, read similar works "to pry into the perplexing mysteries of my mentality." Her reading list included "works by Havelock Ellis, Lombroso, Freud, Stekel, Jung, Brown, Bousfield and others." These were the books being read by the Katoomba authors and discussed during their bushwalks and evening soirées. Such titles were not readily available in the local subscription libraries or bookshops. Dr Dark probably obtained them for the group. I found in Frank Walford's papers copies of the *Medical Journal of Australia* from the 1930s, which carried regular articles on mental illness. It is likely that Dr Dark subscribed to this and passed copies around the group. The question of whether madness was hereditary, and the then current debates about 'nature versus nurture' and eugenics are central preoccupations of both *Twisted Clay* and *Prelude to Christopher* and to a lesser extent of *Salute to Freedom*. The women of these novels dread the encroaching loss of sanity, which they regard as possibly inevitable because of their genetic inheritance. These questions were more than philosophical for Eleanor Dark, as her mother had suffered from a severe mental illness.

Walford's original title for his book, *Twilight*, perhaps left it more open to interpretation as to whether the 'darkening' of the mind of Jean Deslines was a result of her heredity or upbringing. His final title, *Twisted Clay*,[16] indicates that Walford wanted to portray Jean's psychopathic behaviour as an inevitable result of her genetic make-up ('nature') and not her upbringing ('nurture'). In contrast, modern psychological studies have elucidated the influence of early dysfunctional upbringing in the formation of the traits of manipulative, cunning, 'amoral', cruel behaviour and lack of empathy that characterise sociopaths. It was perhaps an unfortunate distraction that Walford made Jean a lesbian as well.

There have been many books, articles and theses that have highlighted the intellectual companionship and support received by Eleanor Dark through her correspondence with other women writers. In fact, she spent much more time rockclimbing, bushwalking and discussing literature with the predominantly male members of the 'Blue Mountaineers' than she did in correspondence with other women writers. That Frank Walford and Eleanor Dark were thinking along similar lines in the 1930s is indicated by a short story that Dark had published in *The Bulletin* in 1934.[17] It relates the solving of a homicide that had occurred on Katoomba golf course. The victim was murdered by the same method used by Jean Deslines on her father: "... killed by repeated blows on the head from some sharp instrument." The murderer turns out to be the town's mayor who, despite being white in appearance, has "... negro blood in him." Dark describes him as having "... the indefinable taint of evil and uncleanness that so often goes with the mixing of bloods which should not be mixed." The murderer's rage against his victim is attributed to "racial instinct" and "atavistic blood-lust". Dark was saying in her own way that he was made of 'twisted clay'

It was no coincidence that two intense novels about disturbed and unconventional women were written in Katoomba at the same time by friends who spend a lot of time walking and talking together and reading the same books. Both novels also include somewhat clichéd elements typical of Gothic literature. Jean Deslines is born during a violent snowstorm and the mental chaos of Linda Hendon's final descent into madness and suicide is mirrored by the lightning and thunder around her.

Eleanor Dark regarded *Prelude to Christopher* as her most important work. Critics today recognise its modernistic stylistic innovations. *Twisted Clay* is certainly the most original of Walford's works. While it is much more conventional in style, it deals convincingly with important psychological themes. It appears to be the first authentic portrayal in English literature of the inner life of an example of the personality type, now so recognisable in real-life horrors and in film, television and books, the sociopathic serial killer. Walford's Jean Deslines is one of the first modern literary 'antiheroes'.

Walford's later life.

Walford followed the success of *Twisted Clay* with *The*

Silver Girl in 1935. He became a regular short story writer for *The Australian Journal*, *The Bulletin* and many other publications.[18] In 1939 Walford's third novel, *And the River Rolls On*, was published in London. His popularity in England reached its peak in 1940, with 10,000 copies of *The Indiscretions of Iole* being sold in five days.[19] From 1941, A.B.C. radio became an important outlet for many of Walford's short stories which were read over the air. The Walford and Dark families maintained a close friendship during the early 1940s with the socialist-leaning Walford occupying executive positions in the local Labor Party branch, to which Dr Dark also belonged. After three decades of criticising local government aldermen in his newspapers, Walford finally ran for election himself in December 1941.[20]

1942 saw the publication of Walford's semi-autobiographical novel, *A Fool's Odyssey* (Werner Laurie, 1942), based mainly on his early years of tropical travels, and the following year the adventure novel, *The Barrier Rat*, appeared. Both Dark and Walford joined the local Volunteer Defence Corps, but Walford moved out of the area to join the Guides and Reconnaissance Unit, under the command of the anti-communist crusader William Wentworth.[21] During his time with Wentworth, and probably angered by Communist-led waterfront strikes that delayed shipment of supplies to Australian troops in New Guinea (where Walford's son was serving), Walford abandoned his socialistic ideas and became an ardent anticommunist.

On his discharge from the Army, his standing in the local Australian Labor Party branch was still high enough for him to be invited to stand for election. However he found that, in his absence, Bruce Milliss, a secret member of the Communist Party, had stacked the local branch, leading to the resignation of many of the old local Labor Party stalwarts.[22] The

December 1944 Katoomba Council election campaign was an extremely bitter one during which Walford denounced Dr Dark and the other members of the Labor Party ticket as communists.[23] The resulting split between the members of the 'Blue Mountaineers' was not only personally traumatic but seriously affected the writing of all the Katoomba based writers.

Dr Dark published only socialist tracts thereafter. Eleanor managed to complete the *Timeless Land* trilogy, but then had an eleven year break from writing before her final novel *Lantana Lane*. She published nothing in the last 25 years of her life. The Lowes had divorced in 1937 and Nina's novels were never published. Eric Lowe published two more, fairly uninspiring, volumes in his family saga. The Lowe's precocious daughter Barbara had had her first short story published in 1929 and later became a prize-winning novelist.[24] Osmar White became a prolific author, continuing to produce a large output of short stories and journalism as well as many books, mainly non-fiction.

Walford's last overseas-published book was a collection of three short stories that appeared in 1945, *The Ghost of Albert and Other Stories* (Werner Laurie, 1945). His novels failed to appeal to post war publishers. He continued to receive rejections over several decades for such titles as *The Nietzschean, Beloved Minx* and *The Immeasurable Moment*.[25] About ten of his novels remain unpublished. In 1954 and 1955 six Walford titles were published by Frank Johnson as part of the 'Magpie Books' series. These were cheaply produced stapled books with lurid covers. The majority were versions of previously published works by Walford. One title *Chain of Violence* had to be destroyed as Gordon and Gotch refused to distribute it.[26] However, his short stories were still being widely published and regularly read on A.B.C. radio.

Walford continually pushed for publicity campaigns to counter the post-World War II decline in Blue Mountains tourism. He worked for many years to create what was later known as Frank Walford Park. He was founder, patron or office holder of many local organisations including the Blue Mountains Historical Society, Blue Mountains Conservation Society and the Pioneer Way Association. He occupied the Mayoral chair for the first time in December 1949, followed by terms in 1956/57 and 1962/63. His popularity and local influence in the local area was at its greatest level in the 1950s. Walford lobbied his wartime commander and friend William Wentworth, then a member of Federal Parliament, to reverse the ban on *Twisted Clay*. In 1960 this was lifted and a Horwitz paperback version published. At this time, aged 78, Walford was still walking between 24 and 32 kilometres per week.[27]

Madge Walford died in 1963.[28] Frank's friends felt that he lost much of his passion for his usual pursuits after his wife's death. He was defeated in the Blue Mountains City Council election of December 1965 after 24 years continuous aldermanic service. Walford continued as patron of various local organisations and gave occasional lectures but did not again participate in any local controversies or produce any more fiction. Walford died on 30 May 1969 and was buried in Katoomba cemetery where some of the gruesome scenes in *Twisted Clay* were set.[29]

Endnotes

1   Birth 1882/4479. Parents Lion Henry Walford and Anna Maides.

2   F. Walford, *A Fools Odyssey*, T. Werner Laurie, London, 1942.

3   *Ibid.*, biographical "blurb", p.5.

4   Walford 1942, op. cit., biographical 'blurb'; E. Wilson 'Alderman Was Once a Brilliant Boxer', *Mountain Gazette*, 16 December 1964;

"Double-Yew", *The Jumbly History of Parramatta*, Frank Walford, Parramatta, 1915.

5 S. Tracey, 'The Great War at Branch Level: The Minutes of the Parramatta Labour League 1916- 1918', *The Hummer*, Vol.3(4) 2000, p.26.

6 *Blue Mountain Echo*, 20 June 1919.

   Anon., 'Advance Blue Mountains', *Blue Mountain Echo*, 6 August 1920.

8 Anon., [F. Walford], 'The Cave Dweller', *Blue Mountain Echo*, 2 May 1919.

9 F. Walford, *Starlight and Haze*, The Mountaineer Printing and Publishing Co., Katoomba, 1919; Scrapbook of published poems 1912–1930s, Walford Family Archives.

10 Rotary Club of Katoomba, *Old Leura and Katoomba*, 1982, p.302.

11 J. Smith, *The Blue Mountains Mystery Track*, Three Sisters Productions, Winmalee, 1990, pp.18-26.

12 F. Walford, *Paths of Dew*, The Author, Katoomba 1927; F. Walford, *New Walks and Sights*, Wilsons Publishing Company, Sydney, N.D. [1927].

13 *Old Leura and Katoomba*, pp.302-303.

14 Anon., 'Invitation Mystery Hike, Opening of Blue Mountain Guide Service', *Katoomba Daily*, 9 August 1932.

15 No surviving copy of *Beyond Ceram* has yet been located. The UK first edition of *Twisted Clay* is copyrighted 1933, but according to the *English Catalogue of Books*, it was published in January 1934.

16 The title was inspired by the sixty third verse of Edward Fitzgerald's translation of *The Rubaiyat* of Omar Khayyam (1859), which Walford prefaced his novel.

17 Eleanor Dark, 'The Murder on the Ninth Green', *The Bulletin*, 12 December 1934, pp. 29-30. This was the first short story that Dark published under her own name. She had previously used pseudonyms.

18 In a letter to Mary Campbell dated 2 September 1957, (private collection) Walford claimed to have had "over 600 short stories either published or broadcast". The Walford Family Archives hold manuscripts or published versions of less than 200 short stories.

19 Frank Walford, 'Notes for Station 3UZ', Walford Family Archives. More than 20,000 copies were sold in total.

20 Anon, 'Katoomba District Poll Result', *The Clarion*, 9 December 1941.

21 F. Walford, *In Khaki*, unpublished manuscript [1940s], Walford Family Archives.

22 F. Walford, *An Appeal by Frank Walford*, [election brochure], The Author, Katoomba, November 1944.

23 *Blue Mountains Advertiser*, 17 November, 24 November, 1 December 1944.

24 Barbara Lowe, later McNamara, used the pen name Elizabeth O'Connor.

25 Manuscripts in Walford Family Archives.

26 Frank Johnson to Frank Walford, 17 June 1954, Walford Family Archives.

27 Anon., 'After 34 Years Book's Ban Lifted', *Blue Mountains Advertiser*, 23 March 1961.

28 Anon., 'Sudden Death of Mrs Madge Walford', *The Clarion*, 4 August 1963.

29 Anon., 'Death of Former Mountains Mayor', *Blue Mountains Advertiser*, 5 June 1969.

THE RECEPTION OF
TWISTED CLAY

JAMES DOIG

ON 6 JUNE 1935 the Comptroller-General of the Department of Trade and Customs wrote to Sir Robert Garran,
Chairman of the Commonwealth Book Censorship Board,
asking him to consider whether Frank Walford's novel
Twisted Clay should be considered a prohibited import
under the *Customs Act*. A few weeks later two members
of the Censorship Board scribbled their judgements on a
sheet of paper. [1] According to Garran, the book was "crude
and repulsive. The so-called 'psychology' in it is cheap fake.
I would ban." J.P. Meurisse Haydon, Professor of French
at the Canberra University College, wrote, "I can see no
redeeming feature in this story of progressive insanity. It
could, I am sure, prove very harmful to a highly impres-
sionable nature. I would certainly ban." *Twisted Clay* was
placed on the prohibited list on 15 July 1935 and was not
released until 19 September 1959.

The novel had been published in January 1934 by the
London publisher, T. Werner Laurie and it is perhaps sur-

prising that it took eighteen months for the Australian authorities to take action. Nicole Moore, in her study of literary censorship in Australia, *The Censor's Library*, calls it a "high-octane mix of sex, crime, and morbid sensationalism," qualities which were certain to bring the novel to the attention of the Book Censorship Board.[2] Certainly the plot, the first person account of a lesbian serial killer, Jean Deslines, seems more akin to controversial exploitation films of the 1990s, such as *Basic Instinct*, than 1930s popular fiction. Perhaps the closest contemporary novel to it is Michael Arlen's social satire, *Hell! said the Duchess: A Bed-time Story*, which was published around the same time (Heinemann, 1934).

Correspondence in Frank Walford's personal archive indicate that the original title of *Twisted Clay* was *Twilight*, and that between December 1932 and February 1933 the novel was rejected by the London publishers, Hamish Hamilton, William Heinemann and Jonathon Cape.[3] Later in the year, T. Werner Laurie accepted the novel and a contract was signed on 19 September 1933 with the book still provisionally titled *Twilight*.[4]

Prior to publication Walford ensured that *Twisted Clay* received positive press in local newspapers.[5] In October 1933, the *Cumberland Argus and Fruitgrowers Advocate* published the following article under the headline, "Local Author's Fine Effort,"

Mr Frank Walford, the well known Parramatta journalist, has had a novel accepted by a London firm of publishers. The title is *Twisted Clay*, and it is said to break entirely new ground. In a letter to Mr Walford, the publishers described the book as "an unpleasant but quite unusual story," which was possessed of "exceptional strength." They added that they were anxious to publish it without delay, and were enclosing a signed contract in anticipation of acceptance. In event of acceptance to the terms they asked him to cable in order to permit an immediate start on the work of publication.

A well-known Sydney journalist, who read the manuscript before its despatch to England, declared that, while he did not approve of "the remorseless dissection of a human soul," nevertheless it was a story of a most unusual type" which displayed "great power."

Briefly, the story concerns a girl who suffers alternating periods of mania and sanity. Her lucid intervals are devoted to evading the consequences of her actions while insane. Those who have read the MS are unanimous that Mr Walford has written a book that will excite attention.

Indeed, T. Werner Laurie does appear to have been excited by the book. According to the *English Catalogue of Books*, *Twisted Clay* was published in January 1934, and between January and March, Werner Laurie spruiked the book in its advertising in the major newspapers of the day: "The publishers feel that this novel will create a deep sensation. The MS was examined by four readers, each of whom foretold it a best seller."[6]

In late January and early February newspapers in the United Kingdom were receiving review copies, and shortly afterwards reviews of the book began to appear, though Walford's claim that a review in *The Times* of London called it "the best book ever written with a lunatic as a central character" cannot be substantiated.[7] On 1 February 1934, the *Yorkshire Herald* described it as "remarkable and deeply interesting," and stressed the serious intent of the author: "There is a great deal more in the book than actually appears in print, and on concluding the story one is led to consider the problems of the present day, with its perversion, sterilisation and mental defectives." On 14 February, the reviewer for the *Aberdeen Press and Journal* called it "a remarkable account of progressive insanity," while *The Western Mail*, under the heading, "Unsavoury," focussed on the horror elements of the novel: "It contains some horrible scenes equal to the worst in *Dracula*," declaring that Walford "is a master of the morbid."

Review copies of the novel, including cuttings of published reviews, were sent to Australian newspapers in March and April, and reviews began to appear in late March, firstly in local newspapers, with positive reports appearing in the *Katoomba Daily* on 27 March and the *Blue Mountains Times* on 30 March, with the latter expressing the view, "possibly *Twisted Clay* is the most ambitious novel yet attempted in Australia."

A glowing review appeared in Australia's leading literary magazine, *The Bulletin*, on 4 April, which called *Twisted Clay* "a masterpiece in its ghastly line," comparing it favourably with the realistic thrillers of Wilkie Collins, Zola, le Fanu and, more recently, Mrs Belloc Lowndes' *The Lodger*. The same reviewer wrote a few months later in an article on "The Australian Novel," that *Twisted Clay* was the best novel of horror he had read.

A review on 20 April for the national newspaper, *The Sydney Morning Herald*, was also positive: "*Twisted Clay*, by Frank Walford, is a remarkable and peculiarly horrible study of progressive insanity…This study in abnormal psychology has been most cleverly worked out, so that its qualities cannot be ignored; but most people will prefer to avoid it." The *Daily Telegraph* reviewed it under the heading "A Modern Dracula," and praised the quality of Walford's writing, like *The Bulletin* reviewer comparing it to le Fanu, and stressing his serious intent, arguing *Twisted Clay* was more than just a thriller.

Unlike *The Bulletin*'s critic, other reviewers were less convinced by the book's claim to realism. Nettie Palmer, in a piece for *All About Books*, a monthly literary review, felt that the book was an ingenious piece of "fantastic horror" but not in the least realistic, while the *Sunday Sun* dismissed it as neither convincing nor worthwhile, and *The Western Mail* of Perth described it as "too far-fetched." The *Woman's Mirror*, pre-empting the Book Censorship Board, declared it to be "a most unpleasant book which may interest psychologists, but will be nauseating to the average reader." In April 1934 the *Blue Mountains Times* reported that the Library Committee was debating whether or not to purchase the book for the public library.

The controversial American publisher, Claude Kendall (whose murder in 1937 remains unsolved), published the novel in the United States in 1934 and began an advertising blitz that saw *Twisted Clay* reviewed in newspapers across the country.[8] The reviews indicate that it created something of a sensation in the United States. The *Lexington Leader* reviewed it under the heading, "Frank Walford writes one of the most amazing books ever printed," the *Dayton Daily News* opened by saying, "This work will probably be regarded as one of the most notable books of the year," and the *Sunday Herald Sun* called it "the finest triumvirate of perversion, horror and murder written this spring."

While most reviewers treated the book as a crime thriller and a study of abnormal psychology, others took a wider view. The *Baltimore News and Post* compared it favourably with *The Well of Loneliness*, and other critics mentioned the lesbian theme. *This Week* of Pittsburg, selecting *Twisted Clay* as the Book of the Week, called it "a modern Dracula," and declared that "for excitement and horror, [it] transcends any of the works of Edgar Allan Poe;" similarly the *New York Mirror* compared it to "Poe and Baudelaire." These reviews were quoted on the back panel of other Claude Kendall books to advertise *Twisted Clay*. No doubt, the popularity of pulp fiction in the United States at this time, with its ubiquitous combination of sex and crime, made *Twisted Clay* more receptive to the American market.

Certainly, the book appears to have sold well. According to a short article in *The Bulletin* following *Twisted Clay*'s banning, by February 1935 the book had gone into two editions in the United Kingdom and three in the United States.[9] The online Australian literature database, AUSTLIT, says that Walford's first three novels, including *Twisted Clay*, sold 20,000 copies overseas.

While contemporary critics noted the serious psychological concerns of the novel – the review in *The Sydney Morning Herald* is titled "Abnormal Psychology," and reviewers tended to call it a "study" or "account" of "progressive insanity" – most realised that Walford's intention was to write a sensational best seller. As H. M. Green wrote in *A History of Australian Literature* (Angus & Robertson, 1961), "*Twisted Clay* is a gruesome study of progressive insanity, but the study is obviously subordinate to a desire to excite and horrify."[10]

Certainly, Walford gave the book serious credentials by having Jean Deslines read works by "Havelock Ellis, Lombroso, Freud, Stekel, Jung, Brown, Bousfield and others."

Havelock Ellis is a particular influence: "I read the night out, only desisting when the rosy shafts of dawn entered my bedroom window. Then I flung Ellis on the floor, and lay thinking. I had absorbed enough to know that I was a Lesbian." The book is steeped in the psychology of "sexual inversion" of the day, which also influenced that much tamer tragedy of lesbian awakening, Radclyffe Hall's *The Well of Loneliness* (1928).[11]

Walford also casts the book as a Gothic novel, and at least one reviewer saw it as stemming "directly from Matthew Gregory Lewis's *The Monk* and Walpole's *The Castle of Otranto*."[12] Jean Deslines birth takes place during a terrible storm, typical of Gothic fiction:

> It was a bitter night when I first drew breath in this bitter world. A westerly gale lashed the Blue Mountains, and snow was driving under the eaves and verandas. The house trembled in the blast; once a resounding crash told that a pine tree had been torn up by the roots, to smash to earth in a ruin of flowers and shrubs. The electrical service was disorganised, and I was ushered into the world by the fitful gleam of candles which flickered and guttered even in the shelter of the bedroom. On the hearth glowed a fire of coke, before which I was washed and wrapped.

But *Twisted Clay* is no pastiche, but rather a playful satire or reinterpretation of the usual Gothic tropes and themes. The Deslines' "bleak old house" in the Blue Mountains is akin to the decaying castle or rambling mansion of Gothic fiction, but in *Twisted Clay* it is transposed to an Australian setting, a "modern" country where there is no tradition of medieval superstition or ignorance. There are no ghosts (except in Jean Desline's mind), hauntings, or vampires, rather entirely modern concepts of psychology, insanity and hallucination. Indeed, the young maiden of the novel is not stranded in an ancestral castle and menaced by a sinister uncle or relative who is after her inheritance or worse, rather it is Jean Deslines who is the menace, who is a threat to all the male characters in the novel.

The novel works because Walford's writing is confident and assured – we sympathise with Jean's plight in much the same way that we can understand the murderous motivations of Patricia Highsmith's Ripley. This is a hard task to pull off, and although we laugh occasionally at dated surface psychology and sexism (for example Jean's transformation by the love of a "real man") she speaks to us as a genuine female anti-hero pitted against the forces of the male dominated establishment.

After the war, Walford tried through his English agent, Innes Rose of John Farquharson, to have *Twisted Clay* reprinted. Werner Laurie appears to have declined the request, perhaps because of the paper restrictions that still applied to British publishers, which reduced their interest in reprinting older works; however it did release the rights for Walford's novels.[13] The Paris publisher, Les Èditions du Chêne, was approached in 1946, but declined to reprint the book in English or a French translation due to a perceived reaction by the French reading public against English translations which had flooded the French market.[14] The following year Walford sent a copy of *Twisted Clay* to the Australian pulp publisher, The Shakespeare Head, which specialised in mystery fiction, but it was not accepted, presumably because the novel was still banned in Australia.[15]

Fortunes improved when *Twisted Clay* was taken off the

banned list in 1959. The novel first came up for review in
May 1958, however the Commonwealth Literature Censorship Board recommended that it continue to be treated
as a prohibited import, however the Appeal Censor
reversed this decision in September 1959 and the book
was released.[16] Walford approached Penguin Books in early
1960 to reprint the book, but they declined. Horwitz Publications, however, jumped at the chance, and published
it in September 1960, though the letter from the Horwitz's
senior editor, Ann Oxenham, accepting the book did advise
Walford that "it may be necessary to tone down some of the
more startling passages – but editing would be very slight
indeed." It is not clear whether the proposed edits were
actually made in the Horwitz edition. In any case, Walford
received an advance of £100 against a royalty of 7½% on
sales and the usual six author's copies. In May 1961 Walford
received a royalty cheque of £32 (after Horwitz reclaimed
its £100 advance) for very respectable sales of 13,427 for
the period to 30 March 1961, and *Twisted Clay* was quickly
reprinted in January 1962. The novel was still doing well in
the late 1960s: Walford received a royalty cheque of $108
in February 1969 for sales of 3,171 apparently in the 1968
calendar year.

Twisted Clay may be a serious book - an indictment of
contemporary attitudes and mores, and a brilliant reinterpretation and inversion of the Gothic novel - but it is also
a rollicking good read, a pulp *tour-de-force* that keeps us
riveted to the last page. Horwitz knew it was on to a good
thing when it reprinted the novel in 1960 with the cover
blurb, "An explosive novel of strange passions," and the
declaration on the back cover: "Just released from the
banned list!"

Editors' note: the text of this edition of Twisted Clay is the complete Claude Kendall edition.

Endnotes

1   National Archives of Australia, CRS series A3023 (correspondence files of the Book Censorship Board), file 1935/36

2   Nicole Moore, *The Censor's Library: Uncovering the Lost History of Australia's Banned Books* (University of Queensland Press, 2012), p. 142.

3   Letters dated 19 December 1932 (Jonathon Cape), 30 January 1933 (William Heinemann), and 2 February 1933 (Hamish Hamilton).

4   Contract in Frank Walford's personal archive. Walford received a £20 advance, royalties of 10%, and six free copies of the book.

5   All extracts from reviews of *Twisted Clay* that follow are from review clippings in Frank Walford's archive.

6   T. Werner Laurie advertising in *The Times*, *The Sunday Times* and *The Times Literary Supplement*.

7   The AUSTLIT entry for Frank Walford makes this claim, but there is no evidence in *The Times* Digital Archive that the newspaper reviewed the book. In its own advertising, Werner Laurie described the book as "the most amazingly clever study of progressive insanity ever written," and reviewers tended to repeat this in their own appraisals.

8   According to the *Catalogue of Copyright Entries* (1935), copyright was registered in the US on 21 May 1934. Copies of about fifty reviews in US newspapers are extant in Frank Walford's personal archive.

9   *The Bulletin*, 6 February 1935,

10   H.M. Green, *A History of Australian Literature* (Angus & Robertson, 1961), p. 1140.

11   See Moore, *The Censor's Library*, pp. 134–143.

12   *Sydney Morning Herald*, 26 November 1960.

13   Letter from Innes Rose to Walford dated 16 August 1946.
      Werner Laurie released the rights of Walford's first three novels.

14   Letter from Les Èditions du Chêne dated 20 November 1946.

15   Letters from The Shakespeare Head dated 19 February 1947 and
      27 January 1948

16   Walford petitioned his local Member of Parliament to request a
      review of *Twisted Clay*. A letter of 28 May 1958 indicates that the
      Literature Censorship Board recommended that the book stay
      on the banned list. A letter of 15 September 1959 indicates that
      the Board had decided to remove the prohibition.

TWISTED CLAY

None answer'd this; but after silence spake
A Vessel of a more ungainly Make:
"They sneer at me for leaning all awry;
What I did the Hand then of the Potter shake?"

CHAPTER I

ALL MY LIFE I have been solitary, isolated from the rest of my sex, like a monolith in the middle of a patch of grass. The River of Life has beaten about my feet, but only the males have made contact. The female element has passed me by, keeping to the centre of the stream like floating leaves, with only an odd one sweeping to the bank at rare intervals, touching me for an instant without staying its progress.

Why do I differ from others of my sex? The difference is not physical. I am typically feminine in shape, with slender, rounded limbs and small, firm breasts. That I am pretty, I know. My mirror and my male friends afford ample evidence of it. Nor would other women hate me so intensely if I were plain. Yet a gulf separates me from my kind. I have gone through life, alone and atypical; and so I am destined to proceed to the journey's end.

My grandmother and her friends attributed my "peculiarities," as they termed them, to the fact that I was a seven months' child, and did all in their power to make my life a hell. They whispered among themselves, and nodded their stupid heads in time to the wagging of their jaws. In public I stared at them insolently. In private I laughed at their ignorance and lack of understanding. Of what moment was the inane cackle of a bevy of old women? Be I what I might, at least I was I, which was all that mattered to me.

How often did my charitable friends and relations narrate the story of my birth! True, they refrained from drawing conclusions in my presence, but the implications were unmistakable. They regarded me as a child of the devil. I learned much from their gossip, chiefly the fact that my mother had been a paranoiac. Possibly that explained something, but it did not explain everything. Some other tag of heredity was involved which eluded me.

It was a bitter night when I first drew breath in this bitter world. A westerly gale lashed the Blue Mountains, and snow was driving under the eaves and verandas. The house trembled in the blast; once a resounding crash told that a pine tree had been torn up by the roots, to smash to earth in a ruin of flowers and shrubs. The electrical service was disorganised, and I was ushered into the world by the fitful gleam of candles which flickered and guttered even in the shelter of the bedroom. On the hearth glowed a fire of coke, before which I was washed and wrapped.

Coming out of the chloroform, my mother raved and screamed, her voice in strange harmony with the tumult of the elements. Then she lapsed into a coma and died peacefully, leaving me to the mercies of her insufferable mother, whose hawk's-bill nose and projecting chin have poked themselves ceaselessly into my affairs. I came to hate her with a hate transcending that of Christians. She was my evil genius, devoid of both charity and understanding. Often I made a mental vow that, when she died, I would steal to her grave at midnight and dance joyously above her rotting bones. The old termagant!

They say my father wept when he realised that my

mother was dead. I do not doubt it. There was a streak of sentimentality in his nature which approximated to weakness. God knows, she had given him little reason to love her in life, so perhaps he considered that something was due when she released him from bondage. Doubtless with a specific amount of sincerity he beat his breast and strewed ashes on his head. It was a fine valediction, and impressed the world immensely. I cannot evade the suspicion that a trifle of hypocrisy was wedded to his sincerity in the matter.

Indulged by my father, and harassed by my grandmother, I lived in the bleak old house on the crest of the Blue Mountains until I grew to womanhood. If my grandmother made my life a hell, I can take to my soul the unction that I repaid her in kind. I missed no opportunity to annoy her. I teased her cat, broke her crockery, concealed frogs in her bed, stitched horsehair into her underwear, drove nails through the soles of her shoes, and mixed sulphate of magnesia with her porridge. I mocked her gods, asked sex questions of her stammering male friends, and swam naked in a creek which I knew was raked by field-glasses from the verandas of the houses which overlooked it. When she raged, I kept icily cool and smiled in her face. She regarded me as a devil incarnate.

One day, when I was twelve years old, she enlisted the aid of a clergyman. With the arrogance of his kind he descended upon the house after I had returned from school, and locked himself in the sitting-room with me, where he began to take me to task for my misdeeds. He had one of those dome-like foreheads which so frequently cover a vacant mind, with a ridiculous wart jutting up just where his brow met his bald head.

The burden of womanhood had come upon me a few

months before and I was in the first flush of puberty; in this, as in most things, I was precocious. I listened to the well-meaning fool with simulated humility, leading him onward until his vanity fructified at the impression which he was making on the formerly incorrigible hoyden. At length, with tears of repentance in my eyes and my head downcast, I came to his side and took his hand, fondling it with my fingers. He proceeded with his curtain lecture, but I noted that his eyes burned and his hand was hot where it rested in mine.

I knew my grandmother as she never was capable of knowing me. I knew that her insatiable curiosity would compel her to peer into the room to see how her emissary was progressing. I awaited patiently the moment when her hawk's nose would be pressed to the window-pane and her greedy eyes would sweep the apartment. In the interim I sidled closer to my mentor, pressing my young breasts against his body. In an ecstasy of joy I felt him flinch away and then strain back against me. He was an easy victim.

A shadow darkened the window, but the clergyman was too perturbed to notice it. Silently I drew his hand about my waist and sank upon his knee, pressing my lips to his. He shivered violently, threw back his head, and made to rise. Then his atrophied manhood awoke and he swept me to his bosom. When my outraged grandmother burst into the room I was screaming and striking him on the face.

That night I lay awake and laughed until the tears streamed down my cheeks. For once I was absolved from blame. She abused the poor man shockingly. He was a disgrace to his cloth, renegade to all the precepts that he preached, a deflowerer of innocence, a debaucher of children!

As one in the grip of a nightmare he stood with bowed

head, awed by the blast of her fury. The simpleton was unable to orient himself. Somewhere, he realised, he had been made the victim of circumstance, trapped in a hideous gin; but the truth eluded his slow wits. "If I could only explain," he stuttered.

"Explain!" howled the beldame. "What is there to explain? I asked you to reason with a wayward child. Like a fool I yielded to your request to interview her in privacy. Little did I suspect your design when you urged me to leave you alone with her. You monster, you beastly seducer, you . . . you . . . you whited sepulchre!"

I almost pitied him as he crawled away with his tail between his legs and a wealth of misery in his eyes. My grandmother actually kissed me as I sobbed on her breast. It was the first spontaneously human action on her part that I could recall.

My father inclined to the opposite extreme. Always he allowed me to follow my own desires, seeking the easiest way out. On rare occasions, driven by my grandmother, he would make a pretence of authority; but a burst of tears, followed by intermittent sighs, invariably routed him and left me in possession of the field. Nevertheless, he loved me and ministered to my wants prodigally. On winter nights, when the dark fell early and the wild westerly winds shook the walls, he would sit by the fire and explain those things which I wished to know. Even at this distance I can recall a hundred such scenes, complete in every detail. With his feet thrust into felt slippers and a blackened briar between his teeth, he would lie back in an easy chair. The firelight played on his homely features, touching them with a nobility which they lacked in severer lights. I would sit on the hearthrug by his side with my head resting on his knee and his fingers playing with my hair. Drunk with a hunger for knowledge, I would sit for hours, scarcely stirring, listening to tales of Rome, Carthage, Greece, Persia, and the rest of the ancient empires.

He confined his discourses mainly to history, and I did not complain. When I sought information on scientific matters, he resolutely turned the subject. For years I was puzzled by this habit; but illumination came one night when I overheard him discussing me with my grandmother. "The child is far too precocious," he informed her. "Sometimes I fear that she carries a mental taint from her mother. Certainly she is not as other children; there is nothing infantile about her, save in a direction which you could not comprehend. It is this infantile propensity, allied with her amazing physical maturity, which frightens me. I live in daily dread that she will develop unpleasant traits."

"It would be difficult to imagine more unpleasant traits than she already possesses," rejoined my grandmother grimly.

Father sighed and turned away. I did not understand his remark until I had turned fourteen, though I pondered it much.

Looking back through the vista of the years I can see myself as I was at the age of twelve. Of average height for my age, I was very slim. It was not the skinniness of childhood, but the slenderness of a woman. My legs and arms were round and shapely, and already I possessed small, firm breasts, quite devoid of that flabbiness which so frequently accompanies the onset of puberty. My hair was jet black and cropped close, lying in straight curls. My eyes were in keeping and fringed with long, curved lashes. My feet and hands were small and well formed. A stranger would have set my age at seventeen, perhaps aided by my extraordinary composure and aplomb. The neighbours united in describing me as "a queer kid." My grandmother considered me a devil. My father ventured no opinion in my hearing, but was wont to study me covertly. For myself, I did not know whether I was child or woman. Possibly I was both, with a touch of the fiend added for good measure.

We lived alone in the great house on the hill, save for a maid named Jenny. She was uneducated, superstitious, and dull of intellect; but her physical proportions were superb. I rightly might describe her as Junoesque, with her wide hips, her ample breasts, and her heavy limbs. She was deliciously feminine, and the greatest delight of my childhood was sleeping with her on winter nights when the winds shook the roof and screamed in the swaying trees. She was so soft, her skin was so white and satiny in texture, and she was so warm!

I remember one night, when I was ten; every detail is impressed on my conscious mind. A foot of snow lay on the ground, and a huge branch had been torn from a pine tree by the weight of its white mantle. A log fire blazed on the hearth; but Jenny and I, who were alone in the house, could not keep warm. We went to bed at eight o'clock, too early to sleep, and cuddled close to one another, and she laughed and hugged me till I gasped for breath, stroking my body with her hands. Hugged to her generous breast I fell into a dreamless sleep.

CHAPTER II

My FOURTEENTH BIRTHDAY was one of the outstanding landmarks of my life. On that day a conversation changed my whole outlook, and guided me across the threshold of womanhood. It is no exaggeration to state that thenceforward I was an adult, despite my years.

Ever eager to please me, my father arranged a birthday party at the house, to which came a pack of tedious relatives armed with a variety of presents which excited my inward merriment. I had outgrown them three or four years earlier. The donors were obsessed by the popular aberration that age is directly related to years; they were unable to conceive that the world contains individuals who develop early. What would they know of gland secretions and their effects on body and mind? They kissed me; wished me many happy birthday anniversaries, and forced their ridiculous toys and trinkets upon me. I smiled, and thanked them, and comported myself with strict regard to the conventions, while inwardly I surged with laughter. When will the world learn that there is no standard for the individual; that slop-made clothes cannot fit all forms perfectly? Still; they were dear people, even if stupid, and I evinced proper gratitude.

The one exception was a cousin, a woman of twenty-three, who was studying medicine at Sydney University.

Several times I caught her eyeing me covertly, and ultimately I found myself alone with her. Months later I learned
that she had maneuvered patiently for the opportunity.

"Jean," she said, "in common with the rest I brought
you a present. If you want to give it to someone else, you'll
find it on top of the dustbin in the back yard, wrapped
in brown paper just as it left the shop. If you can't bring
to mind a child whom it would please, pitch it into the
street for someone to pick up. It is certain to gravitate to
some quarter where it will be appreciated."

I gazed at her long, and she smiled. "You're no longer a
child," she commented. "A blind woman could see that."

I jerked a thumb over my shoulder. "They can't see
it."

Again she smiled. "They're worse than blind; they're
stupid."

"And disgustingly complacent," I added.

"And disgustingly complacent." She stirred the carpet
with her foot. "What do you intend to do, Jean?"

"Get married, and escape from this dungeon."

She wrinkled her brows. "You couldn't do that without
your father's consent; the law is strict. Legally you are a
child, whatever your mental development. Tell me honestly,
kiddie is there a man?"

I shook my head.

"I thought not" She paused. "And I'm inclined to
think there won't be."

Involuntarily I glanced into a mirror above the mantelpiece.

"Oh I you're pretty enough. I don't doubt that men will
come seeking you. The trouble is the reverse; you won't
be attracted by them."

"Why not?"

She gazed at her feet, and ignored the question.

"Why not?" I repeated.

Slowly she lifted her eyes to mine, but did not speak. "Why not?" I insisted.

Still she hesitated.

"Play the game," I urged. "Why shouldn't men attract me?"

"Because . . . Oh, damn it! I've talked with your grandmother. She made much clear to me which she did not understand herself."

"Do I understand it?"

"I'm afraid you don't."

"H'm! *Could* I understand it?"

"Ye-e-es." She drawled the word hesitatingly. "Yes, doubtless you could understand it, given certain knowledge."

"Can you supply the knowledge?"

"I'd prefer not to."

"Why?"

She smiled slowly. "You're disconcertingly direct and laconic in your questions. Please leave it at that. I'd prefer not to; that's all."

"So I'm to linger in ignorance about something which distinguishes me from my fellows. Because you lack the courage to explain what is clear to you, but a mystery to me, I'm to be a social pariah, vainly wondering why I am different from my kind."

"There is no need to remain in ignorance. I merely said that I did not wish to enlighten you."

"Then, where am I to seek the light?"

"Read."

"Read what?"

"Psychology, for one thing."

"Where may I get the books?"

"At any library."

"Thanks," I commented ironically.

She stared at me gravely. "We'd better join the others."

"They might talk psychology, and embarrass you."

"They're more likely to talk dolls," she rejoined maliciously, and laughed as I coloured. "Don't let us squabble," she pleaded, and passed her arm about my waist, to withdraw it suddenly as I snuggled against her. She left me abruptly and returned to the drawing-room.

I sought a settee in the lounge-room, and surrendered myself to introspection. What was wrong with me? Why did I not respond to the attentions of the opposite sex? It was not from lack of opportunity, for God knows young men sought me. But I hated them to touch me. I shrank from their endearments. I begrudged the time spent in their company. My father encouraged their presence, and I bore with them to please him; but they irritated me. After they had gone home I would sit silently by the fire for an hour and then creep into bed with Jenny, hugging her splendid body to mine. What was wrong with me? I must obtain those books on psychology, and ascertain.

Having made this determination, I rose wearily from the settee and entered the drawing-room. My cousin was talking with my father by the hearth, and my grandmother was the centre of a group of relatives. The sudden hush in the conversation, as I approached, revealed that I had been the subject of discussion. Plainly she had been recounting my misdeeds.

"Don't let me interrupt your lecture, Grannie," I exclaimed. She hated the diminutive, and I knew it; but I also knew that she would not resent it before the others, and derived pleasure from the knowledge.

An aunt broke into a confused laugh. "Nonsense, Jean," she said. "We were not saying anything that you might not hear."

"I'm sorry," I replied. "I thought Grannie had been telling you what a wicked child I am."

"Nothing of the kind."

"Thank you, Grannie," I said meekly. "I'm so anxious to please you to-day; and I'm sure I'll be good to-morrow, because I'll be so engaged with all my beautiful presents. How may I thank everyone for the hosts of beautiful toys I have received?"

My grandmother maintained her composure admirably, though I thought she was about to have an apoplectic stroke when I sidled to the rear of the group and protruded my tongue at her.

After tea the young men began to arrive. They were father's contribution to the party; grandmother had selected the relations. They looked horribly stiff and unpleasant in their carefully creased clothes, and a distinct odour of mothballs impregnated the air. Their hair was laid smooth with oil, and each had executed a "part" with mathematical precision. Some wore it at the side, and some down the centre. In each instance its exactitude betrayed that creation had been a prolonged work of art. I wondered if their bodies had been scrubbed as carefully as their necks.

The exception to this ordered perfection was a lanky youth of nineteen, son of a local bank manager. His breath reeked of coarse pipe-tobacco, where those of his companions were redolent of scented cigarettes. His clothes hung in untidy folds, where theirs were creased with care. His hair rose in a bluff shock of dry spikes, where theirs were greased and straightly divided. He was a natural oasis within a tortured Dutch garden of rectangles. Singling him out as the least irritating of the fawning idiots, I permitted him to lead me outside into the night.

A young moon was low in the west, just visible above the row of pines along the fence. Above it a planet shone red, and the dome of heaven was dotted with a myriad white points which shrank and twinkled as I gazed. A soft wind whispered in the trees. The night was keen, but not uncomfortably cold; and we strolled through the perfumed air of the old garden. It was the violet season, and their heavy breath was abroad.

Some magic of the night stirred my latent womanhood and I made no protest as my companion slipped his arm about my waist. I felt no elation, no excitement of any description. My pulses beat no quicker than if he had attached me to him by a piece of string. But there was an entire absence of repulsion, and I felt quite jubilant at the knowledge. My cousin had been wrong: in due course I should marry and fulfil my destiny—perhaps not to the audacious hobbledehoy who now possessed me, but at least to someone. . . .

He led me to a seat and pulled me down beside him. No word was spoken, but his hand tightened on my waist. My head sank on his shoulder. So we remained seated for an indefinite period. I felt languid and peaceful, ready to remain motionless for an age; but he spoilt it. His hand lifted until it closed upon my breast, and his lips sought mine. The spell was broken. I sprang to my feet and slapped him viciously on the cheek. Dismayed, he fled to the house, where I followed at a more leisurely pace.

What was wrong with me? Was my cousin right after all? I must procure those books on psychology!

CHAPTER III

Two DAYS AFTER my birthday party I went to Sydney and procured a number of works on psychology and psychoanalysis. I experienced considerable difficulty. At the public library they gave me a paper to fill in. It required a wealth of detail, including my age, and had to be countersigned by a responsible person. I learned that I would be unable to obtain books on advanced psychology without parental consent. As I did not desire my father to know of my intention, this restriction made the library useless for my purpose. I crumpled up the form and tossed it away in the corridor.

A bookshop, to which I went, proved unwilling to send a false account form to my father. They would forward any books which I required, but the invoice must display the actual volumes ordered. The attendant began to question me sharply when I suggested the ruse to deceive father, and I thought it best to let the project drop. I retreated in an uncomfortable air of suspicion.

In this dilemma I remembered an uncle in a Government office. "Father asked me to buy him some books," I explained, "but I forgot to get a cheque from him. Could you lend me £5? He will post you a cheque when I return."

My uncle rallied me on my forgetfulness, perpetrated a few inane jokes on the folly of lending money to importunate

16

relatives, and produced his cheque-book. Within half an hour I had found another bookshop, selected my requirements, and was in a taxi-cab bound for the railway. In the parcel were works by Havelock Ellis, Lombroso, Freud, Stekel, Jung, Brown, Bousfield, and others. The names of the authors had been obtained by painful scrutiny of a catalogue.

I told my father that I intended to study botany, and he accepted my assurance without suspicion. I chose that subject because I knew that he was ignorant of it. He was a man of exceptionally wide reading, but in the demesne of natural science his bent inclined to the animal kingdom. Unless he developed an unexpected whim to dip into botany, I was safe. I explained that the urge to study botany had seized me suddenly while in the city, and that I had borrowed from my uncle. Dear old daddy swallowed the lie, read me a mild lecture on the iniquity of borrowing, and discharged the debt by the morrow's post. I now had the means at my command to pry into the perplexing mysteries of my mentality.

I read the night out, only desisting when the rosy shafts of dawn entered my bedroom window. Then I flung Ellis on the floor, and lay thinking. I had absorbed enough to know that I was a Lesbian. A vein of fear permeated my thoughts. I shrank under the bitter knowledge which had come to me. Throughout the day I slunk in shadows, fearful to face normal men and women in the sharp light of the sun. My eyes were shot with blood from the long vigil of the night, and dark circles showed under my sockets. Jenny was dismayed at my evident illness, and even my grandmother grew sympathetic, an anomaly which was sufficiently remarkable. In the afternoon I fell asleep and rested until dinner-time. A cold shower, following this needed repose, restored my vigour and something of my self-respect. My father noticed nothing amiss at the evening meal.

Immediately after dinner I returned to my books, but thenceforth was more circumspect in my study. I ceased at twelve each night, and took care to secure sufficient sleep. At the end of a week I had mastered the rudiments of the science, and knew myself for what I was beyond all doubt.

At first the knowledge sat heavy on my soul. I regarded myself as something unhealthy, a gross abnormality which should have been strangled at birth. I imagined that others eyed me askance, that children shrank from my presence; that I exuded a fetid miasma which disgusted heterosexual people. I studiously kept away from Jenny, causing that affectionate but stupid girl to weep secret tears as she conjectured how she had offended me. I was distraught and miserable, prone to attacks of pessimism which threatened hysterical climaxes. I began to lose flesh. Permanent rings of black underlay my eyes. I harboured thoughts of suicide. I remembered having read an article by Professor Haldane, in which he stated that boiling alive, over a slow fire, was one of the easiest deaths known. I filled the copper, turned the gas low beneath it, and clambered in. The intrusion of my body caused the water to overflow, making a dreadful mess on the floor of the laundry; but that detail did not trouble me. I waited for the water to heat, and destroy me.

Then I remembered that Haldane had said that the addition of a little sodium chloride hastened the effect. Wet and dripping, I jumped from the copper and dashed upstairs to the kitchen, returning with the salt-jar. Emptying its contents into the water, I clambered in once more. I had removed my shoes, and soon the bottom of the copper grew uncomfortably warm to my feet. I tried to elevate them, but the only effect was to change the points of contact to my knees. Finally the heat of the vessel became too great to be borne, and I was forced to relinquish my project long before the water had attained sufficient temperature to affect me.

My grandmother burst into the laundry while I was climbing from my unique bath. I learned from Jenny, later, that the old lady had discovered the pool of water which I had shed in the kitchen while reaching for the salt-jar. She followed the wet trail to the laundry, on fire with indignation.

For a moment she stood in the doorway, gaping in amazement. There was excuse for her unwonted dumbness, as I must have presented an astounding spectacle, perched on the edge of the copper with one bare foot feeling for the floor and its fellow doubled beneath me on the cement coping, while the water streamed from my clothing.

"What are you about now?" she screamed, suddenly finding her tongue.

I could not resist the impulse to annoy her. "I was trying to boil my dress and underclothing," I replied innocently.

"To boil your dress and underclothes?" she stuttered. "Do you usually boil yourself with them?"

"Not usually, but this time I thought I might wash myself at the same time. Sort of killing two birds with the one stone, you know."

"Are you mad?"

"Not unless madness is hereditary. Do such things descend from one's grandparents?"

"Come out of there at once, you wretched child. I'll tell your father the instant he comes in."

I descended obediently and hurried upstairs to the

bathroom, where I discarded my drenched clothes and donned dry things. Then I lay on my bed and thought. I felt better. The mystification of my grandmother had put me into better humour. I realised that I did not wish to die, and thanked the Fates that the bottom of the copper had grown hot before its contents. Possibly the shock of having nerved myself to perish, followed by that of an unexpected reprieve, had united to clear my mind of its ghosts. I reflected that possibly forty per cent, of women were as myself, even if ignorant of the fact. For that assumption I had the irrefutable figures of experts to support me. Even Jenny, big, white, stupid Jenny, what was she? What was —,the wife of a certain Government official? What were — and —, and —? Only too well did I realise what they were, in the light of my newly acquired knowledge. Seeing that I was by no means unique in my abnormality, what reason existed for desperation? To the contrary, as primitive forms of life universally were bi-sexual, was it not probable that we, the pariahs, were true to type, and the rest unconscious aberrations? It was a comforting thought, and I nourished it.

At tea-time my father investigated the complaint of my grandmother. As such inquisitions were almost nightly occurrences, he did not treat my latest misdemeanour too seriously. "Grandma tells me that you have been annoying her again, Jean," he said reprovingly.

"What's the matter with her now?" I inquired wearily. His eyes twinkled. "She says that you tried to boil your clothes before you removed them."

"They were old clothes, daddy, and I was having a lark. I lit the copper and jumped in to see how long I could stand it."

He looked serious. "That was a particularly dangerous

thing to do," he explained, and went on to recount Professor Haldane's experiments. I dared not inform him that I was aware of Haldane's amiable habits of boiling himself alive and drinking noxious fluids. To have admitted it would have been to place myself in a decidedly anomalous position. So I was compelled to listen to the details with assumed horror.

"You see how you have played with death," he concluded. I climbed on his knee and buried my face in his shoulder. "Don't talk about it any more, daddy. It's horrible."

I read Bousfield that night, and learned that I was deficient in feminine hormones; that was the primal cause of my trouble. It was possible that I might excite my oppressed femininity if I consorted with the opposite sex; such things had happened. I resolved to make the experiment — but with whom? I shuddered as I contemplated the oiled hair and creased trousers of my male acquaintances. Their embraces would stifle me. Well did I know that kisses and embraces would be the price I must pay for their company. In any case, these endearments were essential to the wakening of my latent womanhood, and must be endured. Who, who, who? The lanky, untidy son of the bank manager, with his bristling hair and disordered clothes; he would be less unendurable than the others! On him must fall the mantle of my saviour. I sought him out, meeting him in the street as if by accident. He escorted me home, and accepted my invitation to stay to tea. My father smiled as he noted the stranger within our gates, and grandmother scowled like a gargoyle. She disapproved of "boys" and sexual precocity.

After dinner we wandered in the garden, the lanky youth and I, drinking in the fragrance of the violets. The moon was entering its third quarter and floated high above us, dimming the stars. We sat on the seat; but he refrained from liberties, doubtless harbouring vivid memory of my violent resentment on the previous occasion. I was forced to take the initiative. I seized his hand and placed it about my waist. For a quarter of an hour he left it there; then it began to work upward slowly, to lie beneath my armpit, whence it edged gently across until it covered a breast. There was no heat in my blood. My pulses remained perfectly normal. I sank my head into the hollow of his neck and nuzzled against him.

Suddenly he was kissing me. Perhaps the quiescent hormones had warmed to activity, for I felt no aversion; I even experienced a thrill of pleasure. He stroked my hair; kissed my lips, my eyes, my nose; squeezed me till I was breathless; and I did not demur. I felt a queer, indefinable fluttering about my heart. My breath came in quick pants. Something stirred within me. I grew somnolent, semi-conscious. As in a dream I felt him lift me bodily in his arms and lacked either the spirit or the strength to protest. Only my lips moved, uttering the single word, "no."

"I love you, Jean."

"No, no!"

"Dearest!"

"No, no!"

"Jean?" And his lips closed on mine.

CHAPTER IV

My lanky accomplice visited the house regularly. In the main, I derived no pleasure from the intercourse; on the other hand, no actual displeasure resulted, and on occasion I experienced that sweet lapse into dreaminess — semi-consciousness even — which had occurred when I first yielded myself to his arms. When I expressed fears, he told me that he knew how to trick Nature; that I had no cause for alarm. Believing him, I continued my reckless course until the inevitable happened.

I never shall forget the day when first I knew beyond doubt that I was pregnant. The weather was bleak and a high wind screamed from the west. Dense banks of cloud obscured the sun. The fallen pine-needles stirred on the ground. For several days I had suspected my condition; but somehow, on that dreary day, I knew. I thought I would faint; but the blood circulated hotly through my brain, and I was denied this temporary respite from my agony. I wept bitter tears. I threw myself on my bed. I cried to the God in whom I had never believed. Having been reared in stark atheism by my father, in that dread hour of trial I had no friend to whom to appeal. I was alone in the universe, trembling on the brink of Avernus. I would have exchanged my most cherished possession for a sister or a mother into whose sympathetic ears I could have poured my woe. My grandmother was impossible. The grim old harridan would have shaken her thin wisps of hair, and informed me that she had known how I would end. The university vacation was in progress, and my cousin had fled north to escape the rigours of winter. There only remained my father; for stupid, loving Jenny would have been of little service in such an emergency.

For days I wept, and conjured my wits, and strove to pluck up the courage to approach him. Then realisation that something must be done spurred me to desperation, and I sought him in his study.

"What's the trouble, child," he asked, as I stood weeping before him.

I stood in silence with the tears flowing down my cheeks.

"What is it?" he inquired more sharply.

For answer I flung myself upon his breast. "Daddy, oh! Daddy!"

He took me in his arms and crooned over me. "Tell me all about it, Jean. Don't be afraid to tell daddy, little one."

"Daddy, I . . . I'm . . . Oh! daddy."

"Tell me, Jean," he enjoined softly.

"Daddy, I'm . . . I'm going to have . . . to have a baby."

Gently he swung me about until my face was turned to his. As I endeavoured to bury my head in his coat, he placed a finger under my chin and tilted my face upward. Then he expelled his breath noisily.

"Ah," he murmured. "I feared it; I feared it. Yet it is preferable to the other."

I stared at him, amazed to detect a gleam of joy in his eye. "Tell me," he asked quietly, "is it . . . was it young Guy?"

I nodded.

"Young blood, young blood," he muttered to himself. "Nature is more potent than the conventions."

"Daddy," I cried, and sobbed in his arms.

"Don't worry, little one," he enjoined, soothing me. "It will all come right. Are you very fond of Guy?"

I shook my head.

"Would you like to marry him?"

"Marry him," I gasped, breaking from his arms. "Oh! no, no!"

He gazed in bewilderment. "Don't you care for the boy at all?" he asked.

I met his eyes. "Not a scrap, daddy. He is no more to me than that kitten on the hearthrug."

"Then why . . . why did you . . . do it?"

I kept silent.

"Tell me, Jean. It is essential for me to know all, so that I may discover the best way out. Why did you permit him to . . . to . . . ?" His voice trailed away into silence.

I sobbed aloud.

"Tell daddy, Jean."

"I don't love him, daddy. I only wanted to . . ."

"To what?"

"To . . . to stimulate my hormones."

I heard him gasp as I hid my face on his breast. Then he turned me about once more, and lifted my face. "Tell me again, Jean," he demanded. "What did you wish to stimulate?"

"My hormones."

"What do you know of hormones?"

"A great deal."

He sighed deeply. "Who told you about hormones?"

"No one. I read about them."

"Where?"

"In books."

"Who gave you the books?"

"I bought them."

"How much have you learned from them?"

"I've learned a tremendous lot, daddy. I've learned where I differ from other girls, why I am a woman at my age, and . . . and what I am. I know why you said you preferred my . . . my disgrace . . . to the other thing."

"You poor kid," he murmured, rocking me on his knee like a babe. "You found that out, and played with fire to try and stimulate your hormones! You poor, luckless kid, striving for the impossible and tumbling from the frying-pan into the fire. As well might you have tried to fell a pine with a feather."

I huddled against him, evading his gaze, and so we sat in silence for an hour. I heard the marble clock in the dining-room strike nine. A little later I heard Jenny ask grandmother whether she would require her any more. I heard the grumpy negative, and Jenny's customary "good night, mum." And still we sat in silence.

Then I heard grandmother stirring, and knew that she was about to switch off the light. I almost smiled as the cat emitted an anguished howl. As certainly as though I had witnessed the incident, I knew that she had trodden on its tail as she crossed to the mantelpiece to wind the clock, which always was her last act before retiring to bed.

Two minutes later her head, crowned by its straggling grey hair, was thrust through the door of the study. She drank in every detail of the tableau which confronted her, and sniffed her disapproval. "Why don't you send that child to bed?" she inquired.

"She'll go when she's ready," snapped my father, and

again a smile almost broke through my grief as I noted her look of amazement at the unprecedented rebuff.

"Perhaps you'd better run along to bed," suggested my father, when she had gone. "I want to think about the position. We can decide our course of action to-morrow night."

"No," I protested firmly. "I mightn't scrape up the courage to approach you again. Let us discuss it now, and have it clone with."

"Jean," he said after a thoughtful pause, "you're no longer a child; I've known that for a year past. I deliberately encouraged you to philander with young Guy, believing that he had attracted you and might prove your salvation. I encouraged it with the full knowledge that this might occur, holding the risk preferable to . . . to the other. It shows what fools we become in our fancied wisdom, and how old Mother Nature refuses to be side-tracked. I'm afraid, child, that you have a thorny path confronting you. God only knows how it will end. All that you can do is to fight, fight grimly, to control your nature. In view of what you have told me about your reading, there is no need to say more. I only want you to understand this, dear: your daddy comprehends to the last farthing, and you will always find him ready and willing to assist you. Never fear to approach him, for he understands, Jean, he understands, you poor, unhappy kid."

I hugged him close. "I'll remember, daddy; but just now we have this other thing to consider."

"Ah," he said, and sat with wrinkled brows while I waited patiently, almost happy in the knowledge that another had taken my burden on his broad shoulders.

"You are quite sure you don't wish to marry him?" he asked at length.

"Please, daddy," I implored.

"All right, little one. I only desired to make quite sure. We won't suggest that way out again. I know just what to do, now, so run along to bed, and don't worry. Just leave it to daddy."

I was curetted a month later, and returned home, blooming, after two lazy weeks in hospital. Save father and a doctor who was his most intimate friend, none ever knew what had ailed me. Even the nurses by some means were kept in ignorance. How, I do not know; but doubtless doctors have their own methods of preserving secrets. Certainly this one had.

Master Guy was given his *congé* two nights after my return. He came to tea, and afterwards took me for the customary walk in the garden. The violets were dead, and the only scent on the air was the musty odour of rotting pine-needles. I permitted him to lead me to the seat, but repulsed him when he attempted to place his arm about my waist.

"You may come to the house as often as you please, Guy," I informed him, "but our intimacy must cease. This is our last stroll in the garden. If you come again, which I trust you won't, we'll spend the evening playing draughts or cards."

The boy gulped. "I love you, Jean."

"The more fool you," I commented callously.

"Don't you care for me at all?"

"I don't."

"Is that final?"

"Irrevocably so."

He rose, and kicked petulantly at the leg of the garden seat. "You're the most changeable little cat I've ever met."

I maintained a contemptuous silence.

"You slap my face when I put my arm round your waist; then you waylay me in the street, ask me to your house, and almost request me to make love to you; now, having led me on, you calmly tell me to go to hell."

"Well?"

He plumped on the seat beside me. "What's come over you, Jean? Tell me you're only fooling!"

"Don't paw me," I exclaimed, as again he strove to take me in his arms.

"Jean!"

"Don't touch me, you . . . you animal." And I ran inside.

"Well," inquired my father, as I entered his study. "I've sent Guy about his business."

"You don't regret it?"

"Regret it! I hate the little beast."

Father sighed. "Always take me into your confidence, Jean," he urged. "Remember that I understand."

"Father's a dear old sport," I confided to Jenny, as I nestled into bed by her side.

CHAPTER V

TWO NIGHTS LATER I first had the dream which has tormented me at irregular intervals since. The details vary, but the central figure remains the same, and the denouement is constant. What it betokens I have not been able to decide; nor have those to whom I have related it been able to furnish explanations which satisfy. As clearly as though it happened yesterday, the details of the initial vision are graven on the tablets of my memory.

I was seated on a package of merchandise which emitted a strange odour, pungent but not unpleasant. Surrounding me were boxes and bales, piled at random. Some leaned perilously, prevented from overturning by the pressure of those about them. In a corner were several crates of live birds, destined for the tables of those who could afford to purchase them. They looked parched and miserable, as though they had been deprived of water for days.

Before me was a quay, looking out to the ocean through rocky headlands, from which high ground swept up and down a forbidding coast. Crowds of men jostled on the quay, making difficult the task of those who carried baskets of oranges and olives from the ships to the sheds on shore. They had to force their way through the pressing throng. I saw Jews, with their fleshy noses and red, full lips; Arabs in their flowing robes; Phoenicians with the

stamp of the sea impressed on their bitten cheeks; Greeks
with their straight noses and upright carriage. But, after
a cursory survey of the heterogeneous array, my attention
was riveted on a Roman soldier who stood motionless at
the entrance to the busy quay. He was of fine stature, his
height exaggerated by the crest of scarlet feathers which
jutted upward from his open helm. A shining breastplate
protected his chest, and brazen greaves gleamed on his
thighs. At his right side hung a double-edged sword, and
on his left arm was strapped an ox-hide scutum edged with
polished iron. Its heel grounded in the dust, a pilum tipped
with a triangular point of steel overtopped his stately helm-
crest. I marked his hawk's-bill nose, his arrogant eye, his
lofty contempt of the motley throng about him. He stood
like a statue, deaf to the babel of tongues. Once he gazed
at me, met my glance, held it for a moment. He surveyed
me from head to foot with calm insolence, ultimately
bringing his eyes back to mine. For perhaps ten seconds
he stared at me without the slightest trace of emotion on
his visage. Then his gaze reverted to the sweating aliens
on the quay. I saw the silken muscles play in his arm as he
shifted his grip on the towering spear.

It must have been about the hour of dusk, but I had no
exact means of determining the time. The sun was out of
sight, and long shadows stretched from the heaps of merchandise. From the soldier's pilum came a thin black line
which passed across my foot. I felt no surprise when I
noted that the foot was encased in a tiny sandal whose
laces crossed on my instep. Slowly the shadows lost their
definity, merging into a blur which encompassed the whole
scene.

From the rear of the shed came a host of pigmies, clad in
mangy furs. They were barefoot, and in the hand of each

was a knife which shone dully in the half light. I watched them curiously, and felt an indefinable ache in my breast. It was not personal concern; a sixth sense informed me that no designs against my own person were meditated. I could not fathom their purpose; but somehow I knew that their action would affect me vitally. Onward they stole, their bare feet making no noise in the thick dust.

Suddenly I realised that their quarry was the Roman soldier. I tried to scream, but no sound issued from my parched throat. In desperation I leapt from my crate of merchandise and rushed forward, signalling frantically with my hands. I was too late! Like a pack of wolves harrying an unsuspecting goat the barbarians were upon my Roman, driving their knives into his back. He lurched forward to his knees, and drove his long spear backward over his shoulder, impaling one wretch on its keen triangle. Then he sprawled face downward on the ground, dyeing the brown dust crimson with his blood. Behind him lay a single assailant, curiously like a bear, writhing upon the steel point in his belly. The rest had fled as noiselessly as they had come.

I found myself wedged in the front circle of the crowd which gathered, staring with unbelieving eyes at the still form which a few minutes before had pulsed with such virile manhood. Then a Greek physician forced his way through the press, and unlaced the fallen man's breast-plate, baring him to the skin. There came a guttural babel from the onlookers, and I almost swooned at the sight. Before me lay no man, but a woman of noble proportions. Her skin gleamed like new ivory in the dusk. Her breasts, half flattened from her recumbent attitude, yet rose like crested mountains. Her wide eyes stared coldly into mine. I screamed, and woke with its echo in my ears.

Since that night the dream has recurred frequently. Its details vary, but substantially it remains the same. Sometimes it is a swarthy Carthaginian who stabs my Roman, sometimes it is a fanatical patriot from the marshes of Germany, sometimes it is a bearded Druid from the Tin Isles, sometimes it is the pack of skin-clad barbarians from I know not where. But always he is slain, and always in death he is transformed into a wide-hipped, white-skinned, full-breasted woman.

Who is this Amazon who haunts my dreams? By what trick of the sub-conscious has she come to play such a tremendous part in my sleeping hours? Is it a fantasy, a grotesque hallucination due to some unsuspected mental trauma; or is it a poignant memory from a long-vanished ancestor, transmitted through the ages by way of the germ-plasm? I do not know; nor are my confidants better informed. True, they make wordy explanations, smothered in a sea of technical jargon, but actually they are as much at a loss to explain the enigma as I.

I only know that in some mysterious manner we are related intimately, my Minerva and I; and sometimes I fear to sleep, lest again my heart shall be torn with the spectacle of her death. Strange woman of my dreams, how white your skin shines in the twilight of that ancient quay, and how nobly your breasts jut upward! Who are you? ; whence do you come? ; and whither do you go? — and I?

CHAPTER VI

My self-esteem had returned. Whether I was seeing myself in truer perspective, or whether familiarity was breeding contempt, is matter for argument; but I had ceased to regard myself as an outcast. I even evinced a tendency to exult at the knowledge that I differed radically from the girls whom I knew. It can be very satisfying to realise that one stands apart from the herd, gazing down upon it from an isolated peak. It matters not that the peak be sterile and uncomfortable. There is rare food for conceit in loneliness, and I gorged it to the full. Better tea and mutton in solitary state than champagne and turkey in a crowd. My roundness of limb returned. My cheeks were tinged with a delicate flush. I sang as I went about the house. The lanky Guy had been banished from remembrance, together with the distressing aftermath of my first adventure in love. I continued to study psychology with the approval of my father, and supplemented it with a brief incursion into Quain's Anatomy. Without question or criticism, daddy purchased any book which I sought, and soon the foundation of a substantial library reposed on shelves in my room. Naturally, grandmother was horrified at the nature of the books which I was absorbing so greedily, and lost no opportunity of nagging father about them.

"You ought to be ashamed of yourself," she would exclaim, "encouraging that precocious girl to read such trash." Whereat daddy would indulge that slow smile of his, and reply: "I have known thousands to be injured by ignorance, but I have not heard of a case where a person has been harmed by knowledge."

"Psychology," she would sniff, "there was no psychology in my day!"

"Quite so," father would agree, "nor were there motor cars, or wireless, or aeroplanes. The world has moved onward a trifle since you wore a bustle and screwed your waist into a diameter of six inches. We have reached a new generation with new concepts of life."

Though I had no inclination toward men, I liked to attract their attention; to know that their eyes were fixed admiringly on me. I wore my dresses outrageously short, and affected coloured garters which showed at each step. Despite the prevailing fashion of flesh, pink, snuff, and shrimp hose, I adhered religiously to black silk, having discovered that a sable hue enhances the contours of a woman's calf, thereby appealing to the male. Possibly I was the only girl in Katoomba who wore black stockings; but I doubt if another caused so many heads to turn after she had passed. From the corners of my eyes, and in street mirrors, I kept tally of those who threw a backward glance as I went by them. When a man stalked on without paying this tribute, I experienced a pang of disappointment. Still, I could take the unction to my soul that few proved remiss.

No longer did I worry over my apathetic hormones. Had a magician appeared, to proffer a magical draught to wake them to activity, I am certain that I would have declined the potion. My efforts to stimulate my femininity had resulted in the creation of an egoism which was proof against worldly buffets. To be myself was the big thing of life; that was the only objective worth striving after. My ego had been quickened from the stupor in which it had languished. I was I. What more to seek?

I was fifteen, and looked twenty, when my father's youngest brother and his wife came to spend a month with us. Harry was a man in his early thirties, blond and big. He had a beautiful straight nose, typically Greek in its absence of an indentation between the eyebrows. His mouth was large, but his teeth were remarkably white and even. His smile was an artist's dream. Gabrielle, his wife, was dark as myself, but lacked my colouring. Her cheeks were a pale olive, looming sallow through the heavy sheath of powder with which she habitually encrusted them. In physique, however, we flew to opposite poles. Where I was slim, she was built on heroic lines, almost deserving the adjective "stout." Her gross calves contrasted to their detriment with the slender curves of mine; and a tendency to bulkiness at the heel was not mitigated by the nude hose which she wore.

On the night of their arrival, Gabrielle and I were seated on a settee. At the opposite end of the room the brothers were gossiping. I saw Harry glance appraisingly from his wife's legs to mine. Idly I crossed my right leg over my left, watching him covertly. His eyes ceased to waver between us, and remained fixed steadily on the generous display. I indulged an inward chuckle; it appeared that even uncles were human. He insisted on kissing me good night when we retired to bed, uttering some nonsense about his pretty niece. But there was nothing avuncular in the pressure of his hot lips on mine. I caught my aunt watching him curiously.

At the end of a week he was my slave. He danced attendance on me, anticipated my needs at the meal table, ran my errands, and otherwise comported himself like a love-lorn ninny. My aunt was furious, and concealed her ire clumsily. Particularly did she writhe when he insisted upon his uncle's due of a bedtime kiss.

One night she came to my room, with a satin dressing-gown about her shoulders. Where it gaped, I caught glimpses of silk pyjamas. She looked even grosser than in her day dresses. Crossing to my bed, she perched herself on the counterpane at my feet, looking down at my dark features on the pillow.

"Jean," she said, "I want to have a good talk with you. How old are you, child?"

"Fifteen."

"Good God! I took you for twenty."

"People do."

"Fifteen! I'm not sure whether it makes it easier or more difficult. I want you to try to understand, dear; and you must never, never breathe a word to another soul of what I am about to say to you. Will you promise me that?"

"Why should I promise?"

"Because I ask you, Jean. I never dreamed that you were such a child; one would not suspect it. However, I think you are old enough to understand me; if you don't, say so."

"Understand what, auntie?" I asked meekly.

"What I am going to say to you. Oh! it is dreadfully difficult. I don't know how to begin. You must keep your uncle at a distance, Jean."

"Keep him at a distance!"

"Yes, for your own sake, for his sake, for my sake, for the sake of everyone." Her voice rose in crescendo as she enumerated the various sakes involved.

"But he is awfully nice to me, aunt."

"That's precisely where the danger lies. He's not a good man, dear; he does not mean you any good."

"What harm would he do me?"

She clasped her hands over her head, and rocked to and fro on the bed like a bereaved negress. "How in the name of heaven am I going to explain to this innocent chit?"

"What, is there to explain?"

"He has fallen in love with you. Now, do you understand? With you, his brother's child!"

"How gorgeous, auntie."

"Jean, Jean, surely at fifteen you can comprehend what I mean. Don't you understand?"

"Oh! yes, but surely an uncle is entitled to love his little niece."

The poor fool writhed in anguish, and I almost pitied her. "He doesn't love you as a niece, or even as a young girl. He loves you like . . . like he used to love me, like your father loved your mother, like you will love some good man in due course. He loves you like that, with the difference that his love is nasty, unhealthy, unclean."

"His breath is quite sweet, aunt. I thought unhealthy people had a bad breath. Sometimes I taste tobacco on his lips, but apart from that his breath is really nice."

"Good God," she breathed, "how can I save this poor Innocent? His breath sweet!" She laughed hysterically.

"I don't understand you, aunt."

"I know you don't, you poor child. I did not dream that such innocence was to be found in the world to-day. Fifteen! and you don't know what is involved when a married man — your own uncle — falls in love with you. Listen Jean! you know that when people marry they have babies?"

"Yes."

"Well, he desires to give you a baby."

"But we're not married."

"That's the tragedy of it. He will wreck your life, make you the scorn of honest people, prevent other men from marrying you."

"I think it would be nice to have a real baby. I'm too old for dolls."

"My God," she murmured again, and began to cry. When she had regained control of her emotions, she leaned across and seized my hand, stroking the arm with her fingers. "Jean," she whispered, "do you know where babies come from?"

"Jenny says they grow inside you."

"Do you know why they grow?"

"I think because . . . because God ordains it."

"No, because man ordains it."

"How wonderful!"

She relinquished the fight, imagining that I was too simple to comprehend what was known to most girls of much tenderer years than mine. "I'm afraid I can't make you understand, dear," she confessed glumly.

I smiled up at her. "I think I know what your trouble is, aunt."

"Do you, Jean?"

"Yes, your hormones are over-active."

"My what!" She almost shouted the word.

"Your hormones."

"What on earth are my hormones?"

"The feminine principle."

"What are you talking about?"

"Your hormones."

"Good God! are you mad?"

"I can't say, auntie. Grandmother thinks I am."

She crushed my hand till it hurt cruelly. "Either you are the biggest simpleton that ever walked the earth, or you are the most artful little devil alive. Which are you?"

"Neither. I am just your little niece — Jean."

"Are you?" she questioned grimly. "You are my little niece, Jean, are you? And what am I? Tell me that."

"You are my dear Aunt Gabrielle, striving to save me from the horrors of seduction; but your concern is more for yourself than for me. If it wasn't your husband who is making a fool of himself chasing a schoolgirl, you would stand by and watch me ruined with complacence. True, you might shed a few crocodile tears after the event, and perhaps read me a curtain lecture on my moral lapse, but you would derive great joy from commiserating with my father and narrating the horrible details to all the old cats in the neighbourhood."

"You little fiend!"

"Not at all. Only little Jean, auntie. Is there any more information which you desire?"

Her face was distorted with rage. Her veins, gorged with blood, stood out like lengths of cord. She flung my hand from her, and gazed at me like a basilisk. "I'll strangle you, you sly, purring devil," she flamed, extending her fingers like talons.

"If you attempt it, I'll scream, and then Uncle Harry will come in and pummel you."

"You fiend, you devil, you arch-hypocrite!"

"Your vocabulary is improving with practice, auntie; but I think it has developed enough for one night. Would you mind retiring? I feel sleepy."

"Oh, you wretch!"

"If you don't go I'll fling a shoe at you. Go back to Uncle Harry, and ask him to give you a baby."

She screamed and took hysterics on my bed, shrieking, yelling, and mouthing unintelligible phrases. So they found her when they burst in. There was father, cool and collected in striped pyjamas; Jenny, with her wonderful arms and bosom bursting from a tight nightdress of linen; Uncle Harry, with his trousers drawn over pyjamas of mauve silk; and grandmother in a lace cap and an old-fashioned nightgown of red flannel. They stared at Gabrielle, and thence inquiringly to me.

"What's the matter?" asked my father tersely.

"I don't know. Aunt Gabrielle came to my room and said Uncle Harry wanted to give me a baby. Then she screamed and threw a dingbat"

Father cast one quick, questioning glance at me, and began to shake the noisy hysteric into sensibility. The others acted according to their lights. Jenny giggled. Grandmother stared from me to the unhappy Harry. He flushed scarlet, stammered a denial, gazed appealingly at me, and then scowled at his wife, who was threshing her limbs and screaming horribly.

When the irate husband, aided by Jenny and grandmother, had escorted the subdued and tottering woman from the room, father crossed to the bed and surveyed me steadily. "What mischief have you been up to now, Jean?" he demanded.

"None, daddy."

"Was that true, what you said when we entered?"

"Quite true. She came here to inform me that Uncle Harry meant to seduce me, and seemed quite peeved when I did not understand what she meant. Then, when

I tried to tell her about her hormones, she carried on like that."

Without a word, he walked to the door, where he stood thoughtfully. Then he turned, came back to the bed, and kissed me softly on the forehead.

"God help you, Jean," he said sadly, and went out.

Uncle and Aunt had gone when I came down to breakfast next morning. I was not sorry. They were a tedious couple, devoid of humour.

CHAPTER VII

THREE NIGHTS IN succession the doctor who had rescued me from the consequences of my folly with Guy, came to the house and was locked in the study with father until long after midnight. I knew that I was the topic of conversation, and grew uneasy. What were they planning? A casual conversation might have no significance; but three successive nights suggested action of some kind. On the third night I crept to an attic window above the porch, listening to their farewell.

"We must decide on something, Murray," said my father.

"I agree with you. The case is serious. Let me see, I shall be free to-morrow after 9 p.m. Would it be too late if I dropped in then?"

"Come at any hour. I'll wait up. You'll find me in the study if it's one in the morning. I'll take a spirit lamp in, and we can brew a jug of toddy. Good night, Murray."

"Good night, Deslines."

To-morrow night! In the study! To decide a course of action! It was essential that I should be there to hear. In these days of freak surgery and burgeoning knowledge of the ductless glands, God knows what ordeal I might be subjected to. Assuredly I must be present at their conference. With this determination firmly fixed in mind, I felt asleep.

That night I dreamed again of my Roman soldier. He was stabbed in the back by a fanatical Gaul, whose features were identical with those of Dr. Murray. The backward cast of the pilum missed the assassin, who laughed hideously as he vanished into the gloom at the rear of the shed. The stark agony in the glazing eyes of the woman who lay dying at the feet of the Greek physician woke me. My pyjamas were drenched as though I had swallowed a sudorific, and I shivered as one with an ague. It was hours before I could compose myself to sleep.

During the day I spied out the study. The sole place for concealment was the window recess. Within it was a low lounge, and curtains screened it from the room. If I could manage to hide behind the lounge before father entered, there was but little chance of my presence being discovered. True, I must endure the ordeal of remaining many hours in my seclusion; but what was such a trivial discomfort, compared with the suspense and mental agony of waiting the outcome of their deliberations?

Just before dinner I entered the study and softly opened the window. Immediately the meal ended I donned a coat, took a book under my arm, and announced that I would stroll down to the School of Arts to select a novel. Father nodded acquiescence. I kissed him good night, grimaced at grandmother, and banged the front door behind me. It was the work of a minute to hide the book under a bush, toss my coat upon a hedge, and steal to the study window. Clambering in cautiously, I closed and latched the window, and laid on a rug behind the lounge, prepared for my vigil.

The luminous watch on my wrist revealed that father entered just half an hour later. He shut the door, glanced at the window, gave an involuntary nod when the motionless curtains disclosed that it was closed, and walked to the fireplace, where he stood with his shoulders against the mantel, staring into vacancy. Ten minutes later he sighed audibly, chose a book from his shelves, drew an easy chair up to the fire, and commenced reading.

Eight o'clock, nine o'clock came and went, and still Dr. Murray had not arrived. The cramps in my legs had long passed into pins and needles, and thence into numbness. I dared no more than to stretch them gently, lest the quick ears of my father should overhear, and this gentle motion was insufficient to keep my blood from stagnating. In vain I turned my toes upward and pinched my thighs. Despite the most desperate efforts a painful numbness developed.

At twenty minutes after ten there came a sharp rap at the study door, and Dr. Murray entered. "Sorry I'm so late," he apologised. "Old Mrs. Maidment had one of her chronic attacks of nothing-at-all, and kept me fussing round her for an hour and a half." He laughed ruefully. "She's easily my best pot-boiler, and I have to humour her. As she's one of the healthiest animals I've yet met, she should keep me in bridge money and tobacco for another twenty years."

He drew off his motoring gloves and greatcoat, tossing them through the curtains to the lounge. I thanked him mutely for the action, as the collar of the coat remained between the dangling curtains, creating a providential gap through which the faces of both men could be seen. He rubbed his hands briskly, and pulled a chair across to the fire.

"Have a cigar," invited father, dropping his book on the hearthrug.

"Thanks." He selected one with care, pinched it

between his thumb and forefinger, bit off the end, and lay back in his chair, puffing ecstatically. "Do you know, Deslines," he commented, "you're an admirable judge of a cigar."

"Damn the cigars," exclaimed father, with the nearest approach to irritability which I had observed in him. "Let us discuss what we are going to do about Jean."

Dr. Murray fingered his cigar thoughtfully, and licked a loose end of leaf into position. "I'm not going to weary you with technical speculations, Deslines," he said. "It is quite apart from the question to consider hormones, or the possible influence of particles of the adrenal cortex on somatic processes. Also, I must confess that I would not be a good tutor. They are questions for specialists, whereas I am a general practitioner. The great point is this: in many similar cases good results have followed the implantation of ovary tissue. Steinach has secured some remarkable successes. He also has experienced some disheartening failures. But the chance exists — and a good chance, too!"

"It would mean a trip to Europe?"

"I'm afraid so."

"And your opinion of the result?"

The doctor shrugged. "It would be on the lap of the gods; but, as I said, the chance is there."

"In my case, would you make the trip?"

"I would, most emphatically. The child is patently abnormal; and she might be transformed into a typically healthy woman. The cost means little to you, which perhaps is an important factor. It is a question of staking the time and expense against the possibility of her future happiness. In your shoes, I would not hesitate."

Father stared moodily into the fire. Suddenly he squared his shoulders, as one who has reached a momentous decision. "I'll do it, Murray. I'd do anything to save her from the terrible destiny which confronts her. Of course, you are aware that there is another possible complication?"

"No," replied Dr. Murray, looking up.

"Yes, her mother, the mental taint! Two alienists informed me that her mother was a paranoiac."

Murray nodded slowly. "I did not think you referred to that."

"The possibility always is there?"

"It always is there. Nevertheless, I think she is quite normal in that direction."

"I'm not so sure," murmured my father. "Sometimes she frightens me; she does such abominable things without rhyme or reason. She seems to extract unhallowed joy from inflicting pain. I don't mean physical pain, but mental. She makes her grandmother's life a hell on earth, and it is not so many weeks since she deliberately goaded into hysterics an aunt who had undertaken a most unpleasant duty on her behalf."

"H'm," commented the doctor, and took to examining his cigar.

"What do you think?" asked father.

"What I already have said. Catch the first practicable boat to Europe, have her psycho-analysed by a competent practitioner, and then try the ovary graft. If good does not result, at least you will have the satisfaction of knowing that you did your best. No man can do more than that, and it will safeguard you against the pricks of conscience."

"I'll do it," said father shortly. "Now, let us talk of something more pleasant."

It was 2 a.m. before the doctor left and daddy retired to his bed. It took me the best part of an hour to restore circulation to my cramped limbs, and I almost screamed with

pain as the blood began to function. Finally my legs ceased
to tingle, and I hobbled upstairs to my bedroom—but not
to sleep. Until Jenny clanged the dressing-bell at 7.30 I lay
thinking; thinking!

The psycho-analysis would be good fun. How I would
mystify the operator by relating imaginary dreams and
fictitious incidents! I would have the poor man distracted
by the end of a month. There also was the tremendous
field of transferred emotion. I would pretend to fall in love
with him, and refuse to be cured of the infatuation. I would
haunt him, both in his consulting-room and in his private
life. It presented almost infinite possibilities. I had no
fear of the psycho-analysis; but the grafting of the ovarian
tissue was quite another matter. Apart from the discomfiture attendant upon the anaesthetic, there was the grave
possibility that it might change me radically. What would
I be, when the foreign substance began to exert its influence? Rather, who would I be? Most certainly I would not
be Jean Deslines. Instead, I would be a kind of synthetic
product, operated by elements taken from another personality. Even my shape might alter. I might grow gross
of body, with limbs like Jenny's. I might develop the
Junoesque breasts of the transformed Roman soldier. I
might become fat, have to take to corsets, and overflow
them like my Aunt Gabrielle. I dared not risk the operation; I dared not risk it!

Yet, how was I to escape it? Too well did I appreciate
the irrevocable mind of my father. Slow to move, he was
irresistible when embarked on a chosen course. Being a
minor, I would have no option but to yield to his inflexible
will; I would be a helpless pawn in the game which he and
his medical accomplice intended playing. To attempt to flee
from my danger would be absurd. In these days of instant

communication, I could not retain my liberty for a month; the police would run me down implacably. In any case, I was not designed for the hardships attendant upon flight from a comfortable home.

What they contemplated was murder, as much murder as if my throat was to be cut; for did they not intend to destroy my identity by changing me into another personality?

Murder! the word suggested another avenue of escape. If I was to be murdered, would I not be justified in slaying my would-be slayer? Self-preservation, the sages declared, was the first law of Nature. And the statutes upheld the principle! The meanest wretch was vested with the right to defend his life against an assailant. Did I not come within the ambit of this ubiquitous law? Was I to stand by supinely, while my ego was murdered at the behest of a single man, whether that man were my father or another? He had entered the lists against me, bent on my destruction. So be it. He would discover that his intended victim possessed rights and intended to enforce them.

In this manner, cogitating on a sleepless bed, I sentenced my father to death. I loved him, after a fashion, and undoubtedly he had proved sympathetic in my tribulations. It would not be pleasant to snuff out the candle of his life. But what was the alternative? I sighed, as I realised that it was my father or I. One was fore-ordained to perish. It must not be I. The decision was made long before I went downstairs to breakfast.

"Jean," said father that evening, when I entered his study to kiss him good night, "how would you like a trip to Europe with me?"

"Are you going to Europe?"

"Yes. Would you like to come?"

"I don't know, daddy. Why are you going?"

"On business, and I'd like to take you with me."

"I don't know that I would like it. Travelling must be very uncomfortable, and there's not much to see really."

"Not much to see!" He gasped his astonishment.

"No. As far as I can gather, all cities are much the same. Some are larger, some dirtier, some wickeder, some soberer; but fundamentally they're all alike — a wilderness of buildings. It would not interest me very much to see Paris, or Berlin, or . . . or even Vienna."

He eyed me curiously. "Why Vienna particularly?"

I shrugged my shoulders "That's where they practise gland-grafts, isn't it?"

"I believe so. What made you mention it?"

"Dr. Murray."

"Dr. Murray!" The inflexion of his voice betrayed his amazement.

"Yes. He told me that you proposed taking me there for a gland-graft."

"Dr. Murray told you that?"

"Yes, daddy. He asked me not to say anything to you about it. And he . . . he tried to kiss me."

"Are you telling me the truth, Jean," he asked sternly.

"Why should I lie about it? I was not supposed to know anything about this trip until you just informed me. If Dr. Murray did not tell me, who did? You can answer that question for yourself, for only you know who was in the secret."

He sank his face into his hands. "Is all the world going insane?" he muttered. "Murray, of all men!"

I stood patiently till he looked up. "You say he tried to kiss you, Jean?"

"Yes, daddy."

50

"When?"

"Last night, about nine o'clock. I was out in the garden. He saw me as he came in the gate, and came across to me. We must have chatted for over an hour. Before he left me, he said that I was to go to Vienna for treatment. Then he ... he tried to kiss me; but I pushed him away."

Father groaned. "We shall leave for England early next month," he said decisively. "You can start making your arrangements."

CHAPTER VIII

Two NIGHTS LATER, about ten o'clock, father burst into my room without the formality of knocking. I was clad in pyjama trousers and a silk slip, preparing for bed.

"Come down to my study at once," he commanded. "As soon as I slip on some clothes."

"Damn the clothes! Chuck something over you, and come down at once."

Obediently I donned a dressing-gown, and followed him downstairs, where he opened the door of his study and pushed me in. Standing by the hearth was Dr. Murray, who greeted me with an angry look.

I knew that a storm was about to break, and experienced a momentary pang of fear; but almost immediately my confidence returned, and I indulged an inward giggle. The men looked so funny with their red faces and depressed brows.

"Tell me the truth about this damned business," thundered my father, for once losing his composure.

"What business?"

"Don't play the fool! You know as well as I what I'm alluding to. What was that cock-and-bull yarn you told me about Dr. Murray and yourself?"

"I told you everything, daddy."

"Did you? Well, now repeat it before Dr. Murray."

"What's the use? He knows all about it."

"I'm not so sure that he does."

"I'm sure, daddy. Look at the guilt in his face!"

"You shameless little devil," exclaimed the doctor, advancing toward me.

Father waved him back. "Is there the slightest element of truth in what I told you, Murray?"

"On my word of honour, it's an outrageous lie, a deliberate concoction to set us at enmity. I haven't seen the girl alone for months."

"Only what I have said before. Consider it for yourself. What time did he say he'd be here last Wednesday night?"

"Nine o'clock."

"What time did he arrive?"

"Ten o'clock; half-past; I don't know exactly."

"Ah! what time did I say he came into the garden?" Father stared queerly at the doctor. "Nine o'clock," he replied slowly.

"How long did I say he remained talking with me?"

"Over an hour, you told me."

"Quite so! He was to see you at nine, and arrived about half-past ten. On the other hand, without any knowledge of your arrangements, I told you that he came to me at nine, and remained over an hour. The times appear to fit without discrepancy. Perhaps Dr. Murray can do more than protest and call me ugly names; perhaps he can explain!"

"I can explain easily enough," averred the doctor, fixing me with a bleak look," but I don't know that I care to do so. If you choose to think that of me, Deslines, after our lifetime's friendship, all I can do is to express my regret at your lack of trust, and leave you. As for that unprincipled little wretch, if I owned her I'd . . . I'd turn her up and spank her handsomely."

"You're not likely to own me," I flashed. "I hate you, you meddlesome interloper. I suppose you consider that you can own any girl whom you endeavour to kiss behind her father's back. Well, you can't own me; and you can't kiss me, either. So don't attempt it again, Dr. Murray!"

"With your permission, Mr. Deslines, I'll retire," said the doctor stiffly, gathering up his gloves and coat.

"Wait, for God's sake, wait!" enjoined my father. "Murray, you are about the only friend I possess; and you can imagine the shock this has been to me. I know Jean is an unprincipled liar, when she chooses; but there are features about this . . . this episode, which are calculated to make any man doubtful. Please help me out, old man. I'm not condemning you; I'm striving to ascertain the truth. Have a little patience with a distracted father."

Without replying, the doctor laid down his belongings and stood impassively; but his eyes did not waver from mine and his face was a fiery red.

"Will you explain, Murray, to oblige me?"

"Certainly I will, when you put it like that. I arranged to be here at nine o'clock; that is admitted. I would have arrived on time had I not received a call to attend Mrs. Maidment shortly after eight-thirty. I was with the old lady till a few minutes after ten. Then I drove here, parked my car against the kerbing, and came straight to your study. The rest you know."

"Suppose we all go down to see Mrs. Maidment, to verify this . . . this very circumstantial tale," I suggested.

As I had anticipated, he stood firmly on his dignity, and refused to acquiesce. "I regret that I cannot annoy my patients by transforming them into witnesses before a tribunal of investigation," he declared.

I sneered. "Naturally," I said significantly.

"Be quiet, Jean," ordered my father. "You refuse to grant permission to have your story verified by Mrs. Maidment," he asked, turning to the doctor.

"I refuse emphatically and unequivocally. You asked for my explanation, and I have given it. Beyond that I refuse to go."

"Wise little man," I confided to the ceiling.

"What do you mean" he snapped.

"I? Oh! nothing. But of course there is always the possibility that Mrs. Maidment may have forgotten about your call, which would be very awkward for you, wouldn't it?"

"You malicious little liar!"

"How gentlemanly of you, and how strictly in consonance with that professional dignity behind which you are attempting to shield yourself!"

"Cease, both of you," cried my father. "How can I decide while you hurl insults at one another like that?"

Dr. Murray bridled. "If you think that I am going to stand here like a schoolboy while you bring me to judgment, you're greatly mistaken, Deslines. I have told you exactly what occurred, and have given my word of honour that my statement is true. More I refuse to do, and I can assure you that there's not another man on earth for whom I'd have gone quite that far. I am sorry that it has come to this pass between us; but I have no intention of kneeling in the dust."

"You have told me the truth, Murray?" asked my father, looking him in the eye.

"I have told you the truth, and the whole truth."

"But the times, man! Were they a coincidence?"

"Either that, or carefully fabricated."

"How did she know about the proposed operation?"

"I cannot say. How did she know about the times? I can only conclude that by some means she overheard our conversation."

"How could she have overheard?"

"I have no more idea than you; but it seems fairly evident to me that she did. Have I ever lied to you, to your knowledge?"

"No."

"Has she?"

"A thousand times."

"Then, who is the more credible witness: a lifelong friend who has always proved faithful and reliable, or a neurotic youngster with a possible mental taint, who makes a practice of deceiving you?"

Father sighed. "I ask your pardon, Murray. I know you will forgive an old friend labouring under a load which often threatens to become unbearable."

"Let us forget it," advised the doctor, and they shook hands.

"Go to bed, Jean," ordered father quietly.

I listened outside the door for a few minutes. "Humour her, Deslines," said the doctor. "Don't believe a word she tells you, however circumstantial her story; and for God's' sake get her across to Vienna with the least possible delay. In the meanwhile, humour her, and keep her out of mischief to the best of your ability."

"Good night, Murray, and many thanks, old chap."

"Good night, old man — and God help you!"

I slipped away in time, and was up the stairs before they entered the hall.

An hour later I stole back to the study. Father was

huddled in his easy chair, gazing despondently into the fire. Without speaking, I crept round behind him and sat on his knee, throwing my arms about his neck and hiding my face in his breast. He stroked my hair gently.

"Jean," he said softly, at length, "why did you lie to me about Dr. Murray?"

"Because I hate him."

"Why should you hate him?"

"Because he desires to murder my identity with his horrid grafts."

"It is for your own good, child."

"Maybe, but it will destroy me. I shall be different. My personality will have vanished."

"Are you so anxious to retain your present personality?"

"I am, daddy. It is myself. If I change it, I shall cease to exist as I am; I shall be someone else. How would you like to submerge your identity, particularly if you did not know just what you were to be transformed into?"

He smiled sadly. "I know it is a frightful problem, Jean; but it is almost certain that your new personality will be a tremendous improvement on that which you possess at present. Have you considered that aspect?"

"I have, daddy, and I don't want to change. I want to be myself, to retain my ego. Need we go to Europe?"

"I'm afraid we must."

"Even if I am opposed to it?"

"Yes, dear, even if you are opposed to it."

"You are determined?"

"Quite determined, Jean. We shall leave early next month."

I sprang from his lap, and stood before him with outstretched arms. "Daddy!"

"Yes, Jean."

"Dr. Murray said, if he owned me, he would thrash me. Why don't you thrash me, to see if it would do any good?"

"Don't be stupid. You're too old to thrash."

"I'm not, I'm not! See, here's your walking-stick. Beat me with it; beat me hard!"

"Go to bed, child, and don't talk nonsense."

With a quick jerk I stripped off my pyjama trousers, standing before him nude to mid-thighs, clad only in my dangling pyjama coat. "Beat me, daddy; beat me hard; beat-me till the blood flows! I want you to!"

"Put your clothes on at once!"

"Not till you thrash me."

"Put your clothes on immediately, and stop this nonsense, or I'll come and dress you, myself. How dare you carry on like that?"

With, a sigh of resignation I drew the trousers on again, and meekly kissed him good night. But I lay awake long, wondering why he would not thrash me. I had longed for him to strike me on my bare legs; ardently I had longed for it. I knew that I would have found pleasure in the strokes, particularly if the blood had come. How different it all might have been, had he but taken me at my word, and trounced me soundly with the cane I proffered!

I cried myself to sleep, for now I was certain that I would need to kill daddy to preserve my identity.

CHAPTER IX

I SPENT THE following week at the library, reading all I could unearth on poisons. My chief discovery was the disconcerting fact that they all left traces for an analyst to find. With some a finger-nail or a single hair was all that was needed for detection. It became obvious that poisons must be eliminated from my plans. There also was the fact that most of them caused agonising deaths. I had no desire to make poor daddy suffer; it was bad enough to have to eliminate him. Still, one's identity must be preserved at any cost.

More violent methods complicated the problem by necessitating disposal of the corpse. In vain I racked my brain through sleepless nights. I could devise no method of death that would appear to have resulted from natural or accidental causes; nor could I formulate a feasible plan of disposing of a body. I was in despair. The days were going, and only a bare fortnight remained before we were to sail. Had I been religious, I would have prayed for some escape from my dilemma. I must have grown morbid through continually brooding on death and the disposal of a body; for, one day, thinking intently as I walked, I turned unconsciously down the road beside the Memorial Hospital, and found myself at the gates of the cemetery.

Why I had taken that particular road is not clear; it must have been due to subconscious guidance.

Finding myself at the gate, it was but natural that I should enter the grounds. There I stumbled across a mound of freshly turned earth, and found inspiration. All became clear in a twinkling; my problem was solved!

In an obscure portion of the cemetery I found a rough shed, in which were stored gravedigger's tools. Picks, mattocks, spades, and shovels were racked neatly along the walls, their handles stained a pale yellow by the decomposed sandstone which comprised the soil of the cemetery. It only remained to develop the details of my plan, and I would be safe — safe, with my father out of the way and my ego secure from annihilation. For the first time for many days I slept soundly, but I dreamed. Again I sat on the bale of merchandise, watching the Roman sentry. Silently, round the corner of the shed, came the fur-clad barbarians. I saw one drive his glistening knife into the soldier's back. I recognised him at once. Save for his diminutive stature, he was Dr. Murray in person. As the Roman plunged forward to his knees, as always, he drove his pilum backward over his shoulder, impaling not his assassin but the man immediately behind him. The wretch shrieked as the triangular blade bit into his vitals, and turned his face in my direction. It was my father! Rushing to the scene, I watched him expire, my agony equal to his own. Then I turned my eyes to the dead soldier, and forgot everything else as I marvelled at her clear skin and magnificent form. I awoke sweating, to wonder why Dr. Murray had stabbed Minerva, and why Minerva had slain my father. What strange trick of fate was it, which bound us all so irrevocably to the dead woman who masqueraded as a man and was but the figment of a dream?

Next morning I scanned the death column of the *Herald*

eagerly, but without success. It was three days before my patience was rewarded by discovery of a notice that an old man had died at Leura on the previous day. Turning to the burial notices, I ascertained that he was to be buried in the local cemetery that afternoon.

The time had come; that night I must put my plan into operation. There was much to do; but the initial step was to canvass the details thoroughly. Nothing must be left to chance, nothing omitted. A single false move would place me in the hands of the law, and the best I might anticipate was imprisonment for the term of my natural life. Every detail must be dovetailed into a perfect whole.

I thought it out, step by step; and it all interlocked. The sole difficulty lay in cajoling my father to drive me to the cemetery by night in the light car. It must be the light car, because I could not drive the big Rolls Royce. How was I to persuade him?

Dr. Murray, father, myself, and Minerva, why were we associated in that distressing dream? Dr. Murray. . . . Dr. Murray. . . . What was it that Dr. Murray had said, when he left the house after that ridiculous inquisition in father's study? "Humour her, Deslines . . . humour her!"

Ah! the answer was supplied. Father would humour me! It was the irony of Fate that the humouring was to result in his own death; but necessity knows no law, and a personality was at stake. Self-preservation was Nature's primal rule.

"You are not enjoying your dinner, Jean," commented my father, as he noted the manner in which I was hacking my food to shreds. I glanced at my plate, to find it a confused mass of chopped meat and mashed vegetables.

I pushed it from me petulantly. "I'm not hungry. How can I enjoy my food, when poor old Mr. Cummings is lying out there in the cold?"

Father stared. "Who is Mr. Cummings, and where is he lying?"

"Out there, in the cemetery. He died yesterday, and they buried him to-day."

"You mustn't let such things trouble you, Jean. Death comes to us all in time. It is but a little thing, when all is said."

"Would you be afraid to die, daddy?"

He laughed. "I'm not particularly anxious to die; but I don't think it would trouble me unduly when my time came."

"Is that honest?"

"Perfectly honest, child. Now let us talk of something a little more pleasant. Your grandmother is horrified."

"Are you really horrified, grandmother?"

She scowled. "Naturally I am. Why must you prate of such things at the dinner table?"

"I won't any more, grannie.'"

"Don't call me 'grannie.'"

"Very well, grandmother."

It was after ten when grandmother retired to bed; but I dared not attempt to put my plan into operation while she was downstairs. I had to wait with such patience as I could muster. The suspense was dreadful. Committing a murder is not easy when one lacks practice. In common with most things, a technique has to be evolved. Facility rarely attends an initial venture in any demesne.

After having allowed ample time for grandmother to complete her simple toilet and fall asleep, I entered the study. There was nothing to fear from Jenny, who habitually retired to rest at nine, and would sleep through the crack of doom.

Father glanced up as I entered. "I thought you had gone to bed, Jean," he remarked.

"I could not sleep to-night, daddy, with poor old Mr. Cummings out there in the cold. He must be so lonely. Take me to see him."

His mouth gaped. "Take you to see him?"

"Yes. Take me out in the car. I want to lay a flower on his grave."

This is sheer nonsense, child. We can't go there tonight. After breakfast to-morrow, if you still wish to go, we'll drive out. Run along to bed now, like daddy's good little girl."

"It's no use, daddy. I must go to-night. Fancy him, all alone, out there in the cold ground. I must go!"

He glanced at his watch. "It's nearly eleven o'clock. We'd be mad to drive there now. Why not leave it till the morning, in the daylight?"

"Because I must go to-night. It almost seems that he expects me."

He gazed at me swiftly. "Very well, Jean, if you're determined. I'll get the car."

"Thank you, daddy. Don't take the Rolls; let us use the little Singer."

"The big car would be far more comfortable. Why not use it?"

"It's too big, and . . . and it has a *spare seat!* He might ride home with us. We don't want him roaming about the house to-night, do we? Please use the small car."

"All right," he said gruffly. "Get a warm coat on, while I run it out in front."

Five minutes later we were seated in the car, purring smoothly along the Bathurst Road in the direction of the cemetery. I passed my hand under the cushion, and felt the handle of the hatchet which I had concealed there during the afternoon. Everything was proceeding according to schedule!

We pulled up at the gate of the cemetery, and went inside on foot. The headstones gleamed eerily in the wan light of the stars, and I could hear my heart hammering against my ribs. It was an unpleasant duty which confronted me!

We experienced a little difficulty in discovering the grave; but eventually we stood beside it. The loose, sandy soil was heaped into a sizeable mound, and two bedraggled wreaths rested on its crest.

As my father stooped idly forward to finger the withered flowers, I drove the hatchet into his skull. He fell without a groan and lay motionless, his head resting on the wreath with which he had been toying. Soon it grew crimson.

Stifling a sob, I hastened to the tool-shed and returned with a long-handled shovel. In half an hour I had excavated a hole some four feet in depth. Another half-hour, and the mound was restored to its original shape; but it seemed to stand higher. Beneath it lay the mortal remains of my father, with the two wreaths — one white and one red — resting on his breast, and the bloody hatchet by his side.

My task concluded, panic overcame me. I raced to the gate; there to remember that I had left the shovel beside the doubly tenanted grave. Summoning the last reserve of my courage, I crept back to the scene, secured the implement, restored it to its place in the shed, and again ran at top speed to the car. For possibly fifteen minutes I crouched on the seat, appalled at the enormity of the crime which I had committed.

Slowly my self-control returned, fortified by the knowledge that the deed had been necessary. Was I not justified in defending my personality against its intending murderer? It was merely that I had struck first. One of us had to perish. I was vindicated by the natural law of self-preservation.

I reached home safely, and restored the car to the garage without being disturbed. But I did not feel safe until I was in bed. Secure in the embrace of the blankets, I reviewed the night's happenings, and realised that I had accomplished my horrible task well. Father had vanished. There would be a nine days' wonder, a more or less protracted search by the police, and a gradual acceptance of the *status quo*. Who would think to dig up one dead man in the search for another? The problem of disposing of the body had been solved beyond peradventure!

Above all, I was saved. I would be permitted to retain my identity. My ego was secure. I had overcome my intending assassins.

Nevertheless, I did not sleep soundly that night. I think I loved daddy.

CHAPTER X

Toward morning I sank into a sound sleep, from which I was awakened by Jenny. "Lor'! there's a terrible fuss about your father, Jean," she said. "His bed ain't been slept in, and they can't find no trace of him anywhere."

"That's strange," I commented. "I never knew daddy to do a thing like that before. I wonder where he is?"

"We're all wondering," she replied, and went out to aid in the search.

My next visitor was my grandmother. "Where's your father?" she inquired.

"How can I say? Jenny tells me his bed was not slept in, and that he can't be found."

"Did you see him last night, after I went to bed?"

"Just for a moment, while I said good night. He was reading in the study."

Thinking it over, after she had departed, I questioned the wisdom of concealing the motor ride. More serious investigation would result when the police were called in; and it was possible that father and I had been seen in the little Singer. It was scarcely eleven when we passed through the railway crossing, and curious eyes must have been abroad at that comparatively early hour. Thank goodness, it was only grandmother! When the police came I would volunteer information about the car.

66

I had not long to wait. Grandmother, after having fussed about the house and telephoned all father's friends, rang up the police station and notified the constable in charge. Within half an hour a sergeant and a plain-clothes officer arrived at the front door, and Jenny and grandmother were subjected to a searching cross-examination. They had to cool their heels while I had my bath and dressed.

When I entered the drawing-room, grandmother and Jenny were seated on a settee, side by side. The latter evidently had been crying, for her lids were red and she was nibbling nervously at a handkerchief. Grandmother wore her grimmest countenance, and scowled at everybody in turn.

"Where have you been?" she snapped.

"Having a bath, grannie."

"Don't call me grannie, you impudent child!"

I sighed resignedly for the benefit of the police. "I beg your pardon, grandmother," I said meekly, and felt that I had won the first move in the game. If grandmother remarked on my omission to mention the motor drive to her, my assertion would be strengthened by her querulous hostility.

"Miss Deslines," said the sergeant, who was standing by the mantel, "you know your rather is missing?"

"So the maid informed me."

"I suppose you have no idea where he might be?" I shook my head. "Not the slightest."

"To your knowledge, he has never spent a night away from home without first having announced his intention"

"Never."

"I understand you were the last to see him last night."

"I think I was."

"Just tell me what happened."

"I went into his study to kiss him good night."

"What was he doing?"

"Reading."

"Did he speak?"

"Yes. He asked me if I was tired. I replied 'No.' He then asked if I would care for a drive with him in one of the cars."

"Ah! And you replied . . . ?"

"I said I was not anxious to go; but, if he desired it, I would."

"You did not tell *me* that," interposed grandmother angrily.

"Oh! grannie, how can you say such a thing? Don't you remember how you were surprised that we used the little Singer; you said it was strange we did not take the big sedan on such a cold night."

"You abominable little liar! Once again, don't address me as 'grannie'"

"I beg your pardon, grandmother. I'll try to remember, though it is difficult after I have been calling you 'grannie' all my life."

"You say you did tell your grandmother" (he accented the word) "about the motor ride?" said the sergeant.

"I did, sir."

"H'm! now tell me about it."

"There's very little to tell. While I was getting my coat, father brought the small car round to the front. We drove down the Bathurst Road as far as Wentworth Falls, and returned. I went straight up to bed, leaving father to put the car in the garage."

"And you have not seen him since?"

"No, sir."

"Did he seem cheerful — in his customary spirits?"

I hesitated. "No-o, not exactly."

"Try and tell me how he differed from usual."

"He was moody, and disinclined to talk. I spoke to him several times on the trip, and he did not reply. Neither of us said a word on the journey home."

"Why not?"

"Well, he seemed averse to talking, so I did not worry him."

"Did he appear to have anything on his mind?"

"I cannot say, sergeant. All I noticed was that he was moody, and did not wish to talk."

"Was he often like that?"

"I never knew him so before."

"I think that's about all I wish to ask you, Miss Deslines. Oh! do you know anything, or of anything, that might explain his disappearance?"

"No."

"And you have no idea where he is now, or where he might be?"

"No, sergeant."

"Or if anything serious has happened to him?"

I extracted my handkerchief, and began to cry. "Do you think anything serious has happened to poor daddy?" I sobbed. "Oh, my God, poor, dear old daddy!"

"I suppose you know that the little hypocrite is telling you a pack of lies," exclaimed my grandmother, unable to contain herself any longer.

"No," replied the sergeant, viewing her curiously: "What lies has she told?"

"About the car."

"I can't see what object she would have in concocting a story of that nature."

"Why did she not tell me?"

"She says that she did."

Grandmother jumped erect. "And I say that she did nothing of the kind."

"Did you tell your grandmother?" asked the sergeant quietly.

I lifted a tear-stained face, and looked at him sadly. "Yes, sergeant. I told her all about it this morning. She said I was telling a lie, because daddy would have used the sedan."

"Why didn't he take the sedan?"

"I don't know. He simply asked me to go in the car. I was surprised, myself, when I found he had taken the Singer."

"Did you express your surprise to him?"

"No. I never question daddy's actions. I love him . . . and we are . . . were . . . are great pals." I broke down and sobbed aloud.

He laid his hand gently on my head. "Don't give way, Miss Deslines; keep your courage up. It will all come right. We'll bring your daddy home safe and sound; I'm convinced of that."

I clutched at his arm. "Please bring him back to me, sergeant; bring him back to me. Don't leave me alone in the house with grannie — I mean, grandmother: Oh! don't, please, sergeant! Can't you stay here while that other gentleman finds daddy? Oh, daddy, daddy, where are you? Get him, sergeant, please get him. But don't leave me alone with grannie — grandmother!"

"Don't you worry, miss," he said. "I'll find your daddy. I'll start looking for him at once. He's not very far away. We'll have him home to tea."

Grandmother left her seat and crossed to us, and I shrank in simulated alarm as she approached. "Don't beat me now, grannie — grandmother; please don't beat me just now. I'll never, never call you 'grannie' again; I promise that I won't. I could not bear to be beaten while poor daddy . . . poor daddy . . . poor daddy, dear old daddy. . . ." I crouched in my chair and gazed at her with streaming eyes.

She stared in genuine amazement. "Have you taken leave of your senses entirely?"

"Yes, grannie — grandmother," I quavered. "If you think so, I must have done so. Please don't beat me; don't hit me with daddy's stick. I'll do anything you wish; only don't thrash me! I'll deny that daddy and I went in the car, if it will please you. I'll tell the sergeant now. I'll do anything you like, as long as you aren't unkind."

"It's a pity you don't get thrashed a bit more," she exclaimed, goaded beyond endurance.

As the sergeant scratched his head thoughtfully, I cast myself at his feet, clutching at them frantically. "I'll say it was a lie," I shrieked. "I'll tell him we did not go in the car. How was I to know you would object to my telling him? Oh, my God! how was I to know? Don't hurt me; don't beat me with the walking-stick. We did not go in the car; we didn't! We walked, sergeant; we just strolled down to Wentworth Falls and back, indeed we did. It was all a lie about the car, a wicked lie to get grannie — grand-mother into trouble. I'm a wicked abominable liar. Don't beat me, gran — grandmother, Oh, daddy, daddy!"

The sergeant vouchsafed grandmother a malevolent look, and lifted me in his arms like a babe. "Calm yourself, Miss Deslines," he advised, "there is nothing to worry about. He placed me gently on the settee beside Jenny, and turned to grandmother. "Have I your promise that you won't interfere with the child to-day," he asked grimly.

"It may interest you to know that I have never laid a hand on her in my life," she snapped.

"Quite so. But have I your assurance that nothing of the kind will occur to-day"

"You have not! She's an unprincipled little liar. I can't fathom what's in her mind, but she is bent on mischief of some sort. It's like your impertinence to ask *me* to promise that I won't thrash her. I tell you that I've never laid a hand on her in my life." She flounced out of the room in a towering rage, slamming the door behind her.

"Please don't leave me, sergeant," I whispered, catching his hand.

"I'm sorry, but we must go now," he said, looking at me pityingly. "If anyone attempts to interfere with you, leave the house and come to the police station. That's the best I can do for you. Don't be afraid. Just run across to the station; we'll protect you." He laid his hand on my head again, and left the house, followed by the detective.

"That blasted old tyrant has got the poor little devil completely cowed," I heard him remark as they walked through the front door. "Good God, did you ever meet such a vicious old beast? She must knock her about damnably."

"Snotty old swine," agreed the detective. "I wonder what her game is, denying that the kid told her about the car ride?"

Jenny burst into a fit of giggling after the police had departed. She was accustomed to my efforts to humiliate grandmother, and suspected nothing more ulterior on this occasion.

CHAPTER XI

IT WAS A nine days' wonder, and then the world settled down to forget that daddy ever had lived. Within a month people ceased to inquire if we had received tidings of him, and by the end of two months his name rarely was heard, even at home. Human beings are like that: they come, and they live, and they go and are forgotten. The forgetting is the least tedious, for people are naturally adept at it.

The only persons in the whole world who bore his memory in mind were myself and Dr. Murray. I often thought of him, after I had gone to bed, wondering if he slept comfortably in the quiet cemetery. It was a lonely place; but he always had been a solitary man with an ingrained disdain of social life. There was none to annoy him there, or disturb his thoughts. He would not have to say, "Keep quiet, child!" or "I wish you would not sweep the hall for an hour or two, Jenny!" Those who were near him would be quiet enough! Then I would turn on my side, double my legs up until my knees almost touched my chin, and fall asleep. I was certain that daddy was happy.

Dr. Murray called on the day following the discovery of daddy's disappearance. I heard him talking to grandmother downstairs. His even voice and the querulous tones of the old woman made a queer duet; but, strive as I would, I could not distinguish their words. The con-

versation reached me as a murmur, now soft and subdued
as the doctor spoke, then harsh and shrill as grandmother
took up the tale. The alternation sounded so funny that
I had to laugh. I could picture them in my mind. Both
devoid of humour, they would be standing face to face in
the hall. Grandmother's angular height and the doctor's
chubby shortness would bring their eyes level. His brows
would be depressed until his eyes were half hidden, and
hers uplifted into a hundred wrinkles which vanished
into her ridiculous grey fringe. Of course, he would be
getting unexpurgated details of my remarkable behaviour
during the inquisition by the police. He would be listening avidly, and thinking hard. I did not underrate him; he
was a dangerous man! I feared him more than the others
combined. The police, without prompting, would be easy
to delude, and I flattered myself that I had spiked my
grandmother's artillery effectively. Jenny's dull stupidity
was a barrier against which the cleverest detective would
hurl his arts in vain. The sole weak link in my armour was
Dr. Murray, with his plump form, his chubby cheeks, and
his cool brain. It was in his power to cause me considerable annoyance. A contest of wits seemed inevitable,
and it behoved me to get in the first blow . . .

Half an hour later Jenny came to my room to say that
Dr. Murray wished to speak to me. I first was inclined to
refuse, to send a message by the girl that I was too dis-
tressed to see him; but reflection disclosed that such an
attitude merely would be postponing the inevitable. He was
not the man to be disposed of easily, and possibly now was
the best time to grant the interview. If I were driven hard,
I could take refuge in hysterics, an escape that would be
denied me after the shock of daddy's disappearance had
been given time to dissipate.

He was waiting in the lounge, standing by a small palm. "Good morning, Jean," he said affably.

I bowed my acknowledgment.

"This is an extraordinary business," he proceeded, watching me intently.

"Dreadful."

"Of course, you have no idea where your father is?"

"No."

"I understand that you were the last person who saw him."

"Yes."

"He took you for a motor trip to . . . where was it?"

"Wentworth Falls."

"And came home with you?"

"Yes."

"And you did not see him again?"

He smiled crookedly. "You're not very discursive."

"Why should I be?"

"Quite so. I realise that caution is praiseworthy."

I gazed at him steadily. "Might I ask what you mean by that innuendo?"

He shrugged. "Nothing. I was only trying to imagine some reason for your reticence."

"Why should I discuss daddy with a stranger?"

"I'm scarcely that, am I?"

"You're worse. A stranger would respect my grief by not intruding at such a juncture. You're careless how you wound in your efforts to satisfy your vulgar curiosity."

He recoiled, coloured, and then smiled contemptuously. "Your father was my best friend," he said quietly. "I intend to ascertain what has become of him. To avert any misunderstanding in the future, I may as well inform you that you cannot force me to lose my temper or my self-control; nor can you induce me to relinquish the search. I think that little explanation should clear the air a trifle."

"So you're going to search for daddy, Dr. Murray?"

"I am."

"How delighted the police will be to secure such an invaluable ally."

"Doubtless. Particularly when I throw a little professional light on yesterday's comedy."

"I am so dense that I don't understand the reference."

"Oh, no, you're not! It seems that you gulled that stupid sergeant properly, perhaps more thoroughly than your unfortunate grandmother realises. It will be my unpleasant duty to make certain things very clear to him."

Such as . . . ?"

"Such as your propensity to tell vicious lies, accompanied by a little light on your ability as an actress."

"Nature designed you for the task, doctor. You're the ideal sneak."

He smiled, a trifle sourly. "My temper is proof against your arts."

"Wonderful man!"

"I'm glad you think so. It confirms my own opinion."

I walked to the door. "With your permission, Dr. Murray, I'll retire. Go and talk to Jenny; she is certain to be impressed by your talents. Men of your type appeal to the half-witted. Jenny is an excellent conversationalist, as she is a good listener. One word of advice: don't scare her with bogy-man threats, as she is exceedingly nervous."

I knocked the palm-stand over as I marched disdainfully to the door, knowing that the crash would bring grandmother past-haste to the lounge. We passed each other in the hall. A minute later the drone of their duet floated to me, and I knew that the doctor would be occupied for at least ten minutes. It was the work of a few seconds to dash to the telephone, muffle the bell with my hand, and ring the police station.

"Sergeant," I whispered huskily, "please come to the house at once. This is Jean Deslines speaking. There has been an important development. Hurry, for God's sake. Don't stop on the road; delay might mean anything."

I congratulated myself on the final sentence as I rang off, again taking care to muffle the bell. It was so deliciously vague, so easy of explanation, yet so potent. It was unlikely that he would delay, even if hailed by Dr. Murray as their cars crossed.

I was waiting at the gate when the police car drove up, for Dr. Murray was still in the lounge with grandmother. Laying a finger on my lips, I beckoned the sergeant and led the way behind a hedge.

"Sergeant," I asked, with my voice trembling, "do you think anything could have happened to poor daddy? I'm so frightened; oh! I'm so frightened. They're in there now, whispering together."

"Who's in there?"

"Dr. Murray and grandmother. Oh, God, what have they done to daddy?"

He lifted one eyebrow, and scratched vigorously behind his ear. "Dr. Murray!" he ejaculated. "You have nothing to fear from Dr. Murray."

I commenced to cry.

"Look here, miss," he said gently, "this business has upset you completely. Why don't you lie down and have a good sleep? That's what you want. Dr. Murray's all right; it's just that your nerves are a bit off."

I wiped my eyes with a handkerchief, and smiled at him wanly. "If all men were like you, sergeant, this would be a good world to live in; but they're not. Oh! if you only knew!"

He adhered to his role of soothing me. "Suppose you tell me all about it, Miss Deslines. Then I'll be able to take steps to fix things."

"Thank you, sergeant; and thank God for one honest man in the world, one strong man to help a defenceless girl in her hour of trouble!"

He squared his shoulders, and twirled his moustache. "Tell me all about it, Miss Deslines."

I glanced apprehensively about me, and then stood beside him, holding his band and nestling against him. "Dr. Murray came to the house about an hour ago, and was closeted in the lounge with grannie — you don't mind my calling her 'grannie,' do you, sergeant? You see, I've called her that all my life."

Call her whatever you like, miss," he replied, squeezing my hand paternally. You were saying that Dr. Murray was in the lounge with your grannie?"

"Yes, they were there for a long time — half an hour, three-quarters of an hour, I don't know how long."

"Yes?"

"Then grannie came out, and sent me in to Dr. Murray, saying that, he wished to speak to me. I went without hesitation, because . . . because he always had pretended to be daddy's best friend." I sobbed.

"There, there, Miss Deslines, don't give way. What happened?"

"He said that I'd acted abominably, in telling you about the motor trip with daddy when grannie wished it kept secret."

The sergeant screwed one corner of his mouth half up

his cheek, and squinted in amazement. "Dr. Murray said that," he gasped.

"Yes, sergeant. And he told me that I was to get in touch with you at once, and say I had told you a lie. I refused, and he began to threaten. He reminded me that he was a doctor, and that his word would carry tremendous influence. If I didn't deny the motor trip, he would call on you personally and tell you that I was — let me try to think of his exact words — oh, yes, I remember! — that I was in the habit of telling vicious lies, and was — I forget the actual word — some sort of an actress."

The sergeant stared at me with wide eyes. "You're quite sure that you're not imagining things, Miss Deslines? You're sure Dr. Murray said that?"

I sighed. "Unfortunately, I'm only too sure, sergeant. When I refused to lie to you, he called grannie in and they threatened to thrash me within an. inch of my life. Dr. Murray tried to grab me; but I was too quick for him and got away. I knocked granule's palm over and broke the pot as I dodged him. She'll beat me for that, I know. What am I to do, sergeant; what am I to do?"

He stood silently, surveying me steadily.

"Daddy and I did drive to Wentworth Falls, sergeant. Truly, we did."

"I know that. You were seen at the level crossing. Look here, miss, why doesn't your grannie want me to know about the motor trip?"

"I haven't the slightest idea. I only know that for some reason she doesn't want it known. Oh! if you only knew how cruel she can be. And now I'm all alone; and poor daddy . . . poor daddy . . . what have they done with him?"

"I know all about your grandmother," said the perplexed sergeant, "but I think you're wrong about Dr.

79

Murray; I've known him a long time. Besides, why should he be in collusion with your grandmother over this mysterious car business?"

"I don't know," I replied wearily. "They were forever whispering to one another behind daddy's back. It's been going on for months. If I went near them, Dr. Murray would begin speaking in his ordinary voice, and say: 'I don't think you have anything to worry about, Mrs. Evans; it's only a cold,' or something like that, evidently to make me think they had been discussing her health. It happened that way several times in the last couple of months."

"Let us go up to the house," said the sergeant thoughtfully. "I'm positive you are astray about Dr. Murray; but we'll see them now."

"No, no," I cried in alarm. "She'd kill me if she thought I had brought you here like this. You must go alone. Let her think you dropped in casually. I could not go with you; I'm too scared of her. You don't know what she would do after you had gone; she'd beat me almost to death. Oh! please, sergeant, don't take me in with you; please don't!"

"All right, all right," he exclaimed testily. "Sneak up to your bedroom, and I'll go to the front door. Don't you worry, miss. I'll just drop in casually and straighten things up for you."

I chuckled gleefully as I fled to the rear of the house. While it was patent that at present he thought my charge against the doctor was the outcome of hysteria, it was almost certain that the doctor's statements would be disbelieved, and that my version would be accepted implicitly before the forthcoming interview terminated. I bade fair to spike the doctor's guns as effectively as those of my grandmother.

Within five minutes I was summoned to the lounge. Grandmother was seated in a corner, with the doctor standing beside her. The sergeant, looking very grim, was facing them.

"Now, Dr. Murray," he said," would you mind repeating that before this young lady?"

"Certainly," said the doctor easily. "I told you that you could not rely on a single statement which emanated from Miss Deslines. She is an inveterate liar of a most malicious order. Her grandmother is aware of the fact; so is — or was, God knows what has become of him — her father. He and I frequently discussed his daughter's unfortunate characteristic. It troubled him greatly."

"Do you know what she has told me about her father's disappearance?" inquired the sergeant.

"Substantially. Mrs. Evans explained what took place."

"And you suggest that she lied?"

"I do, most emphatically."

"About what?"

"About the car journey. I am inclined to think it was a fabrication. If her father took her to Wentworth Falls that night, why did she not tell her grandmother? Plainly it was an afterthought, prepared for your edification."

"For what reason?"

The doctor shook his head slowly. "I can't imagine; but there is a deep scheme underlying it somewhere."

"Would it surprise you, doctor, to learn that we have corroborative evidence of the car journey from an independent quarter?"

"It is rather surprising to me; but it does not alter the position. It merely reverses matters. In that case she wilfully deceived her grandmother about it, which is the same thing. Why was such an important fact suppressed at the outset?"

"I can't say," said the sergeant shortly. "The young lady says she did tell her grandmother."

She did nothing of the kind," snapped grandmother.

"Did you tell your grandmother?" asked the sergeant quietly, turning to me.

"I did, sir."

"You abominable little liar," she exploded.

"If you will permit me, sergeant," interposed the doctor. "I have studied this young lady's case from early childhood. She is queer mentally, and takes a malicious delight in telling unnecessary lies, particularly those calculated to make other persons uncomfortable or embarrassed. On the other hand, I can assure you that Mrs. Evans may be believed implicitly. I would stake my professional reputation on her trustworthiness."

The sergeant frowned at the ceiling for a space. "Thank you, doctor," he said at length in a thick voice.

"I trust I've made myself clear?"

"Admirably so. You've made many things clear. I'm very much obliged. I was quite in a fog, but you've cleared it up."

The doctor could not resist the impulse to flash a glance of triumph in my direction. I could have hugged him for the weakness when I noted that it had been observed by the watchful sergeant.

I was waiting by the hedge when he came out. "What do they intend?" I sobbed, hanging on his arm. "There's something I can't understand going on. What . . . what if they intend that I should disappear like poor daddy?"

"I wouldn't have credited it," he said, "if I hadn't heard it with my own ears. I would have laughed at the bare idea of Dr. Murray's being in anything crooked. I can't see a foot in front of me yet; but I will, by God! I will before I've finished."

I clung to him. "I'm terrified, sergeant."

He stroked my head gently. "Look here, miss! Don't you ever breathe a word about having spoken to me. Do you understand?"

"Yes," I whispered.

"And another thing: if either of them offers to lay a hand on you, bolt into the street and then claim the protection of the first person you meet. Ask him to take you to the police station. I'll see that you're protected."

"Thank you, sergeant," I murmured, and kissed him on the lips.

CHAPTER XII

THE MONTHS CAME and went, and the lilac season arrived. The scented florets spangled the trees, impregnating the air with their breath. Clusters of the bloom stood in a vase on my window-sill, that I might delight in their beauty by day, and inhale their fragrance as the night air drifted in. I always loved lilac.

One morning, when the sun peeped into my room, and insects buzzed about the scented bloom on the casement ledge, I thought of daddy, lonely and neglected in the distant cemetery. He had shared my passion for lilac, and now he lay where it was denied to his eyes. It was possible that its scent might be able to penetrate the glebe and touch his nostrils. Intrigued with the thought, I hastened to the bathroom, stood for a few seconds under the shower, and slipped my clothes on. Half an hour later I was in the cemetery with a bunch of lilac in my hand.

It was the first time that I had visited it since that dreadful night, and I shuddered involuntarily when at length I stood beside the mound which hid more than the rest of the world knew. Either the earth had consolidated much, or my imagination had exaggerated the height of the tumulus, for it now was comparatively flat. The relatives of its legitimate tenant had erected a sandstone slab at its head, on which a marble tablet set forth his virtues and the dates of his birth and death.

Across the path, a woman was praying beside a newly turned heap of earth. Its pathetic absence of length disclosed that its occupant was a child. She kept lifting a handkerchief to her eyes, and once I heard her sobbing aloud. I wonder why people weep over their dead?

Turning my eyes to my father's grave, I fell into thought. Could his gaze pierce the yellow earth, to see me standing there with my floral offering? If so, did he understand that I had struck without malice, purely in self-defence? One might harbour resentment against him who had slain wantonly; but no reasonable person—and daddy had, been eminently reasonable—could protest against obedience to the first law of Nature.

"I'm sorry that it had to be, daddy," I whispered, and cast my flower above him. Perhaps he smiled in his sleep as I did so. He was a man of infinite understanding.

From the grave I went to the tool-shed. As before, a row of implements was racked neatly against the wall. Among them was a long-handled shovel, its point slightly blunted by use. Was it the self-same shovel that I had employed in my nocturnal labour? I presumed that it was. There were not so many graves dug in Katoomba that the life of shovels would be limited, and only a few months had elapsed since daddy fell asleep. I fingered its stained handle, speculating on the important part it bad played in my life. Were I but to use it purposively for a brief while, what a wave of excitement would sweep the community! There would be policemen and detectives, hosts of newspaper reporters, Dr. Murray with triumph in his pale eyes, grandmother with a grimmer scowl than ever, my sergeant with frank amazement on his countenance, and Jenny with her stupid face puckered into wrinkles of awe, all gathered about me and the poor bones I had disinterred. It was truly wonderful, when one considered it dispassionately, what turmoil a simple shovel was able to occasion. It could aid in the saving of a personality, or set the world into throes. One would not suspect its potency, when gazing without understanding at its worn point and discoloured handle.

A young rabbit, with its ridiculous tail shining white in the early sun, hopped to a tiny hillock, and sat making its toilet. Its great brown eyes were soft and pensive. Altogether it made an appealing picture, and I stood watching it with a smile. Trustfulness always appeals to me. As I watched its antics, there came a sharp report from my left, and the little creature leapt high in the air, to fall in a grotesque heap and wriggle its limbs feebly. It struggled desperately to its feet, strove to run, and then pitched on its side, motionless. At the same instant two boys came running, one of whom bore a light rifle in his hand.

I felt the tears hot on my cheeks, and dashed to the little victim, clutching it to my breast. I pressed its warm fur against my face, caressed its silken ears with my fingers. But the heart no longer pulsed; my efforts were useless; it was dead.

Laughing with glee, its murderers came to me. "Not a bad shot, from that distance," commenced he with the rifle, stretching out his hand for the broken body.

"You little beast," I exclaimed, "how dared you shoot the innocent little thing?"

He giggled. "Hand it over," he commanded. "It's mine."

"Go away from me."

"You give me my rabbit."

I hugged it to me. "I won't."

His companion had crept behind me, and with a sudden snatch swept the rabbit from my grasp. The boys fled in company, shouting derisively.

The woman, who had been praying beside her dead, appeared at my side. "Don't cry, dear," she begged.

"It was so tiny."

"So was my little one."

"And so warm."

"Was it warmer than she?"

"And its hair was so soft."

"Not so soft as hers."

"And it was killed so suddenly."

"Ah! she lingered in agony for days."

We left the cemetery in company, our hands twined about each other's waists. At the gate of the Memorial Hospital she kissed me good-bye, and turned toward Leura.

In front of the Drill Hall I came upon Dr. Murray, changing a wheel on his car. The flat tyre on that which was resting against the mudguard betrayed that he had sustained a puncture.

"Good morning, doctor," I said blandly.

He ignored me.

"Punctures seem to be a craze with you."

He screwed the nuts home.

"The last time we met, you were trying to puncture my reputation. You seem to have met with better success this morning,'

He lifted sombre eyes. "A wheel has a conscience."

"How considerate of it! Have you convinced the sergeant yet?"

He stared at me curiously. "I'm convinced that you are destined to wind up on the gallows."

"For murdering you?"

"Possibly. I've little doubt you'd welcome the chance."

"They'd never hang me for it, little man. Any jury would bring in a finding of justifiable insecticide. They would commercialise me — stick a gaudy label on my back and take me round to rid the world of mites such as you. I'd be the vogue, advertised in the papers, with illustrations of fat little men, devoid of brains, falling dead at my approach."

"I promised you that I would keep my temper," he said evenly, and set about screwing the discarded wheel into the clamp at the rear of his car. I watched him scrub his hands with a piece of cotton waste, rub them on a tuft of dewy grass, and wipe them carefully on a second piece of waste. In silence he entered the car, and set the engine purring.

"Aren't you going to offer me a lift?" I inquired.

"I am not."

"Wise little man! Never take risks with potential insecticide."

He drove away, but I had the satisfaction of noting that his face was red.

"Where have you been?" asked grandmother tartly, as I entered the breakfast-room.

"Mourning a rabbit, and pulverising an insect". She stared at me.

"You see, it is the lilac season."

She lifted her hands helplessly.

CHAPTER XIII

A GREAT SHOCK was in store for me. My grandmother, doubtless acting on the suggestion of my evil genius, Dr. Murray, made application to the courts for an administrator to control daddy's estate, and the appointment of a guardian for myself. After a little delay, Dr. Murray was chosen to administer the estate, and I found myself saddled with dual guardians in himself and my grandmother, appointed *durante minoratate*. I consulted a solicitor, and learned that my guardians possessed the power of parents. I was completely in their hands until I attained the age of twenty-one.

I soon discovered, in what manner they intended to exercise their new authority, for I was summoned to a consultation in the lounge on the night following the enaction of the decree which had delivered me into their power. The grim scowl on grandmother's face, and the unholy triumph which flickered in the eyes of the stolid doctor, warned me that I must guard my every action and weigh each word I uttered. I had offended them both too seriously to hope for mercy or consideration. It was unlikely that they would resist the impulse to end my freedom.

"Jean," said the doctor," I presume you know the reason of this interview?"

"Yes."

"Have you anything to say?"

I lifted my brows. "What should I have to say?"

"I thought that possibly you might have some suggestions to put forward."

"None."

"Very well, we have."

"Naturally."

"Naturally, as you remark," he said ironically. "We consider that you have been running wild far too long, and—"

"Can't we eliminate the sermon?" I broke in. "Believe me, I know by heart all the platitudes which you are about to inflict on me. I know how shockingly wicked and disrespectful to my elders I am; and how I have worried my affectionate grandmother; and how I have read books calculated to make her fringe curl, instead of poring over nice, moral tales about brainless dolts devoid of red corpuscles. Let us cut out the moralities, guardian, and get down to what grandmother wouldn't dream of styling tin-tacks."

He preserved his serenity. "I'm inclined to agree with you, Jean. It would be useless to offer good advice, or to expect you to conduct yourself like a normal person. We have no desire to resort to harsh measures, but your activities must be curbed. How far we will be forced to go depends upon yourself."

"And if I'm tractable?"

"Then we'll get along nicely."

I studied my shoe. "Doctor," I said at length, meeting his faded eyes, "would it not simplify matters greatly if you stated your intentions regarding myself?"

"It is a fair request," he admitted. "First, you are to be sent to a boarding-school. While you are there, I shall make arrangements for a locum, so that I can leave my practice and take you with me to Europe."

I drew a quick breath. "To Europe! I suppose that means Vienna?"

He nodded gravely. "It means Vienna, Jean."

I had feared it from the outset. Now that I was completely in his power, the little fiend was determined to carry out his hare-brained plan of an ovary-tissue graft. After all my tribulations, and my heroic elimination of daddy in defence of my identity, I was to be led to the slaughter like a lamb by this phlegmatic little man whom chance had endowed with a parent's authority. If ever my wits were to serve me, now was the time. I could not hope to effect the disappearance of a second guardian without mishap. My only ally was guile. If it should fail me, all would be lost. The first move obviously was to temporise; the more time I won, the better would be my chances of success. I must discover Murray's weakness. Every man possessed a faulty link in his suit of mail, which made him vulnerable. My problem was to find the defective link.

"I realise that I am in your hands, doctor," I said meekly. "I have no desire for this operation; but I am willing to bow to your decision. The fact that it was daddy's wish influences me greatly. I am ready to go to school when you say I must go, and I am ready to accompany you to Europe.

I can say no more. May I go to bed now? I am tired."

"Just let me say this, before you go," he insisted quietly. "I have had a long discussion with your grandmother. We will not interfere in the slightest degree with your personal habits. You may retire, or rise, at any hour you please. You may choose your own wearing apparel. Within reason you may decide your own amusements. You may read any books that you wish. Those are matters for you, and in them you will be a free agent — always within reason, as I said previously. On the other hand, we are determined to order your life in certain directions. You will be subjected to discipline in specific matters which I need not detail, as you are as well aware of them as we. They include proper schooling and the simple little operation — quite devoid of danger — which will correct your abnormality. Now that you understand the position, you may retire to your bed or ·do just what pleases you."

"I'm not a fool, doctor. I know when I encounter an authority which is unyielding. You've made your attitude clear, and considering everything, it is not unfair. Will you now allow me to define mine?"

He nodded, with his eyes fixed gravely on mine.

"I know that I've been troublesome. Perhaps it was due to absence of proper control. I don't know. As henceforward I'm to know the bit, for my own sake I prefer a snaffle to a curb. Having no choice in the matter, I'm prepared to knuckle down to control. Your commands and those of grandmother will be obeyed, if not willingly, at least cheerfully." I laughed sheepishly. "If I'm a good child, will you call it pax?"

"Gladly."

"Will you shake hands on it?"

"With pleasure." He extended his hand, and we gripped hard.

"And you, grandmother! Will you kiss and make it up, if I promise not to annoy you in future?"

For answer she turned her wrinkled cheek, and I dutifully pecked at it with my lips.

In my room I changed into pyjamas, threw a dressing-gown over my shoulders, lit a cigarette, turned on the electric radiator, and thought! My grandmother would be simple. Her mentality was low. She lacked initiative. She was devoid of the requisite force of character to dominate me. Dr. Murray, however, was a vastly different proposition. He was cold, determined, and admirably restrained. He loomed like a monolith, hard on every side. Yet common sense told me that he must possess some weakness. There is a flaw in the hardest stone, a fault in the strongest chain. The difficulty lies in detecting it! What was the little doctor's weakness, and how was I to discover it? In vain I dissected him. The mental effort only served to exaggerate his invulnerability. Threats would prove futile. Personal violence would be impossible in the face of his watchfulness. Hysterics and tears would break like ripples on the rock of his professional lack of sympathy. I must find his hidden weakness. What was it?

Over my second cigarette I gained an idea. What was the weakness of every man? — Sex! Why should my implacable guardian be immune from the chronic affection of his fellows? Was it even probable that he was immune? Could not my steel strike fire from his flint? Hitherto, he had seen me at my worst. He viewed me as an irresponsible hoyden, a mischievous liar, and a pervert. But was that estimate irrevocable? He had the scientific mind, and it was unlikely that any of his concepts would be fixed. Such men only hold ideas as transitory substitutes for the truth which will come later. They formulate, or accept, theories to enable them to pick their steps in a mad world; but at best they know them to be theories, which must be kept plastic. They are ready to change their views, modify them radically, or even fly to the opposite pole. Always Truth marches ahead of them, though they hope to overtake her on the morrow.

Yes, I reflected, it was improbable that Dr. Murray's views on anything, even on myself, were petrified. His life's training was against dogmatism. Despite himself, it might be possible to compel him to amend, or perhaps recast entirely, his opinion of me.

My first essay, I decided, would be directed against the unstable ramparts of sex! He was between forty and fifty, a dangerous age. True, he possessed a wife; but that factor was immaterial. It might delay fruition of my plans; it would not inhibit them. The ancient description fitted his wife excellently: she was fair, fat and forty, a dowdy piece, with lank hair, full cheeks, and dark pouches under her porcine eyes; unattractive physically, and ossified mentally. She would prove an ineffective buckler against my youth, good looks, and agile wits.

During the ensuing few weeks I studied my guardian minutely. I was careful to concede unprotesting obedience to my grandmother, coupled with meek deference to himself. My conduct was irreproachable. I even consulted him before I purchased books.

Grandmother was both amazed and delighted. "It only shows what a little firmness will do," I overheard her confiding to the doctor.

He shook his head doubtfully. "I'm frankly astonished," he admitted, "but it is early to prophesy. It may be just a passing phase, or. . . ."

"Or what?" she inquired, as he hesitated.

"Or a scheme."

"I don't think it is that."

"Perhaps not; but I don't intend to be caught napping."

That night I resolved to play my next card. His doubt was encouraging. It was something to have broken through his former inveteracy. Despite himself, the training of a life was operating to my advantage. He was incapable of sclerosis of thought.

On his next visit, I deliberately stayed up. Half an hour after her usual bedtime grandmother admitted defeat and left us, yawning prodigiously. The doctor and I were left together in the little lounge. A cheerful fire of coke glowed on the hearth, painting golden tones on the single palm that drooped in a corner. The light transmitted through the silk cover of the electric globe was almost cathedral. From without came the whisper of the night-wind in the pines, varied by a spasmodic rattling of the window in its frame. The cat, a huge, unsexed creature, purred on the hearth rug, at intervals stretching his paws lazily.

For five minutes nothing was said; but sly glances into the mirror above the mantel revealed that he was watching me intently.

"Ah," I sighed at length, "this is heavenly."

"It certainly is cosy."

"So warm and languorous."

He looked at his watch. "By Jove! I had no idea it was so late. I must be going. Anyhow, it is time good little girls were in bed."

"Don't go yet, please. I just couldn't leave this fire."

"Stay as long as you like, Jean; but I have a wife at home, and patients to attend in the morning."

"Just another ten minutes."

"Why do you wish me to stay?"

"I don't know; but somehow I like to see you there. You look so strong and capable. One has a feeling of security when you're near."

He laughed. "I did not think I conveyed the impression

of strength. I'm under no delusions about my size and lack of muscular development."

"Pshaw! Those are the prerogatives of an elephant."

He extended his arms. "I'm rather undersized, you must admit."

"So was Napoleon. Is bulk the test of a man?"

"I suppose it isn't."

"Well, don't disturb my dreams with nonsense," I reproved lazily, and stretched my legs outward to the blaze until my skirt was drawn well above my knees. In the mirror I saw his eyes take fire.

"A short while since, you were not unduly keen on my presence," he commented.

I turned my eyes to his. "Wasn't I, guardian?"

"If you were, you managed to conceal the fact fairly successfully."

"That's scarcely the same thing, is it?"

"Now, what this devil do you mean by that?"

"The first blind man was Adam," I murmured, "and men have been blind ever since."

"What are you talking about, Jean?"

I rose and crossed to the settee where he was seated, standing before him. "I suppose you imagined that I hated you?"

His eyes stared into mine unwaveringly. "I suspected it more than once," he said drily.

Suddenly I kissed him full on the mouth, and ran from the room, evading his frantic clutch. In the security of my bedroom I heard him come to the foot of the stairs, and return to the lounge. It was a full hour before he went. I knew that he had been waiting my return, and hugged my pillow in ecstasy. I had found the joint in his armour!

CHAPTER XIV

I DID NOT see Dr. Murray for over a week, and viewed his defection as auspicious. If he were angered with me, undoubtedly he would have been at pains to call and express his reproof; such was his nature. His absence betokened that he was pondering the position, and I founded my hopes on the proverb that he who hesitates is lost. While he wrestled with his problem, I exploited the hours to conciliate my grandmother. I obeyed her behests without grumbling; went out of my way to serve her; performed numerous petty duties unbidden; all of which gave her pleasure. She was overjoyed with the transformation.

"I can't imagine what has come over you, Jean," she remarked one day. "You've developed into a most lovable girl. I hope you intend to keep it up."

"I'll do my best, grandmother," I replied. "Since poor daddy left us I've been doing considerable thinking, and I realise what a little beast I've been in the past. I owe much to you and Dr. Murray, which I can only repay by making your task of guardianship easy. He's a dear man, and you're a dear, too!"

I hugged her impulsively, and she actually blushed. She always was an undiscriminating fool! So far as she was concerned, there would have been little need to purchase her good offices with hypocrisy; but I had to tread most warily in my seduction of the doctor. If I had warmed to him, and continued to treat his co-guardian with disrespect, he certainly would have suspected my genuineness. He was a cold person, with a disconcertingly worldly mind. My altered conduct toward my grandmother was excellent corroborative evidence of my reformation—a powerful ally in the task of undermining his preconceptions. I meant to leave no stone unturned in my fight to preserve my identity.

Ultimately, as was inevitable, Dr. Murray arrived to dinner one night. I preserved a discreet silence during the meal, contenting myself with monosyllabic replies to such questions as were addressed to me. I avoided looking at our guest, and managed to blush twice when he spoke to me, first having assured myself that my grandmother's attention was directed elsewhere.

At the conclusion of the meal I pleaded a headache and retired to my bedroom, leaving my guardians alone. I resolutely refused to meet the doctor's eyes, adopting the simple expedient of holding a handkerchief to my forehead as I said good night.

I was not surprised when he called again next evening. We were in the lounge, grandmother was ensconced in an easy chair, and I was sitting on the rug at her feet with my head on her knee. I saw the pleased surprise in the doctor's face as he noted our intimate attitude. He little dreamed that I had calculated on his visit, and that the tableau had been carefully posed for the occasion. I jumped up hastily as he entered, and sank demurely into a chair.

As before, grandmother permitted herself to be outstayed, and retired. My effort to accompany her was frustrated by the doctor, who declared that he wished to speak to me.

"I'm rather tired, doctor," I pleaded. "I did not sleep too well last night. My head was troubling me. I really think I ought to go to bed now."

"Display a little courtesy," he joked. "You cannot both desert a guest like that."

"It won't harm you to sit up a little longer, Jean," said grandmother. "I can't keep my eyes open. Entertain the doctor, dear."

"As your guardian, I bid you to remain," he ordered with a smile. I obeyed meekly, twisting my hands nervously and gazing everywhere but at him. The fish had nibbled, and I did not intend to frighten it by striking too soon.

We must have sat in silence for several minutes. He cleared his throat noisily several times; but I stared intently at the fire. "Jean," he said at length.

I did not reply.

"Jean!"

"Yes." I still gazed at the fire.

"I want to speak to you."

"Yes?"

"Look at me. How can I talk while you keep your face averted like that?"

I looked up with my cheeks stained red. "What do you wish to say?" I whispered.

He coughed uneasily. "Last time . . . that is to say, on the last occasion that I was here, you . . . er . . . you remember what occurred as we parted?"

I nodded, and took to fidgeting with my hands.

He drew up his chair beside me. "Your conduct was somewhat amazing. Don't you think so?"

"I suppose so," I breathed, and made a sudden dash for the door.

He caught me with ease, and stood holding me about

the waist, I could feel his ridiculous heart hammering through my dress, and he was breathing thickly.

"Don't," I gasped. "Please, don't!" and wriggled from his arm.

Watching me warily, lest I should escape, he tugged the settee across to the fire. "Sit down," he ordered. I obeyed, and he sat beside me, tugging at his trousers to prevent their knees from bagging.

"Why did you kiss me, Jean?" he demanded.

"I . . . Oh! I don't know. It was just a . . . a joke. You are my guardian, you know," I added hastily.

"Only your guardian," he queried, his breath hot on my cheek.

"No, oh God! no!" I cried, and flung myself on his breast, burying my face between the lapels of his coat. He crushed me to him vehemently. His breath came and went in quick gasps. I felt him shivering violently. Suddenly he was smothering me with kisses, and emitting queer, inarticulate sounds.

"Do you love me, Jean?"

I strained against him.

"Since . . . since when?"

I lifted my head and looked into his eyes, holding his face between my hands. "Always, I think, always. Oh, my dear!" I pressed my lips to his, and he drank their wine hungrily.

"Once you hated me," he urged, thirsty for a denial.

"Never, never!"

"Then why did you treat me so cruelly?"

"Because . . . because you persisted in treating me as a child. Because you ignored me. Because . . . because . . . Oh! there were a thousand reasons, you strong, blind, innocent man."

He thought for a moment. "That was why you said that

Adam was the first blind man, and men have been blind ever since?"

I covered my face with my fingers. "Don't remind me of that, or I'll hate you. I blush every time I think of it."

He set to kissing me again. It was horrid; but one needs must pay the ransom of one's identity! I can see him now, his pale eyes burning with strange fires and his florid cheeks redder than Nature had made them. He was a tempestuous little man when the safety-valve was unscrewed. I had not suspected the existence of such deeps under his outward calm. In truth I had uncovered the flaw in his harness. It was long after midnight when I succeeded in driving him from the house.

He became a regular visitor, concocting excuses to deceive grandmother. She, poor simple soul, entertained no suspicions, and made him welcome. I submitted to his kisses, but steadfastly refused more intimate favours. He languished; he burned; he implored; but I was unyielding. I appreciated the value of deferred sweets. I had no intention of allowing myself to cloy his palate. For what he received, I meant to extract the full price; it included elimination of the boarding-school and abandonment of the trip to Vienna.

"Jean," he said, nearly a month after my bogus confession of love, "I have been talking seriously with your grandmother. We are in complete agreement that a remarkable change has come over you."

I ogled him through downcast lashes.

"She cannot explain the change. . . ."

"Can you?" I asked provokingly.

He kissed me. "You and I possess certain inside knowledge which is denied to your grandmother. However, she appreciates the improvement, and we have decided that there is now no occasion to send you to boarding-school."

I sat on his knee and flung my arms about his neck. "You sweet man! how can I thank you for that?"

"Jean!" he flamed.

"Don't spoil everything," I pleaded, breaking from his grasp. "Please don't!"

He had not mentioned the Vienna operation; and I was too wise to broach it myself. All concessions must emanate from him. My position would be weakened tremendously if I sued for favours. I must play my cards with care, patiently awaiting the hour when trumps would be dealt me in full measure. Of my ability to triumph I had no doubts. Given that you know an opponent's weakness, while he remained ignorant of yours, the end is as inevitable as the succession of the seasons — provided the play is not ruined by a clumsy move. I was not likely to fail. In this grotesque contest I had adopted an invariable rule: when in doubt, don't!

Each day witnessed my arch-enemy deeper in the toils. The lust to possess me was undermining his self-control. I doubt if he would have married me, had such a contingency been possible, for his scientific mind was at work subconsciously throughout the episode. I am convinced that vague doubts troubled him; but nightly they were consumed in the fire of his passion, leaving his mind vacant for love to riot untrammelled. Many a fool has ignited the grass in a paddock, to discover the flames beyond his control. So he burned, and panted, and embraced me; but ever I held him at a distance, denying the logical outcome of our liaison; and ever his desire expanded, burning the barriers of caution, duty, and habit in a holocaust which threatened ultimately to destroy himself.

By the end of the second month my task had assumed desperate proportions. He was a man distraught. Complete possession of my body had become a mania. With the waters of Tantalus an inch from his lips, he was unable to restrain his ardour. Several times he had attempted to force me. And still the subject of Vienna had not been mentioned!

I perceived that I must adopt another plan of campaign. His scientific training was creating unconscious inhibitions; he still contemplated the dreaded operation!

Or was he intrigued with the prospect of the long journey, on which he and I would be thrown together without danger of interruption?

I realised my peril, and decided to act. I went to the police station and interviewed my sergeant, twiddling my thumbs and devastating him with languishing glances.

"Sergeant," I whispered, after a calculated silence, "I am in terrible danger."

He gaped at me.

"You know that the court appointed my grandmother and Dr. Murray my joint guardians?"

He nodded.

"Grandmother has been splendid; she is completely changed. She no longer thrashes me, and has been quite ... quite human and affectionate. But the doctor — " I broke off and lifted a flushed face. "Oh! how can I tell you? It's so horrible. H ... he is making love to me." I buried my face in my hands, and sobbed.

"Making love to you?" The sergeant gasped his astonishment.

"Yes, sergeant," I whispered. "He kisses me, and has tried ... tried to ... to ... Oh, my God! how can I tell a man?"

His face became grim. "Do you mean to tell me that your guardian is misusing his position to force his attentions on you?"

"Just that, sergeant. He's horrible . . . and so . . . so insistent. I'm afraid to be left alone with him for a minute; and . . . and I lock my door every night."

He rose, and began to pace up and down his tiny office. "You realise exactly what you are saying?" he inquired.

"Only too well," I affirmed sadly.

He tortured his forehead into innumerable wrinkles, and thought hard. "If there was any corroborative evidence . . ." he exclaimed.

"It could be obtained readily enough. The little beast is certain to come to-night. He comes every night, now. If you and another witness could only hide somewhere, where you could see and overhear, you would soon be convinced."

"It's most irregular," he protested.

"Consider my terrible danger, sergeant. As my guardian, the man has such shocking privileges."

"I'll risk it," he muttered. Then, to himself, but quite audibly: "Poor little devil! She needs protection."

After the evening meal I met the pliant sergeant at the hedge. He was accompanied by a young constable. I smuggled them to the veranda, where they posted themselves by the window and began their vigil.

The night went, as most nights had gone for weeks past. About ten grandmother kissed me, apologised to Dr. Murray, and retired to bed. I was sunk in an easy chair, and Dr. Murray occupied the settee.

For a few minutes we retained our respective positions, and no word was spoken.

"Jean," he called suddenly. "Come over here, darling."

I turned my head. "Please speak a little louder. My ears have been buzzing all day, and I find it difficult to hear."

"You must be waxed up," he commented. "Drop into the surgery to-morrow, and I'll syringe them for you. If you can unearth a bottle of peroxide of hydrogen I'll drop a little into them at once; it will assist greatly."

"There's none in the house. Jenny spilt it yesterday."

"Never mind it just now. Come and sit beside me." I obeyed, and he kissed me ardently. Then he swung me upon his knees. "How much longer need I wait?" he asked, and kissed me again.

"Don't, please don't," I implored, gazing up at him with yearning eyes. Then, too low for the eavesdroppers to over-hear: "You scorch me. My strength flies when I am in your arms. Hold me tight . . . tighter!"

He went mad. He smothered me with hot kisses. He strained me to him. He stroked me with passionate fingers. I fought desperately, for the benefit of the watch-ers, pushing at his face with mock panic which transformed my resistance into caresses. Then I screamed.

He thrust me from him in amazement, at the same moment that the sergeant burst in the french windows that gave ingress from the verandah.

While my guardian stood with dropped jaw and an absurd look of dismay frozen on his vapid face, I ran to the sergeant and threw myself on his breast. "Save me," I pleaded, "save me from this man."

"I'll protect you, miss," he replied grimly. "Call your grandmother!"

I dashed obediently from the room and ran upstairs to grandmother. Stupid from sleep, she threw a dressing-gown over her flannel nightdress and followed me downstairs. The tableau which met her view dispelled the humours of sleep.

"Whatever is the matter?" she exclaimed.

The sergeant answered her. "Miss Deslines was forced to come to the station this morning, to secure police protection against her guardian. Constable Smithers and I took up positions on the veranda, where we could see what happened in this room."

"Yes," she gasped; and again, "Yes?"

"Well, Mrs. Evans, we saw enough to show that this man is anything but a fit guardian for a young girl. He made her sit beside him; he started kissing her; and then he attempted worse things. We saw enough to send him to gaol, if you wish it."

"Good God!" ejaculated grandmother, turning to look at the unhappy doctor. His face was striking evidence of the justice of the sergeant's accusation. His faded eyes bulged like miniature balloons. His cheeks were a fiery red. His expression embodied guilt, dismay, and vindictiveness. Like a whipped cur, he stood speechless, wrung by the sudden knowledge that I had tricked him. Too late he saw the gin into which he had walked open-eyed. He foresaw the ruin of his reputation, his expulsion from the profession to which he gave allegiance. In a single cataclysmic moment, the structure of his life had crashed upon his devoted head.

"You treacherous little fiend," he cried, shaking his fist threateningly.

I screamed again, and huddled against the sergeant.

"Don't mind the cowardly brute, miss," he said. "You're quite safe now." He turned to grandmother. "Do you give him in charge, mum? It's a serious offence to molest a ward."

Having achieved my object, I was averse from extremes. Besides, who could foretell what might be elicited in the desperate fight that the victim of my stratagem would wage in the struggle to re-establish his place in the world?

"No, no," I cried. "I don't want my shame published to the world. I could not face a court, with crowds of curious onlookers and awful questions from lawyers. I could not; oh! I could not! Let him go. He has been punished enough. Think of his wife, and her disgrace! Think of me! Think of all concerned! What benefit would we derive? Let the beast go!" I shuddered dramatically, and wept on the sergeant's tunic.

"I'm not certain that I have the power to let him go," he said doubtfully. "I'm inclined to think that he has committed a criminal offence."

"Sergeant," I whispered through my tears, "you said it was irregular to spy on him. Can't you and this other gentleman pretend that you came here unofficially? Please, sergeant! You have nothing to gain; and I . . . I have much to lose. Please let the horrid little animal go!"

He turned to my grandmother. "What do you think, mum?"

She looked her grimmest. "I think he ought to be hanged; that's what I think!"

"Do you want him arrested?"

"Please, grandmother!"

"Let him go," she said with an effort, "but on the distinct understanding that he's not to come near this house again, or speak either to myself or my grand-daughter."

"I don't know what to do," mumbled the sergeant. He thought for a moment. "Will you relinquish your position as this young lady's guardian, if I consent to take no action?" he asked.

"It is not very likely that I would consent to retain the office," rejoined the doctor, who had recovered his self-possession.

"You will resign formally," persisted the sergeant.

"By God, yes," he exploded. "It is almost impossible for me to explain matters . . ."

"I agree with you," said the sergeant drily.

'"Almost impossible to explain," he proceeded. "Nevertheless the day will surely come when you will all realise just what this . . . this exceedingly clever young lady is. She's a fiend from hell, with the morals of a tomcat, and utterly unscrupulous. She would seduce an archangel."

"That will be enough from you," snapped the sergeant. "Get out of this while the going's good! I'd give a stripe to lock you up right now. You're a disgrace to your profession."

Snugly tucked in my bed, with grandmother's kiss warm on my brow, I gave myself over to laughter. The tears ran down my cheeks until the pillow was wet. Grandmother shook her head pityingly over the damp slip next morning, imagining that I had cried myself to sleep. She was a. simple soul.

The doctor's guilty face! — I wriggled with glee. His popping eyes! — God, it was funny. His burning cheeks! — What an exquisite revenge. His humiliation, his knowledge that he had been cheated, his impotent writhings, his fallen conceit! — I stuffed the sheets into my mouth, and almost smothered with stifled mirth.

CHAPTER XV

AFTER THE DISCOMFITURE of my troublesome guardian, my dream began to torment me. Night after night I woke in a bath of perspiration, with the memory of the glazing eyes of the Roman Amazon searing my brain. I feared to sleep, and devoured books until my lids closed despite me and I sank into fitful slumbers with the electric light blazing.

On the third night I rose and walked to the window: The air was clear as crystal and shot through with the quavering light of stars. Like a great, white stream, the milky way crossed the sky, spangled with dim nebulæ. Then it was that I first heard The Voice!

While I stared at the still river of suns, there came the silvery note of bells. I was amazed at the unexpected sound, and scanned the garden. It lay in deep gloom, for there was no moon and the shadows of the trees were profound. Sneering at my credulity, I lifted my eyes once more to the stretching girdle of stars. Again I heard the bells, softly musical. I listened raptly. Then came The Voice!

"Little Jean," it said, "are you listening?"

"Yes," I whispered.

"You have done well, Jean. You have vanquished your enemies and vindicated your ego."

"Who is speaking?" I demanded. But there came no

reply; only the bells tinkled sweetly for an instant and grew silent. I pinched my thigh, and assured myself that I was awake. It was no dream; from somewhere in space a voice had approved my conduct! I returned to bed, to dream of the dying Minerva; but on this occasion her eyes did not laze in death. Instead, they dispatched a glance of undying love, and she smiled through the blood which issued from her mouth. I slept till morning, and woke refreshed.

My cousin arrived next day, fresh from a third-year triumph at the University which carried an exhibition. She sparkled with undisguised glee, and hugged me merrily. Later, she came to me in more serious mood. Her eyes were troubled, and a sequence of tiny wrinkles had appeared in her forehead.

"I have been talking to aunt," she said. She always styled my grandmother thus.

"Yes, Myrtle."

"She has told me about Dr. Murray."

"She had no right," I protested indignantly.

"Tush! child, it's only in the family. Why should I not be told?"

"She had no right," I persisted.

"Anyway, she did; so what's the sense of arguing?"

"Still, she had no right."

"I am wondering. . . ." She hesitated. "I'm wondering if there are features of that incident with which aunt is not acquainted."

"I wonder," I said mockingly.

She eyed me gravely, and sailed off on another tack. "Have you been reading psychology, Jean?"

"A little."

"H'm! Was it enlightening?"

"Oh!- yes."

"Did you learn much?"

"Naturally."

She frowned. "I didn't mean that exactly."

"How quaint! I thought you did."

"Jean, play square. Did it make anything clear to you?"

"Is that another mystic question, or do you mean it this time?"

She gave it up. "You're incorrigible, Jean. I wish I knew the truth about Dr. Murray. You see, I happen to know that his reputation stands very high in the medical world."

"What does that prove?"

"Nothing, perhaps. Still — why can't you tell me?"

"If you'll only stop your mysterious beating about the bush, and tell me in plain English what you're driving at, I may be able to relieve your curiosity. What do you wish to know?"

"The whole truth about your relations with Dr. Murray."

"Don't tell me that he's been seducing you, and you're jealous! That would be too delicious."

She appraised me quietly. "You're a spiteful little brute, Jean."

"So Dr. Murray said."

She flushed angrily, and went inside.

I heard The Voice again, that night. As before, it was heralded by the tinkling music of bells.

"Little Jean!"

"Yes. Oh! yes."

"Sleep and dream, Jean; dream of your Minerva. Study her closely. Strive to recognise her features."

I crept into bed and lay shivering. For long, sleep refused to visit my lids; but ultimately I slipped into dreamland. She was killed again; stabbed in the back by a ghostly figure with rectangular outlines. I stared at the assassin. It was a book, with the single word, "psychology," emblazoned across it in gold. Two nebulous legs supported it, and a mask of a head trembled indefinitely into the shadows which swathed the scene. As she weltered in her rich blood she smiled in my direction, and I recognised the features of my cousin, Myrtle! True, it was an expanded, grosser Myrtle, but undeniably she; a Myrtle grown taller, thicker, fuller-breasted. Suddenly her eyes assumed that unforgettable glaze, and I woke.

I forsook my bed and stole into my cousin's room. She slept. Her breast rose and fell rhythmically with each breath. One deliciously round arm was curved under her head; the other stretched downward on the quilt, naked and white. Her face was placid and unlined; her nose gloriously straight; her lashes dark and curled. Beyond doubt it was Minerva, or her avatar, reduced in size, refined, and deliciously feminine!

I trembled violently. Strange feelings stirred within me. Flashes came and went before my eyes. The pulses hammered in my temples. I breathed in suffocating pants. Suddenly I grew cold as an icicle, and quite composed. Noiselessly I tiptoed to the bed, pulled down the clothes, and crept in beside her. She did not stir. I took her in my arms.

"Who is it?" she gasped.

"Only I."

She sat up. "What are you doing here, Jean?"

"I could not sleep."

"Go back to your own bed."

"If you wish it." But I did not move.

She slipped slowly under the bedclothes and stretched out beside me. "What on earth is wrong with you, Jean?"

"I don't know. I could not sleep."

She pillowed my head on her arm, and it came to rest on her shoulder. "Tell me about Dr. Murray."

"He's a beast."

"And what am I?"

"You're Minerva."

"Who's Minerva?"

I kissed her. "The dearest, sweetest, most delicious woman in. the whole world. She died, but is alive. She was lost, but is found. She was denied, but is given."

"I don't understand you, Jean."

"I don't want you to understand. I want you to love me." Tightly embraced, we fell asleep.

I woke with the first flush of the dawn. Rosy shafts were radiating upward from a lake of gold on the horizon. The gums glistened, and dew-drops sparkled on the pine-needles. I turned and gazed at the sleeping girl. Was this Minerva—this suspiring slip with the clear skin and dreaming lashes? Where were the hooked nose, the firm mouth, the dark complexion? She had bewitched me. I recalled that, even in my throes of the night, I had remarked the straightness of her nose. By what enchantment had I been deluded to confuse her with my glorious Minerva?

I took her in my arms, and a generous warmth enveloped me. I was dreamy, in a state of partial coma. My body seemed to float in space. I had drunk of something more potent than hashish!

CHAPTER XVI

WHEN I WENT to my room that night daddy was sitting on the bed. He was hatless, and in the back of his skull was a deep gash from which protruded masses of a dull grey, spongy substance. His clothes were stained with yellow soil, and his hands looked thin and frail. On his lap lay a wreath of withered flowers, stained crimson. He looked up with the old slow smile as I entered.

"I was beginning to grow impatient, Jean," he said, idly fingering the dead flowers.

I shrank away, my heart hammering and my breath burning my lungs.

"Are you afraid, Jean; afraid of daddy?"

I merely stared, with my legs trembling under me.

"You did ill, child," he reproved.

"It was you or myself," I rejoined, made bold by panic.

"Oh, that? Pah!" He snapped his fingers. The sound rang like a pistol shot. "I was not referring to that. You had a perfect right to defend yourself. I harbour no grudge."

Relieved, I crossed the room and stood before him. "What is troubling you, daddy?"

He fingered the back of his head, pushing the spongy emission into the orifice. "Why did you not patch my wound? A handkerchief stuffed into the opening, a strip

114

of sticking-plaster, even a pad of leaves—anything would have served to exclude the earth. You failed sadly, Jean."

"I was in haste."

"Could you not have spared one minute for him who was to lie for all eternity?"

"I did not think of it."

He shook his head gravely. "The universal fault of youth: act first and think after! You tumbled me into that hole with my wound uncovered. Earth found its way in, and is clogging my brain. I have difficulty in concentrating; my wits tend to grow addled. You did ill, child." He picked at the hole in his skull and extracted a lump of dirt, matted and congealed, gazing at it solemnly for a moment before casting it on the floor.

"You see?" He lifted interrogating brows.

I nodded.

"What do you propose to do?"

"I don't understand."

"About this." He indicated the wound, from which spongy matter again was oozing. He pushed it back petulantly. "You must do something."

"What can I do?"

"Protect the wound. Stop my brains from seeping out. Prevent the dirt from entering. It is simple enough."

I procured a clean handkerchief. "Let me bind it now, daddy."

He smiled pityingly. "Do you imagine it is quite as simple as that?" he asked.

"Why not?"

He laughed until the injured brain-tissue leapt in and out like a grotesque jack-in-the-box. "Ho, ho!" he roared, "the little simpleton imagines that she can dress it here."

"Why not?" I repeated.

"Because it is a physical impossibility. I look substantial enough, I dare say; but I'm not; I'm merely a mass of ectoplasm, a materialised figment, the essence of a dream."

I felt the sweat break cold on my forehead. "What am I to do, to help you, daddy?"

"Dress my wound. Protect me from the dirt which hopples my wits. Keep my brains from leaking."

"But how — how?"

"Dig me up. What other course suggests itself? Dig me up, and fix me comfortably. Wash out the dirt. Stop the hole. You owe me that, at least."

I shrank away, wide-eyed. "I would not dare. Oh, daddy, I would not dare!"

"Dare you refuse?"

"No," I breathed, "no."

"I shall expect you, Jean. Don't be long, child, for I suffer."

Before my eyes he vanished — melted into an intangible vapour that curled upward to the roof and was gone. I was alone in the room, staring through the window at the stars. I dragged myself to the casement and thrust my head into the cool night, drawing quick breaths like a swimmer who has been submerged for the span of his endurance. The stars twinkled and winked, and the Milky Way stretched above and beyond like a river of light-points.

Again I heard the soft tinkle of bells, followed by The Voice.

"You must obey him, little Jean. There is nothing to fear. You must make his sleep comfortable. Choose your own time; wait your opportunity. But you must exhume his body, sponge his wound, and stop the hole in his skull. Then

116

cover him again with the soft, clean earth. It is an inescapable duty."

A shooting star flamed across the sky. "See," came The Voice. "Do you know what that is? It is a hormone, seeking a place to rest. Every night they search patiently, and when a babe is born they pierce its chest and effect lodgment. This knowledge is given to few. Men talk learnedly of hormones, and write dreary treatises about them; but how many know that they come from the sky, disguised as meteorites?"

I licked my lips, which were dry.

"There are countless billions of them stored in the Milky Way. It is a vast girdle of hormones, strung together on invisible threads of ether. As they ripen, they break off and set out to fulfil their destiny. Never forget the hormones, little Jean, for they are the dynamos which drive the human race!"

The Voice ceased with a subdued clash of bells, and I crept into bed fully dressed, where I lay thinking . . . thinking. Later I kicked my shoes off, stuffing them over the end of the mattress with my feet. Ultimately I fell asleep, to dream of Minerva. She perished with her eyes bright, and an understanding smile on her lips. As she lay still, a brace of hormones flashed down the sky and impacted on her eagle-billed nose. They vanished from sight immediately, penetrating the skin without injuring it. But the hook had been beaten from her nose; in death it was as straight as that of Myrtle.

Omnipotent hormones!

I rose and entered Myrtle's room. She was awake, and stirred as I drew near.

"What are you doing here, Jean?"

"I am lonely."

"Good God, child, why are you not undressed?"

"Am I not?" I glanced down at my rumpled dress.

"Have you been to bed?"

"Like that?"

"What on earth were you doing?"

"Talking to daddy."

"*What!*" She sat erect like a figure on springs. "Has your father been here?"

"Yes, Myrtle."

"Where has he been?"

"Sleeping."

She gazed at me strangely. "Are you suffering from hallucinations, Jean?"

"No. He was there, and spoke to me. We talked for a long time."

"What about?" she asked sceptically.

I shook my head cunningly. "Just a little secret."

"Can't you tell me?"

"Not even you."

"Where is he now?"

"He's gone."

"Where?"

"Back to the place where he sleeps. He won't come again, provided I do something for him."

She stared fixedly. "I'm frightened about you, Jean. You are so queer, so . . . so mysterious, and you say such uncanny things."

I smiled at her. "Do you know anything about hormones, Myrtle?"

"Precious little."

I wagged my head. "I knew that."

"Did you? May I ask what *you* know about them?"

"Everything."

"Do you, indeed?" she commented sarcastically. "You must be a very wise young person."

I nodded complacently.

"Just what do you know of them?"

"Where they originate, how they operate, how they are transmitted. I know all there is to know about them."

"Then you must possess knowledge which certain scientists would give their souls to know."

"It is precisely because they have no souls to give, that they don't know."

She shrugged her white shoulders under the blankets, sending waves rippling across the woollen fabric. "You're a strange little fish, Jean. Get into your nightie and come to bed with me. Damn hormones!"

CHAPTER XVII

THENCEFORTH THE VOICE determined my actions. It ordered my life in almost every detail. At first I only received its messages at night, always heralded by the low music of invisible bells; but after a few weeks I began to hear it by day. It whispered in my ear vibrantly, so distinctly that I grew afraid lest it might be overheard by others. Strangely enough, I did not hear the bells during the daylight. Either they were mute, or absent. Possibly the sun's rays neutralised their vibrations; I had read of such things.

When the date of a fancy-dress ball drew near, I was completely under the domination of The Voice. It echoed in my ears almost perpetually, guiding, advising, ordering! I was its slave, the creature of an anonymous whisper.

Myrtle and I discussed the forthcoming ball much, striving to decide upon appropriate dresses.

"You would look sweet as 'Night,'" she suggested.

"With a black dress, spangled with stars, and the moon on your breast, you would be the belle of the ball."

"I don't care for it; it's too hackneyed."

"A Spanish señorita, then, with a sweeping black robe and a silken shawl to add a touch of colour."

"Why do you wish to garb me in black?"

"I don't know. I'm sure either costume would suit you." I objected obstinately.

Three days before the ball, she came to me triumphantly. Her cheeks were flushed, and her eyes sparkled. "I've got it," she exclaimed. "A friend of mine in the city is sending us costumes from the wardrobes of himself and his wife. They are actors, and we may rely on his taste."

I grimaced. "I want to choose my own dress. Has he told you what he proposes?"

She drew a letter from her pocket and scanned it. "You are to be a slave girl. You will wear a long robe of transparent white silk over flesh-coloured tights. A wrought gold band will encircle your head, and a collar of pearls will be strapped about your throat. Sandals, laced high over the instep, will serve for footgear. He says they are admirable for dancing; not a bit clumsy. It is a great pity you cannot braid your hair into two plaits; but your curls will do."

I felt suddenly faint, and caught at the back of a chair for support. She had described in detail the costume that I wore in my dream!

"And you," I murmured, "what will you wear?"

She laughed gaily. "Oddly enough, I'm to be a Roman legionary. I shall wear a brass hem, capped with a plume of scarlet feathers; a corselet of mail; brazen greaves on my legs; and carry a tall spear. Oh! yes, and a small shield will be strapped to my left arm. I suppose the shield will be a nuisance. If so, I shall leave it under a seat."

She wrinkled her nose thoughtfully. "I wonder if I'm too small to look the part? I've a suspicion that I'll be lost among all that ironmongery."

"No, no," I said hoarsely, "you'll look the part to perfection."

"How do you know?"

"I'm confident of it. We'll be guided by your friend. The dresses are chosen!"

They arrived on the evening before the ball, carefully wrapped in tissue-paper, and crated. We tipped the carrier to take them upstairs to Myrtle's room, and soon the garments were spread about the furniture. I recognised every item. What coincidence was this? What monstrous fantasy of Fate was being enacted for our benefit? In what manner was my slim, straight-nosed cousin related to the hawk-billed Amazon of my recurring dream?

I looked superb in my diaphanous drapings. My mirror informed me as much, even if Myrtle had not exclaimed with pleasure and hugged me passionately.

"You perfectly gorgeous kid," she cried. "I feel inclined to get a stick and thrash you. No one has a right to look so alluring."

"Do," I urged, smiling.

"I'd like to; but you'd be all bruises. We'll have to postpone the whipping."

"What a pity!"

"I almost think it is." She kissed me.

I retired to touch my cheeks lightly with colour. When I returned, half an hour later, she was dressed. The severity of the open helm accentuated the purity of her features. The scarlet plume suited her complexion excellently. Her virgin form looked wonderfully supple and yielding under its shining armour. The burnished greaves fitted her swelling thighs as though they had been moulded to them. She was sweetly beautiful and gloriously alive, pulsing with virile womanhood. I gasped when I saw her.

"Will I do?" she inquired with mock anxiety.

"Do? — You'll devastate the ball-room."

"Then there'll be a pair of us, for you look simply delicious."

We stood side by side and admired ourselves in the mirror. Unless it lied, I was a worthy partner for my cousin. I certainly looked my best.

We created a minor sensation at the ball. We had agreed to dance the first number together, and held to our decision in spite of the importunities of eager suitors. As we glided round the hall, to the rhythmic music of a jazz waltz, we were the cynosure of all eyes. My dark slimness and my cousin's more robust blondness were perfect foils, whereby each gained in attractiveness without diminishing the appeal of the other. The effect was heightened by our striking costumes. Myrtle's scarlet crest was a focal point from which arrested glances swept downward to our toes. As she had prophesied, we were "the hit" of the evening.

The extraordinary sequence of coincidences which had marked the occasion, culminated during the final dance, which again we trod together. The orchestra broke into the strains of an almost forgotten waltz which had been the rage some years before. I found myself humming the words as we swayed to its dreamy music:

"We made a promise, and sealed it with a kiss,
In that little Spanish town. 'Twas on a night like this!"

A little Spanish town! Was it perchance a town standing behind a dusty quay? Did it look out to the sea through rocky headlands? Ages ago, in the dawn of history, had a Roman soldier yielded up his life there, to become transformed in death into a glorious woman? Who was Minerva? Who was I? Who was my stately cousin, now decked in the habiliments of a dead woman? What mysterious drama was being enacted? What was this *catena* which stretched through two millenniums of time, and linked a seaport town in the old world with a mountain town in the new?

A cowboy and pantaloon insisted on escorting us home, and demanded farewell kisses as a reward. The pantaloon's breath was faintly charged with onion. I hoped, for Myrtle's sake, that his companion had displayed more discretion in his choice of viands.

The Voice was whispering in my ear as we walked up the drive. "Kill," it urged. "Minerva must die. Her destiny must be fulfilled. Kill!"

I shuddered at the knowledge that I must slay my cousin.

"Are you cold? "she asked.

"Yes, dear, so very cold."

"I'll warm you up. Come to my bed when you get your things off."

She would warm me up! God! the irony of it! Me, who had been decreed by Fate to re-enact the tragedy of that old Spanish town that stared seaward through gaunt headlands! Me, who had found her after millenniums of separation, only to lose her again! She would warm me in her white arms, and hold me to her generous bosom! I shook like an aspen.

"Poor kid! you're chilled right through. I'll race you upstairs."

Standing before my mirror, removing the gilded band from my hair and the imitation pearls from my throat, I considered the position. The Voice had spoken, and its orders must be obeyed. A dual duty had been imposed on me by my mentor. I must exhume poor daddy to cleanse the dirt from his brain, and I must slay Myrtle as she had been slain ages before. The more I pondered the task of easing daddy's discomfort, the less it repelled me. I pictured him, sleeping in his strait bed, with the insidious dirt permeating his brain and making thought difficult. Undoubtedly I had been remiss in exposing him to such a fate. It would have been so simple to have protected the hole in his skull from the inroads of foreign substances. All that was involved was a few hours' work with a shovel. Then he would be able to think clearly once more and beguile the tedium of his long sleep. I owed him that much — and it would be done!

But the other duty! I stared at my reflection in the mirror. Through the thin fabric of my dress my limbs showed slenderly pink in their tights. The band had gone from my curls and the stiff necklet from my throat; but the sandals, with their crossed straps, still encased my feet. Truly, I was an intruder from another age — a fragment of flotsam cast on the beach of the twentieth century. I sighed. That other fragment, linked to me by bonds more powerful than steel, was to be thrown back to the Sea of Time to drift at the mercy of unknown currents. Perhaps, in some era of the future, we would be jettisoned once more to continue the drama that seemed destined to have no end. The task was hideously repellent, but who was I to bid defiance to The Voice which ordered my actions? My cousin must die! But first I must minister to daddy's comfort.

Clad in a nightgown of cream silk, whose open neck exposed one firm breast, Myrtle entered my room.

"Good gracious, Jean, aren't you undressed yet?"

I shivered. "Not yet, dear."

"Hurry up, child! You'll have your death of cold. You're chilled to the bone now. If you moon there any longer you'll be down with pneumonia."

I hastily stripped off my things and slipped into

pyjamas. "Not, those, Jean. Wear your nightie; it's more feminine."

Meekly I obeyed, and she smiled happily.

Twice I heard the muffled note of bells that night. But The Voice did not speak. I was not surprised; it had said all that was necessary.

CHAPTER XVIII

FOR A WEEK I procrastinated. I had resolved to execute
the commands given me, but I was awaiting final orders.
During this period the bells ceased to chime and no whispers came to my ears. Plainly my mentor concurred in the
delay. Myrtle and I roamed the hills and gullies, attended
the picture theatre, danced together at Echo Point, and
were inseparable. Our idyll kept us in a state of rapture,
and the days and nights fled with astonishing rapidity.

One afternoon, as we tramped homeward from
a picnic at Minnehaha Falls, The Voice was heard. "To-
night," it whispered, "to-night you must exhume your
father. Cleanse his wound and bind it, and lay him to rest
again."

From the moment that darkness settled upon the mountains the bells chimed ceaselessly. Faint, but vibrant, they
tinkled their fairy notes, reminding me of my duty. I did
not fail them. Maintaining a pretence of reading, I sat in
the lounge until grandmother went to bed. Half an hour
later Myrtle yawned and tossed her book upon the mantelpiece.

"Coming to bed, honey?"

"Not just yet."

"Don't be long, then."

"I'll come soon."

She blew a kiss from her finger-tips and retired.

Ten minutes passed before I procured my coat and went out quietly by the side door. A young moon was just vanishing behind the hills and the stars shone with unusual brightness. They furnished enough light by which to see, without revealing unduly. It was unlikely that I would be detected at my labour. I accepted as an omen the fleeting passage of a hormone, which suddenly blazed into being on my left and vanished in a flickering trail of fire.

At the cemetery I lost no time in procuring the shovel and soon was digging steadily. The task was the reverse of easy. During the months since daddy had been laid to rest, the earth had consolidated to a surprising extent. Gravel, intermingled with the soil, prevented me from sinking the shovel deeply. I was forced to confine my excavating to a sequence of scratches, lifting but a quarter of a spade of earth at a time. It was tedious work, and by 2 a.m. I was down less than three feet. My strength was failing. My breathing was growing laboured. Blisters which had developed on my palms and thumbs were breaking. I halted and leaned upon the shovel.

While I stood this, there came the soft tinkle of the bells. I groaned aloud, imagining that the sound was intended to spur me to activity. But, before I could grasp my implement and resume work, The Voice whispered sympathetically in my ear.

"You have done well, little Jean. You may cease now. Leave everything as it is; none will disturb it. Return home and I shall instruct you when it is necessary to complete your task."

Emitting a prolonged sigh of relief, I laid the shovel beside the partially opened grave, and fled home. The bells jangled intermittently as I went.

Passing along the hall upstairs I noticed Myrtle's door ajar. On tiptoe I crept in and switched on the light. She stirred slightly, but did not wake, and I stood watching her. Suddenly her eyes opened. She stared blankly for a moment, then sat erect, glancing involuntarily at the clock on her dressing-table.

"Where on earth have you been till this hour?" she exclaimed.

"I've been for a walk."

"With whom?"

"By myself."

She scanned me narrowly, and her eyes widened as she noted the state of my dress.

"Jean, you're smothered with dirt."

"Am I?" I queried carelessly.

"You know that you are. What have you been doing?"

"Nothing."

She gasped audibly. "Who was with you, Jean?"

"Are you jealous?"

"Who was with you?"

"Nobody. I was alone."

She sprang from the bed and seized me by the shoulders, shaking me viciously. "You're a damned little liar. Who was with you?"

I swung away from her grasp. "I tell you I was alone."

She gazed at me steadily for several seconds. "Will you tell me what you were doing?"

I attempted to embrace her.

"Don't come near me with that filthy dress."

I tore my outer garments off, and stood in my slip and bloomers. For a space we remained, staring at each other. Then I took her in my arms and kissed her.

"Own up that you were jealous," I whispered, stroking her head.

"You're a tantalising little devil, Jean. Can't you tell me what you were up to?"

"Not even you, Myrtle. The secret is not mine to tell anyone; but I give you my word of honour that I was alone. It was just . . . just something that I had promised daddy."

She clutched my hand tightly; then swept her fingers along it and gave a little cry. "Good God!" she muttered, turning my blistered palms upward. "What have you done to your hands?"

"I can't tell you, Myrtle. Truly, I can't."

"You've been digging."

I made no comment.

"Your poor hands are all blistered."

I kept silent.

"Oh! well, keep your secret!"

"I must, Myrtle.

CHAPTER XIX

THE VOICE HAD been wrong; the disturbed grave was discovered next morning by a municipal official, who at once communicated with the police. Soon the cemetery was the venue of a jostling crowd, kept back from the partially opened grave by a squad of constables. A small army of newspaper reporters prowled about, and special police officers searched diligently for clues. They measured footprints, photographed finger-marks on the handle of the shovel, examined the headstone through magnifying glasses, held colloquies away from listening ears, and eventually deputed two detectives to run the culprit to earth. The Press, lacking more substantial fare at the moment, gave the incident unmerited prominence. The daily papers blossomed into streamer headlines, and advanced fantastic theories about the motive which had animated the nocturnal digger. One journal ascribed it to a lunatic. A second canvassed the ruling rates for skeletons and declared that body-snatching had inspired the work. A third invented some apocryphal small boys, imbued with a spirit of mischief. A usually staid periodical excelled itself by dipping into esoteric medicine and hinting at the presence of a necrophile in the community. Obviously the editor had perused an article on the subject at a recent date, and was anxious to air his knowledge. He had not paused to ask himself why a necrophile should seek to exhume a body which had been buried for months.

So those concerned made their investigations, and advanced their theories, to the huge enjoyment of the morbid. Curiously enough, neither police nor Press conceived the simple idea of completing the unfinished task of excavation. Their imaginations halted at theory and supposition; common sense was not allowed to intrude. Convinced that the grave contained but one corpse, they centred their activities about its presumed occupant and the actual evidence of digging.

God knows where their theorising led them; but their only tangible discoveries were three: the digger had been a person of indifferent physical strength; he or she was unaccustomed to the use of a heavy shovel; he or she had worn high-heeled shoes. From these premises they reasoned that the work had been performed by a girl or woman of slight physique who wore a number two shoe. A close scrutiny was made of suspicious strangers who answered the description; but none thought of prosecuting inquiries in the home of the wealthy Deslines family. The lonely old house on the hill was not disturbed by prying eyes.

Yet there was one person who did not harbour delusions. Myrtle, with the memory of my home-coming on the fateful night fresh in mind, knew that I was guilty; but even she did not suspect the truth.

Having devoured the morning paper, with its ridiculous theories, she sought me in the garden. I was lying on a couch of pine-needles in the shade of a towering giant which exuded a faint odour of turpentine. From its penumbra stretched a lake of sunlight, bordered by the shadows of other trees and shrubs. An island of flowers rose in its centre, spreading incense about it. Bees, with garnered gold on their thighs, flitted among the blooms. A thrush whistled liquidly on a bough. It was idyllic, and I was enjoying it to the full when my cousin burst into the peaceful garden with the paper clutched in her fingers.

"Have you read the paper?" she inquired by way of prelude.

"No."

"I think it will interest you."

I grimaced. "What's the Government been doing now?"

"I did not know you were interested in politics."

"I'm not."

She eyed me covertly. "Someone tried to dig up a grave in Katoomba cemetery two nights ago."

"How extraordinary."

"Isn't it?" She read from the paper, holding it out-spread before her: "Investigations disclose that the malefactor was evidently a woman, apparently of slight physique."

I picked pine-needles from my hair.

"I wonder who it could have been, Jean?" She folded the paper deliberately, placed it on the ground, and sat on it.

"I'm not a seer."

"You are not accused of it; but I thought you might have some idea."

I yawned. "Not the slightest in the world, Myrtle."

She fingered her lower lip thoughtfully. "Jean," she whispered after a pause, "where were you that night?"

"In bed, I suppose."

"But it was the night when you came in at all hours of the morning, covered with dirt and with your hands all blistered."

"Are you suggesting that I had been out at the cemetery, digging up a grave?"

"If not, where were you?"

"That's my own secret, Myrtle."

She gazed at me steadily. "Why did you do it, Jean?"

I cast pretence to the winds. "I can't explain, dear. You would not understand."

"Am I as dull as that?"

"It's not a question of dullness. Without a complete knowledge of the circumstances, none could understand; and I'm . . . I'm pledged to secrecy."

She tore a shred from the margin of the paper and began to nibble it. "That night, you . . . you said something about a promise to your father. Was it the truth?"

I nodded.

"Is he alive, Jean?"

"I don't know."

"Previously, you told me that he had been in your room."

"That is so."

"Then he must be alive."

"I suppose so."

She closed her eyes and remained deep in thought for several seconds. Then, opening her eyes suddenly: "Jean, is he in that grave?"

"Don't be stupid. That's old Mr. Cummings' grave."

"Then why need you dig him up? What is the relation between him and your father?"

"I can't tell you, Myrtle; it's not my secret. Daddy explained everything to me, and I promised him that I would do certain things; that happens to be one of them. Don't question me, dear. You must trust me."

She sighed, and stared at me with blanched cheeks. "I'm frightened, Jean."

"There's no occasion to be."

She ignored the interjection. "I'm scared stiff! Not that you will be suspected, but because . . . because . . ."

I broke a pine-needle in two and tossed the fragments away. "Because . . . ?" I repeated inquiringly.

"Because . . . because it's all so mysterious and unaccountable; and because . . ."

"Yes?"

"Because . . . I doubt your sanity!"

I giggled. "I'll be doubting yours, if you go on like that."

Her eyes were grave. "I'm not joking, Jean. I wish to God that I was! This mysterious business about your father, which necessitated desecrating the grave of a total stranger, coupled with other things, is worrying me intensely. I can't see daylight anywhere, or make head or tail of it."

"Then why worry about it?"

"Because I can't help it. I am wondering what is to happen next. It frightens me."

I rose and crossed to her, stirring the edge of the paper with my foot. "Myrtle," I said seriously, "the explanation is ridiculously simple. If I could only explain, you would laugh at your present fears."

"Then why don't you?" she said petulantly.

"Because I'm bound by a solemn promise. Trust me, dear! There is nothing to fear, and the circumstances are not so . . . so bizarre as you imagine. It is only that your perspective is distorted by lack of knowledge. Believe me when I assure you that the explanation is so absurdly simple and obvious that it is a marvel you remain in the dark. I'm sorry I can't make it clearer; but I'm in honour bound."

She rose in her turn and faced me, staring directly

into my eyes. "I'm frightened, Jean," she declared, and shuddered.

"The more goose you," I rejoined, lightly, and laughed at her.

That night the bells chimed ceaselessly, vibrating in my ears until my head began to buzz in sympathy. I fell asleep to their insistent music. In the middle of the night I was wakened by the low whisper of The Voice.

"Things have gone awry!" it said. And again: "Things have gone awry!"

I made no reply, but listened intently.

"You must complete your task, little Jean. The grave will not be guarded to-morrow night. Return, and ease your father's pain. He expects you. The dirt is penetrating deeper into his brain with the passage of each day. Cleanse his wound and protect it against injury."

I lay awake till morning, planning and pondering. Once a dark shadow obscured the window, and I thought I could detect daddy's face outlined against the night. But he did not enter, and the shadow passed. Through the casement came the gleam of stars, and twice hormones flashed across the visible sector of sky, seeking infant breasts to enter. I almost cried aloud when the wailing "mo-poke" of an owl rose on the night, to jeer at myself when I recognised the source of the eerie noise. I was distraught, semi-hysterical, borne down by the weight of a nauseous duty which could not be escaped. The sole gleam of joy which illuminated the dismal vista of my thoughts was the fact that The Voice had made no reference to the destruction of Myrtle. I do not think that I could have endured the command to stab her. There are limits to human strength.

In the grey light of the dawn I left my bed and studied

myself in a mirror. My cheeks were pale and sunken; black, cavernous hollows underlaid my eyes, and nests of tiny wrinkles had appeared at their corners. Even my hair was dry and lifeless, its curls evincing a tendency to lankness. I looked old and haggard.

Myrtle shook her head sadly when I came to the breakfast table, and avoided my eye. She, also, looked pale and morbid, as though exhausted by a sleepless night. We made a dismal pair; as we maintained a valiant pretence of eating.

CHAPTER XX

AT INTERVALS THROUGHOUT the day The Voice sounded in my ears. It confined itself to laconic injunctions to remember. "Don't forget," it would whisper, or "Remember to-night," or "Your daddy suffers," and similar terse phrases. By the time darkness swept over the land, I was in a pitiable state of nervousness, ready to jump at the vaguest shadow. The banging of a door, the cry of an animal, the creak of chafing boughs in the garden, reached my ears with the tumult of a thunderclap and induced an almost irresistible desire to scream. My wonted self-assurance seemed to have melted before a wave of neurotic impulse. I was a writhing bundle of nerves, stretched to the tautness of a banjo-string and responding to every vibration.

Reviewing the night from the perspective of distance, I am amazed that I displayed the courage to execute my allotted task. I find it strange that no thought of disobeying The Voice crossed my mind. My belief in its omniscience had been weakened by the discovery of the violated grave, after its assurance to the contrary. Yet, despite its egregious error, and the condition of my nerves, at no juncture did I contemplate disobedience. I had a duty to perform, and that night had been chosen for its execution! Those two facts obsessed my mind to the exclusion of independent thought. I was the abject slave of The Voice.

Immediately dinner was over, I hastened to the cemetery and procured the shovel from its shed. Then, by the wan light of the stars, I commenced digging. On this occasion I felt no fatigue; nor did the blisters, which rapidly formed beneath their unhealed precursors, give me pain. They came, and they burst, and thin trickles of blood ran from them, but they occasioned no discomfort. I worked steadily, and found the removal of the loose earth, previously excavated by me and later thrown back by the authorities, absurdly simple. Within an hour I had reached the compressed soil which underlaid it. I seemed to float in space. My body had lost its weight. My breath was admirably even. I dug methodically, only pausing at intervals to wipe the blood from the handle of the shovel with my skirt. I had found that it grew slippery if denied this attention.

Suddenly the shovel drove against something which refused to yield. Again and again I tried to thrust it downward, but without success. Casting the implement aside, I knelt by the hole and peered into it; but the light was too meagre. I was forced to clamber in. Still nothing was discernible. Scratching the loosened earth with my fingers, I encountered a piece of cloth. Then I knew that I had reached daddy!

My pulses did not quicken, and my heart beat normally as I climbed from the hole and sought my handbag. Extracting an electric torch, I slid into the hole again and switched on the battery. Sticking it firmly into the wall of the grave, I proceeded to uncover daddy's face, scratching the soil out with my hands and casting it behind me after the manner of an animal. At length his head was bared, jutting stiffly outward over a shallow depression which reached as far as his shoulders. I drew the torch from its bed and flashed it directly on his features, to recoil with a cry of horror. Through the sandy covering which encrusted his face I could discern the terrible corruption which had taken place. His eyes had vanished completely, leaving gaping sockets partially filled with dirt that had been converted into a horrible liquid. His skin was blackened and eaten into hideous holes, and through shrunken lips his teeth protruded like those of a vampire. I gazed in the manner of one who had been hypnotised, holding the rays of the torch against his devastated features.

Suddenly weariness overcame me, and the palms of my hands began to burn as though they had been touched by flame. I shuddered as if stricken by an ague, and dropped the torch. Still alight, it threw a circle of luminescence on the ragged walls of the grave, exaggerating the inequalities until they loomed like peaks and dales. I felt my senses reeling.

The subdued chiming of bells rang faintly in my ears. Then, from a tremendous distance, came The Voice.

"Be brave, little Jean! You have done well. There is nothing to fear from your daddy. Wash his wound and protect it. Then you may go home to bed. Don't fail him, Jean; he depends on you. Be brave!"

My head ceased to swim and vigour returned to my limbs. I drew a deep breath and flung my curls back from my brow. They were drenched through, but whether with dew or sweat I could not tell. Flattening them across my head, I clambered from the grave and procured a small towel which I had brought in my bag for the purpose. Moistening it under a tap, I returned to the hole and jumped into it.

Employing the wet towel, I scrubbed the back of daddy's head thoroughly. Then I returned to the tap, washed the towel, and set about cleansing his wound. Water must have penetrated it, for the skull appeared to be filled with a fluid which reeked with an abominable smell from the putrefying Mr. Cummings.

A third time I visited the tap, and returned with the towel wet but sweet. I bound it tightly over the hole in daddy's skull, to prevent contaminating dirt and stenches from entering. Then I scrambled from the grave for the last time, and sank in a faint beside it.

The music of bells called me back to sensibility; but I must have stared uncomprehendingly at the stars for minutes, ere I realised where I was. Before I could move, The Voice addressed me.

"Your task is ended, little Jean. Go home to bed and sleep!"

I gazed at the fallen torch, whose rays passed across the open grave and illuminated a distant headstone. Subconsciously, without recourse to reason, I felt that the hole should be filled in.

"I am tired. Oh! so tired. Need I return the dirt to the grave?"

"Go home, child. Leave everything as it is. You have done well."

Mechanically I gathered up the torch and my handbag, and fled from the scene. How I reached home I never knew. I remembered passing through the cemetery gates; then came a complete hiatus until I found myself at the top of the stairs, about to steal along the hall. I ached in every bone. My hands throbbed pitiably. My head expanded and contracted in alternating movements which threatened to drive me mad. And in my nostrils lingered that disgusting stench which had emanated from old Mr. Cummings as he rotted a few inches under daddy. How daddy endured it was beyond comprehension. Why did he not remove himself to a sweeter resting-place?

I must have removed my clothes and donned pyjamas, for the first thing that greeted my eyes, on waking next morning, was a heap of earth-stained clothing in a corner. Myrtle was standing over me, shaking me fiercely by the shoulders. Her eyes were wide with fear, and blazed into mine.

"Have you been there again?" she whispered huskily, shaking me as a terrier shakes a rat.

"Let me sleep."

"What have you been doing?"

"Let me sleep. For pity's sake, let me sleep!"

"Your clothes! My God! look at your clothes!"

"Please let me sleep."

She plunged a hand under the blankets and seized my wrist, drawing my hand into sight, and cried aloud at its appearance. It was masked with mingled blood and dirt which had congealed into a crust of hideous import.

"Oh, my God!" she whispered dully; and again: "Oh, my God!"

I felt myself sinking into slumber; but she shook me into wakefulness—shook me fiercely and remorselessly.

I struggled feebly. "Let me alone. I want to sleep." She grew gentle. "Tell me all about it, Jean."

"There is nothing to tell. I'm tired."

"Were you at the cemetery?"

"Yes."

"My God! Why?"

"Because I promised daddy."

"What did you promise him?"

"I want to sleep."

She was implacable. "What did you promise him?"

"To bind up his wound, so that the dirt wouldn't addle his wits. He could not think clearly."

She dropped my hand and shrank away, gazing at me wildly. "You promised to bind up his wound," she gasped. "What wound?"

"The wound in his skull. His brains kept oozing out, and the dirt kept creeping in. It stopped him from concentrating."

Staring at me strangely, she backed to the door and vanished. I heard her sobbing as she ran along the hall. Then, as I fell into a delicious sleep, there came the sound of a key turned hurriedly in a lock.

I woke with my mind icily clear. Never had my wits been more alert. A few seconds served to reveal the appalling danger in whose shade I stood. After all my scheming and acting, culminating in the disposal of my father, a few hours' madness had caused me to sacrifice my hard-won security. In my folly I had betrayed myself beyond repair. The violated grave would be discovered before noon—possibly had been discovered already. Daddy's remains would be identified without difficulty. The police already were in possession of finger-prints and other evidence against me. The fact that daddy had been murdered would necessitate inquiries at home, and inevitable exposure would be my portion.

Wholly sane, and determined to fight desperately for my salvation, I leapt from bed and dressed myself as quickly as my battered fingers would permit. I left the stained and bedraggled clothing, which I had worn during my maniacal labours, in the corner where I had hurled it when disrobing. I realised that concealment of my action was impossible. The sole hope lay in adopting a bold course, and trusting to my youth and guile to preserve me.

I went straight to the telephone, rang the police station, and asked for the sergeant in charge who had proved such a pliant accessory previously. He was on the wire almost immediately.

"Sergeant," I whispered, "come to the house at once. This is Jean Deslines speaking. My father has been murdered, and I have irrefutable evidence in my possession. I am afraid to speak much on the telephone. Please hurry!"

"I'll come at once, Miss Deslines," he replied, and rang off.

My next step was to visit Myrtle. She still was locked in her bedroom, and I had tremendous difficulty in inducing her to admit me.

"I am perfectly sane, Myrtle," I whispered through the keyhole. "I don't blame you for having doubts, for God knows how it would have been possible for you to have decided otherwise. The truth is, that I *was* half insane this morning, owing to the fact that poor daddy had been murdered by his best friend. I went through hell last night, seeking evidence; and it is a miracle that I found the strength of mind to carry it through without going mad in reality. But I did, dear, and I triumphed. The fiend who struck daddy down will pay the penalty of his crime on the gallows."

I heard her approach the door. "Who killed your father, Jean?"

"Dr. Murray."

"My God!"

"It's true. I suspected it from the outset; and now I know. A chance phrase gave me the clue, and I made a solemn vow to my dead father that I would avenge his death. Open the door, Myrtle. There's nothing to fear."

After a dismaying delay, she yielded to my importunities and unlocked the door. I slipped inside and closed it again.

"Don't be afraid," I admonished, as she gave a startled cry. "All that I have told you is true. I have rung up the police, and they will be here any minute. Look at me, dear. Do I look mad?"

Reassured by the critical glance which she cast at me, she came to my side. "What does it all mean, Jean?"

"I haven't time for details. You'll hear the whole story when the sergeant comes. Possibly I was foolish in acting personally instead of notifying the police; but, you see, I was not sure. I was fearful that they would regard my story as too bizarre for belief—would imagine that the loss of my father had turned my brain, so I decided to furnish the evidence myself before enlisting their aid." I shuddered ostentatiously. "My God it was an awful ordeal, Myrtle. If you only knew the hell I endured in that lonely cemetery, disinterring a body, you would pity me. I'm inclined to believe that I *was* half insane when you woke me this morning . . . Oh, Myrtle, Myrtle!" I threw myself on her breast, and sobbed.

She fondled me tenderly, running her hands through my unwashed curls, in which the dirt still lingered. When at length I raised my eyes to hers, I had the satisfaction of realising that at least one important witness had been convinced. I had small doubt of my ability to deceive the sergeant. He was a congenital simpleton, already strongly prejudiced in my favour.

Awaiting his arrival, I canvassed the position: I was under no delusions about my recent madness. The chiming bells, the mysterious Voice, the ridiculous belief that shooting-stars were hormones, told me in trumpet tones that my reason had been impaired. The hereditary taint, transmitted by my mother, had almost proved my undoing. However, by a lucky fluke, I had recovered in time, for there still was an excellent chance of extricating myself from the consequences of my mania. But I would need all my wits about me. A single false step would destroy me irrevocably.

It was unfortunate for Dr. Murray that once more he was to become my scapegoat; but there was a measure of poetic justice in the fact, seeing that his desire for a gland-graft had caused all the trouble. Nor did I fear that he would be haled to the gallows. The worst that he would be called upon to endure would be a disconcerting suspicion. No jury would convict him on the evidence which I could concoct. True, he probably would be ruined profession-ally; but what was that comparatively trivial penalty com-pared with lifelong imprisonment in a mental hospital for myself? The more I pondered the possibilities, the more I felt that I could bear with equanimity any punishment that accrued to the meddlesome doctor. Besides, he was a plump little man; and I detested fat!

When the sergeant rang the bell, I had completed the details of my defence, and was eager for the fray. But I did not delude myself that an easy task confronted me.

CHAPTER XXI

HE WAS SEATED in the lounge, and rose as I entered.

"Sit down, sergeant," I said. "I have a strange story to tell you; one that will strain your credulity to the utmost. However, by the time I have finished you will be convinced that the world contains one fiend who should end his life on the gallows." I wiped my eyes on a lace handkerchief.

"You say your father was murdered, miss?"

I nodded. "I think it would be best to let me tell my story. When you have heard it, you may ask any questions you please. Will that suit you, sergeant?"

"I think it would be the best way."

"Sergeant, you remember how Dr. Murray treated me?"

"I'm not likely to forget that."

"Do you remember, also, what I told you about his constant whispering to my grandmother, behind daddy's back?"

"I do."

"Well, when daddy disappeared I was suspicious of him. I connected the whispering with it. I have since discovered that my suspicions were unfounded; my grandmother is quite innocent. What they found to whisper about, I don't know; but I am satisfied that it was not about poor daddy's death. In that relation Dr. Murray acted alone."

The sergeant shuffled his feet uneasily, and opened his mouth; but before he could speak I waved him into silence.

"After that dreadful night when you saved me from him, I thought and thought over daddy, knowing how the doctor hated him. Then, one afternoon, I came face to face with him in the School of Arts."

"Face to face with whom?" inquired the sergeant.

"With Dr. Murray. I think he had been drinking, for his face was very red and his breath just reeked of spirits. He stared at me horribly and began to chuckle. I tried to push past him; but he stepped in front of me. It was during the dinner hour, and no one was about.

"'Where's your interfering policeman now?' he sneered.

"I was angry at the slighting manner in which he referred to you and asked him where my father was. At that, he made a clutch at me. I pushed him on the chest and he fell on one of the seats, striking his head against its back. The blow stunned him. He lay there, quite unconscious, and I was terrified almost out of my wits for I thought that had killed him. I felt cold all over. Then he began to mumble, and I caught daddy's name.

"'As a personal favour, Deslines,' he muttered, 'would you run me across to the hospital? I strolled over, and it would be a damned nuisance either to walk to the hospital or go home for my car. It would oblige me greatly, and would only take you a few minutes. I won't be stopping there.'

"I stared at him in amazement, then gradually began to realise the significance of his words. He had induced daddy to take him in the car after we returned home that night. I listened eagerly; but he remained silent for what seemed like hours. Every minute I feared that someone would come in; and just as I had made up my mind to leave, he spoke again.

"'They won't think of digging up one dead man to find another, Deslines,' he mumbled. 'You're safe till the Day of Judgment.'

"Then he opened his eyes and stared at me. Fearing further trouble if I stayed, I left as quickly as I dared, and hurried home.

"I did not sleep a wink that night, sergeant. A sixth sense told me that he had murdered my daddy, and had revealed his secret while unconscious on the seat in the School of Arts. But how was I to discover the truth from a few mumbled phrases? I pondered his words all night, repeating them over and over to myself, but I was no wiser when at last I fell asleep.

"Enlightenment came next afternoon. All day I had been repeating his words, and suddenly I realised just what they meant. 'They won't think of digging up one dead man to find another'! There was only one interpretation: my poor father had been buried with someone else! But with whom? I set myself to puzzle it out."

I paused, having suddenly thought of Myrtle, who I had promised should hear my story.

"Would you mind if I called my cousin?" I asked. "She is rather an important witness, having been more or less in my confidence from the outset."

"Get her, by all means," he concurred.

I ran to the foot of the stairs, and called softly. She came at once, and sat down beside the sergeant.

"Where was I? Oh! yes, I remember. I thought, and

thought, but without success. Then I had an inspiration. Obviously, Dr. Murray had not killed two men, so where was he to find a dead man with whom to bury daddy? There was only one place — in a cemetery! It also was obvious that it must be the local cemetery, otherwise he would need to carry a . . . a corpse" (I sobbed dramatically) "a long distance."

I paused to wipe my eyes, and gloated inwardly at the tense attention of my fool of a sergeant. Again wiping my eyes, I proceeded. "I went to the local newspaper office and hunted through the files. As I had anticipated, I learned that a Mr. Cummings had been buried that very day. I was convinced that my daddy lay in his grave."

The sergeant gave a muffled exclamation; and Myrtle gasped.

"You guess the rest, I know," I said. "For weeks I tried to pluck up courage to verify my theory; but it was such a dreadful task for a young girl that I faltered. Then I spurred myself by kneeling down under a pine tree one night — daddy always loved the old pines — and making a solemn vow to my dead father that I would expose his murderer."

I turned to Myrtle. "You remember how mystified you were, when I told you that I had made a promise to daddy?"

"Yes," she murmured. "I remember only too well."

"I thought you would. But even after I had made my solemn promise, I found it almost beyond my power to goad myself to action. Day followed day, and still I delayed."

"No wonder," interjected the sergeant. "Why didn't you inform the police?"

"I thought of that. My God! How often did I think of it; but what had I to tell them? A few words muttered by an unconscious man! Was I to ask them — to ask even you? — to move on such meagre evidence, disinter a dead man, and incur the displeasure of his relatives? Would I not have been laughed at, perhaps regarded as a lunatic? Also, if the police did act, to find my suspicions unfounded, what would be my position? The more I reflected, the more it was brought home to me that I, and I alone, must test my theory.

"While I was trying to screw my courage to the test, I had a very vivid dream. I thought that daddy came to me with a great hole in his chest, from which blood was running." (Again I interrupted my narrative to shudder for the benefit of my audience.) "He said nothing; just gazed at me sadly. It made a tremendous impression on me.

"I was too distraught just then to realise how natural such a dream was, in view of my perpetual concentration on the subject of his death. I told my cousin about it at once; I could not wait till morning, it had affected me so much. I went immediately to her room."

"That is so," volunteered Myrtle with a nod.

"Shortly after this, I acted. I went to the cemetery, found a shovel in a shed, and began to dig. But my strength failed before the task was completed. I was so exhausted that I could not even return the earth to the hole. I just had to run away and leave everything as it was. My poor hands were a mass of broken blisters, and my clothes were ruined. My cousin noticed my condition, and accused me of having been the culprit who disturbed a grave. That, of course, was after she had read the papers. I made no attempt to deny it. My conscience was clear; all I had to do, in event of emergency, was to explain everything.

"Following the uproar over the disturbed grave, I

lived in hope that the police would dig deeper; but they merely filled in the hole, leaving me where I had been at the outset. I waited until my hands had healed a little, then went to the cemetery again last night to complete my task. I dug, and dug! It seemed to me that never had a grave been made so deep. Then, just as I was beginning to despair, the shovel struck something. I was afraid to look, and stood shaking in the dark for a long, long time. But again I screwed up my courage, and turned my torch downward. I had no difficulty in identifying daddy's . . . poor daddy's . . . poor daddy's clothes. I think I went mad with grief. I jumped into the hole, and scraped the dirt away from his head with my fingers."

Here I sobbed hysterically, while Myrtle clasped my waist and the sergeant patted my head, both uttering soothing words which they might have addressed to a child. But I had my part to play, and clung to them desperately as I sobbed. When I judged that this pantomime had lasted long enough, I dried my eyes and proceeded with my story.

"His face, sergeant . . . his poor, dear face . . . How can I tell you? . . . But he was still my lost daddy, and I fondled his head. I was horrified when my fingers entered a terrible hole in the back of it. I shrieked aloud, and I think I must have fainted, for I can remember nothing till I found myself wetting a small towel under a tap. I had brought it to wipe my hands on, when the work blistered them. I had missed such an aid dreadfully on my first visit, and was careful to include it on this occasion. I washed his dear head as well as I could, then rinsed the towel and tied it over his wound. You see, even in my distracted state I could not bear to think of him contaminated by contact with the bare earth. Most persons . . . are laid to rest in

. . . in coffins, which protect them, while poor daddy had been thrown into a hole like a dead animal. Oh! it was horrible to think of. It is horrible to think of even now!"

Again I broke down, and again the dear fools comforted me.

"There is little more to tell. Somehow I reached home, completely exhausted, and got to bed, where I slept until my cousin woke me early this morning. I was stupid with pain and terror, and my hands ached frightfully."

I turned the palms upward for investigation, and he gasped at their condition.

"As soon as my senses were restored, I rang you up and told my cousin everything."

I ceased, and a prolonged silence ensued. Myrtle came to my side and placed a supporting hand about my waist, while the sergeant pondered.

"It certainly is a most extraordinary story, Miss Deslines," he said at length. "I am amazed that you found the courage to go through with it. Of course, you should have notified me in the first instance. You had no right to tamper with a grave; it is a rather serious offence.

"Now, don't worry about that," he exclaimed hastily, as the tears gathered in my eyes. "There is not going to be any trouble over it. The world will admire your pluck and persistence; and I can assure you — unofficially, of course — that you won't get into trouble. You just leave everything to the, and it will all come right. We'll have Dr. Murray by the heels in short order. The man is a fiend. In all my experience I've not met his equal, and that's saying something. But now I've got another duty to perform. I must take down your story and ask you to sign it. Before doing that, I have to warn you that there is no need to say anything, and that anything you do say may be used against you."

I gave a little scream, and Myrtle hugged me to her breast.

"Don't worry over that warning, Miss Deslines," he cried. "It is merely part of my duty. I know that you did not kill your father. But I am forced by the regulations to warn you; it's merely a formality. Now let us get the story in writing."

Myrtle procured pen and ink, and he laboriously transcribed the tale, which I signed.

He patted my head at parting. "You're a game little thing, miss. You deserve to see your father's murderer hanged."

CHAPTER XXII

THE EXCITEMENT WAS intense. Daddy's body was removed to the morgue, and buried two days later on an order from the coroner. The hatchet found beside him was tested for finger-prints. The result was negative; evidently its long burial had destroyed incriminating evidence. Crowds thronged the cemetery, surveying with morbid interest the now famous grave. Our home was besieged by reporters and police. I was forced to narrate my story a dozen times, and was careful always to include the incident witnessed by my accommodating sergeant when Dr. Murray had attempted to force his attentions on me. I was deliberately creating atmosphere against possible developments. In event of suspicion being directed to myself, I wished to have certain preconceptions firmly established in the minds of the jurymen.

Such a wave of sympathy with me swept the State that felt quite safe. The Press was unanimously on my side, referring to me as "The Girlish Heroine," "The Heroine of a Graveyard Vigil," and similar fantastic names. I was photographed in a hundred attitudes. One enterprising Sunday newspaper went to the length of suggesting that I should pose in the clothes which I had worn when digging, with a shovel in my hand. I refused, fearing that acquiescence might detract from my popularity. It was most important that I should be regarded as the innocent victim of a man's lust and unscrupulousness — a man who first had murdered the father, and then had attempted to force his unwelcome attentions on the grief-stricken daughter.

My story was exaggerated and distorted to afford recreation for the multitude. Murray was portrayed as a fiend incarnate. True his name was excluded religiously from the narratives, but the inference was plain. They managed to introduce his portrait in their columns as the guardian who had relinquished his authority. One daring weekly sheet openly stated that his resignation had taken place under duress, following an interview with a police official. He was "cut" by his acquaintances, and his patients sought a less notorious physician. He became a pariah, and then a recluse. By the end of a fortnight he had ceased to frequent the streets, and remained in the seclusion of his home. My bold stroke had vindicated my judgment. Even the Attorney-General, in response to questions asked in Parliament, stated that no action was contemplated by the Crown over the violation of the grave. This prosaic announcement appeared under such captions as "Katoomba Heroine to Escape Prosecution," "Brave Girl Immune from Trouble over Grave Incident," "Authorities Sympathise with Father's Avenger."

Throughout the hubbub which centred about me I preserved a meek demeanour. I wore deep black, hid my features behind a veil in public, spoke in monosyllables when addressed, made full use of tear-dimmed eyes, and otherwise exercised my ability as an actress to enhance the favourable impression which prevailed. I doubt if a jury would have convicted me, had the Crown produced a dozen eye-witnesses to testify that I had slain my father.

I was safe, safe! I had extracted my affairs from chaos, and now trod in ordered security.

Thus matters stood when the coroner's inquiry was held. It was regarded as a *cause célèbre*, and the court-room was thronged with the inquisitive and the morbid. Outside, people who had been unable to force their way into the limited confines of the court clustered in hundreds.

I was not represented by a solicitor. I realised that greater latitude would be accorded me if unadvised. Besides, I had more faith in my histrionic ability than in the forensic oratory of the greatest advocate in the land. My pliant sergeant conducted affairs for the Crown, and a solicitor from Sydney represented Dr. Murray.

There was a stir when I entered the witness-box. It crystallised into whispering as I removed my veil at the request of the coroner. I had taken the precaution to sit up during the preceding night; this had created dark rings under my eyes. My hair had been carefully teased into curls and waves with a damp comb. My cheeks had been made pallid with powder. I wore my most woebegone look. I must have looked pathetically girlish, with the sides of the tall witness-box concealing my figure and only my white cheeks and black eyes, underlaid with dark circles, showing above its coping. To heighten the effect I took care to speak in a husky whisper.

"Just tell his Worship your story, as you told it to me," commanded the sergeant.

"Take your time," advised the coroner sympathetically, as I broke into subdued sobbing. "I'm sorry that it is necessary to upset you like this. Just take your time, and tell me everything in your own way."

I described in detail the events that took place on the night of daddy's disappearance, proceeding to the appointment of Dr. Murray and my grandmother as my joint guardians. During the recital the court was enveloped in a hush where the drop of a pin would have resounded like a clap of thunder. The first interruption came when I reached the incident with Dr. Murray in the lounge.

"I object," boomed his solicitor. "It is not relevant. My client is not on trial. This court is only interested in the actual events which attended the death of William Charles Deslines."

"I will note your objection," said the coroner, after a pause. "I may state that I do not consider myself bound by the strict rules of evidence. They pertain to higher courts. My concern is to determine the cause of the death of William Charles Deslines. The witness in the box is a child, unrepresented, and naturally distraught. I intend to give her every latitude. It is for me to sift the relevant from the irrelevant, and record my finding."

"I ask your Worship to note my objection."

"I have done so."

"I thank your Worship."

In hushed tones I continued my story, and had the satisfaction of seeing Dr. Murray writhe, as all eyes were turned to him when I told of my visit to the sergeant and the subsequent denouement in the lounge.

The hypothetical meeting in the vestibule of the School of Arts completed his demoralisation. His face became a vivid red. His ears coloured in sympathy. The veins protruded on his temples. These stigmata of temper were interpreted by the onlookers as evidence of guilt. I believe that he would have been lynched forthwith had a leader arisen to suggest it.

Tensely the big audience hung on my graphic description of my two journeys to the cemetery. I employed all the arts at my command in its narration. I made dramatic pauses to wipe my eyes. I burst into fits of bitter sobbing. I spoke daddy's name in a reverent undertone which bespoke uncontrollable grief. Almost to a man my auditors were with me; the sole exceptions were Dr. Murray and his counsel.

In vain the latter protested against my evidence. "The surmises of this young lady are scarcely evidence, your Worship."

"I am granting her full latitude. Later I shall decide what is evidence."

"It is grossly unfair to my client."

"He will have an opportunity to refute her statements when he enters the box."

"Will your Worship allow him similar latitude?"

"He will be permitted to deny such assertions as relate to himself."

I concluded on a dramatic note, exposing my torn hands to the public gaze. There were murmurs of pity and sympathy when the indurations and raw areas on my palms were surveyed. I felt that I had done well.

There was yet the ordeal of cross-examination to come. Dr. Murray's solicitor, with pages of notes exposed on the table before him, rose, cleared his throat, and remarked: "If your Worship pleases."

At a nod from the coroner he began:

"You say that Dr. Murray forced his attentions on you against your will?"

"The sergeant and a constable saw him."

"I'm not asking you that. Please answer my questions as shortly as possible. Did you not encourage Dr. Murray?"

"No."

"Was he not in the habit of kissing you, with your consent?"

"Yes. Poor daddy always kissed me good night, and when Dr. Murray began to do the same thing I considered it was right, seeing that he was my guardian."

"It did not strike you as wrong for a girl of your years to be kissed by a married man?"

"No, not under those circumstances."

"What age are you?" interposed the coroner.

"Fifteen, sir." I heard gasps in the audience.

"Is anything to be gained by following that line of argument," asked the coroner. "It is totally irrelevant."

"My client is virtually charged by this witness with seduction and murder. His position is very serious."

"And do you think it would affect the former charge to any extent if it could be shown that a child of fifteen had been a consenting party? In any case, Dr. Murray is not on trial here."

"Very well, your Worship, I'll come to the alleged meeting in the School of Arts." He turned to me: "You said you encountered Dr. Murray in the vestibule. Is that correct?"

"Yes."

"What day was it?"

"I can't remember."

"Ah! you can't remember the date when Dr. Murray, according to your statement, virtually confessed that he had murdered your father? Do you ask this court to believe that?"

"Yes."

"Would you not think that such an important event would be impressed indelibly on your memory?"

"It was! It is! I shall never forget him, lying back on

the seat all white and still, and mumbling that daddy was safe till the Day of Judgment."

"Never mind that," he ejaculated testily. "Just answer my questions. Can you recall the date?"

"No."

"Would there be any record in the books of the School of Arts to bring it to memory?"

"No. I did not enter the School of Arts. I ran away just after Dr. Murray spoke."

"Now, I suggest that it is all a lie; that you deliberately concocted this story for your own ends, whatever they may be."

"Concocted it!" There was undiluted amazement in my voice. "Why should I concoct such a terrible thing?" I paused to wipe my eyes. "And if I concocted it, how did I come to find poor . . . poor daddy in the grave? Does that look like a concoction? Who put him there? How did Dr. Murray know he was there? How did Dr. Murray know he was dead, even? How . . . how . . ." I broke down and sobbed without restraint.

"I really can't see how you are assisting your client by persisting in this line of cross-examination," said the coroner.

"I wish to afford you every opportunity to refute certain statements which have been made; but, as you remarked yourself, Dr. Murray is not on trial. In any case, you must accept the witness's answers. Dr. Murray will have ample opportunity to present his case when he enters the box."

"Very well, your Worship," rejoined the solicitor sourly. "I'll not trouble this — er — unsophisticated young lady anymore." He sat down, and gathered his papers together.

"Just one question, before you stand down," said the sergeant. "You did not kill your father?"

"I? Did I kill daddy? Oh, my God! he was the only soul on earth who loved me; the only soul whom I loved. Oh, daddy, daddy!" The tears streamed down my cheeks.

"Miss Deslines," said the coroner gently, "the sergeant does not mean to be unkind. It is necessary to answer his question. Just say 'yes' or 'no.' Listen carefully! Did you kill your father?"

"No, no, no! Oh, my God! no! Poor, dear old daddy! Why should I kill him?"

"That's all," he said kindly. " You may leave the box. Just take a seat there," pointing to some vacant chairs on the opposite side of the room, inside the railing.

Necks were craned, and a buzz of whispering arose, as the sergeant assisted me to one of the chairs, where I readjusted my veil and sat meekly.

My grandmother was the next witness. With her jaw thrust out, and her absurd hair brushed back, she took complete charge of proceedings. In vain the sergeant attempted to ask questions, and the coroner strove to restrain her. She ignored them both, rambling on at a furious pace. The deposition clerk worked arduously at his typewriter, his fingers fairly flying; but he must have discovered it difficult to set her story down on paper. She was incoherence itself. The unfortunate Dr. Murray came in for severe castigation. He was a seducer, a liar, and a murderer. She brushed the solicitor aside contemptuously when he protested, and perforce he joined the impotent listeners, who had bowed to the fury of her eloquence.

There were no questions when she had finished. Plainly all were glad to see her leave the witness-box. She had not shed much light on father's death; but she had intensified the feeling against Dr. Murray. I almost discovered the mind to pity the fat little pawn in this Homeric battle of wits. He was so hopelessly compromised.

The sergeant had to bellow "Silence!" several times, before order was restored, when Dr. Murray entered the box. People moved in their seats, shuffled their feet, whispered to one another, and craned to view the monster. He was commendably cool; but blood suffused his cheeks and neck, and beads of sweat glistened on his forehead. He knew that the gin was closing inexorably.

"Dr. Murray," said his solicitor, "you have heard the previous witnesses. What comment have you to offer?"

"It is a tissue of monstrous lies."

"Did you kill Mr. Deslines?"

"The question is absurd. Most emphatically, no!"

"Was he your friend?"

"My greatest friend."

"In your opinion, who did kill him?"

"Don't answer that question," interposed the coroner. "We are not here to listen to surmises. Keep to what you know; don't discuss what you may think."

"Is there any truth in the statement about the alleged meeting in the School of Arts?" continued the solicitor.

"Absolutely none."

"Have you, at any time, met Miss Deslines in the vestibule of the School of Arts?"

"Never."

"Did you try to seduce her in her house?"

"You remember the occasion when the police burst in the door of the lounge-room?"

"Yes."

"Tell his Worship, shortly, what preceded their arrival."

"I really can't see the use of this," protested the coroner.

"Your Worship promised us opportunity to refute the assertion made by Miss Deslines."

"Very well, I'll permit Dr. Murray to proceed, though I confess I cannot see how it will advantage him. As far as I can gather, the police are alleged to have found him in a compromising position. How much the question whether the child was a consenting party affects the issue is for you to determine; but I trust the time of this court won't be wasted unduly."

"We will not press the point," commented the solicitor. "Possibly the opportunity to clear my client's reputation will be afforded in another jurisdiction. We will wait till then."

"I think you are wise," said the coroner quietly. "Have you finished with your witness?"

"I have nothing more to ask him, your Worship."

"Have you any questions, sergeant?"

"Only one, your Worship. Dr. Murray, have you any knowledge of the circumstances attending the death of Mr. Deslines?"

"No."

"Of your own knowledge, are you in possession of any facts that would explain how he came to be done to death in Katoomba Cemetery, or buried there?"

There were many witnesses. The sergeant gave evidence about the discovery of the initial attempt to open the grave, followed by what he had found there after his interview with me. The Government Medical Officer explained that death had been caused by a blow on the head with a sharp instrument. The hatchet produced was capable of inflicting such a wound. Grandmother was recalled to furnish details of daddy's insurances. An expert testified that the handle of the hatchet was innocent of finger-prints. It was dreadfully monotonous and uninteresting.

In recording his finding, the coroner read at length from a sheet of foolscap, on which he had been writing industriously for several minutes. I preserved a copy when it appeared in the newspapers next morning. It read:

"The evidence submitted to me to-day, touching the death of William Charles Deslines, presents many extraordinary features. Much of it is irrelevant, and therefore inadmissible. I am delivering my finding on statements which are strictly admissible at law. In the main, the discarded evidence is mere conjecture, suspicion, and deduction. On the evidence before me, subject to the foregoing deletion, it is apparent that the last person known to have seen the deceased alive was his daughter. She left him in the car and went upstairs to bed. There is nothing to show that anybody else saw him again until his body was exhumed in the dead of night by his daughter. It seems certain that he was killed by a blow with a sharp instrument, presumably the tomahawk which was found beside him in the grave at the cemetery. I find that William Charles Deslines was foully and wilfully murdered by some person or persons unknown."

CHAPTER XXIII

Flushed with victory, but preserving my staid demeanour, I left the court with Myrtle and my grandmother. We had to face a battery of cameras and fight our way through an inquisitive throng, all eager to catch a glimpse of the girl who had played such a prominent part in a most unusual case. They clutched my hands, tore the veil from my face, cheered frantically, and otherwise comported themselves like savages. I endured it complacently, for was it not a spontaneous tribute to my masterful acting? I had won their sympathy and regard, turning imminent disaster into a regal triumph. My arch-enemy had suffered a deadly wound, and must lurk in hiding lest he be torn to ribbons by the incensed mob. He even was in grim danger of arraignment on the charge of murder. The police almost certainly would dog his footsteps, seeking evidence to complete his destruction. A bold design, executed without faltering, had rescued me from the pit. The folly of my temporary dementia had been dissipated. My heart surged with joy, and I experienced difficulty in maintaining my pose of shocked grief. Nevertheless, I did not commit the blunder of regarding Dr. Murray too cheaply. He was a dour little man, for all his pink plumpness, and no one can graduate in one of the higher professions without making powerful friends.

That I was justified in my doubt was disclosed three days after the inquest, when I received a visit from a detective-sergeant of the Criminal Investigation Branch. He was a tall, florid man of possibly forty years of age, with a swarthy jowl and the comic-opera name of O'Flanagan. I learned later that he was considered one of the most astute officers in the service.

"I am sorry to worry you so soon after your trouble," he apologised. "But duty is duty, and I have no option."

I sighed wearily. "I had hoped that the matter was ended, and I would have a little peace."

"Naturally, Miss Deslines. However, I shall not bother you much. I merely wish to confirm the reports received from the officer in charge of the local station. Perhaps the simplest method would be for you to tell your story, just as you told it to him before the inquiry."

"Is it necessary? I told everything in my evidence."

"It is quite necessary; otherwise I would not be here. Of course, I can't compel you to say anything against your will; but you will make things easy for both of us if you will consent."

I thought for a moment. "I have no objection, Mr. O'Flanagan. I merely had hoped that I was done with the painful affair forever."

"Naturally, Miss Deslines," he repeated, and extracted his watch, a heavy silver hunting-piece. During my narrative he amused himself by flicking its front case open and shut. It was a most irritating habit; but possibly the trick was designed for just that purpose, and I kept my temper. I had not the slightest intention of being goaded into saying anything stupid.

"H'm," he commented, when I had finished. "It reads just like a detective novel."

"Really?" My voice expressed polite surprise at the criticism.

He smiled genially. "Don't take me the wrong way. I meant nothing beyond the fact that the circumstances are most unusual."

"I did not dream that you did, Mr. O'Flanagan."

"Naturally."

The ridiculous word appeared to be his constant adverb. Here, also, I must guard against irritation!

"You know," he remarked, "that was a smart bit of work on your part, when you deduced the hiding-place of your father's body. You actually had very little to work on."

"Do you think so? To my mind, it revealed everything, once I had grasped its significance."

"That's what amazes me. For a young, inexperienced girl to weld such links together is almost miraculous. You are exceedingly clever, Miss Deslines."

I accepted the compliment without comment.

"I greatly doubt whether I could have solved that particular problem, myself."

"Naturally." I could not resist the temptation, and had to fight down a grin when he smiled crookedly.

"Yes, you're clever, Miss Deslines."

"I appreciate your opinion, Mr. O'Flanagan; but I'm afraid you'd find it difficult to convince my friends and relations."

"Dr. Murray has no doubt about your cleverness," he said, turning the fingers of his left hand to him and picking at his nails.

"I don't value his opinion. He's an abominable little man; and . . . and he killed my daddy."

O'Flanagan dropped his hand to his knee and looked up. "I am not so sure of that, Miss Deslines."

"Indeed! then who did?"

"Ah! that's the problem we have to solve; and it's not going to be easy."

I shook my head. "Dr. Murray killed him, Mr. O'Flanagan. He betrayed himself that day at the School of Arts. He's guilty as hell."

"H'm!"

"Ask the local sergeant for his opinion. I have not discussed the matter with him; but he has the advantage of knowing a little about the doctor, and I know what his verdict would be."

"Naturally."

"Do *you* know the doctor?"

He examined his nails critically. "Not very well."

"Naturally."

He laughed, and rose. "I must be getting along, Miss Deslines, and will say good-bye. I admire your sense of humour very much. You are a captivating antagonist."

He left me pondering the word. Antagonist!—a captivating antagonist! Was it possible . . . ?

I feared to complete the question.

Day followed day; the winter had come again; and still Dr. Murray remained at liberty. I had heard nothing further from Detective-Sergeant O'Flanagan; but the silence had not tended to ease my mind. Obviously the man had been suspicious, and was prejudiced against me. I feared his apparent inertia more than overt action. He was a dangerous foe.

In desperation, driven by tormenting doubts, I resolved to interview the sergeant. I found him seated in his office, compiling returns.

"You're looking quite your old self, Miss Deslines," he commented.

"I'm feeling almost my old self," I admitted. "Has there been any new development about . . . poor daddy ? "

He shook his head. "Not a thing."

"Is Dr. Murray to go scot free, after having committed such an atrocious crime?"

He scratched his chin thoughtfully. "You and I know he is guilty; but the trouble is evidence. So far, there's not a thing to go to a jury. Even your own evidence merely concerns a few words mumbled by an unconscious man. It requires something stronger than that before a man can be arrested, let alone sent to the gallows."

"The coroner knew he was guilty. Why did he let him go?"

"He couldn't possibly commit for trial on the evidence before him. The Attorney-General would have refused to file a bill, and he'd most likely have been rapped over the knuckles. He had no option, miss."

I sighed. "I suppose I'm unreasonable; but it seems terrible that daddy's murderer should go free."

"It's damnable, miss; and that's the plain English of it, if you'll excuse the expression."

"Excuse it!" I laughed grimly. "It doesn't half express what I think about it."

He wagged his head sympathetically.

"I had a visit from a man named O'Flanagan a little while ago," I said carelessly. "He told me he was a detective-corporal or something, from Sydney."

"Detective-sergeant, miss. He's one of the best men in the C.I.B."

"How thrilling! He said he did not believe Dr. Murray was guilty."

The sergeant bridled. "That's the worst of those plain-clothes fellows; they get notions before they investigate, and don't trouble to ask men who are on the spot and in touch with the details."

"I suggested that he should interview you about it."

"What did he say to that?" he asked eagerly.

"I can't remember his actual words; but he sneered at you, and let me understand plainly that he regarded you as a fool."

"Did he use the word fool, miss?"

"No, he didn't. I want to be quite fair. He merely conveyed that impression. I wish I could remember just what he did say."

"There's no need, Miss Deslines. I know O'Flanagan, and I know that he considers all uniformed officers fools. I'd almost give a stripe to show him a thing or two."

"Why don't you?" I whispered.

"Eh?" He gave me a startled look.

"Why don't you concentrate on getting evidence against Murray? You have the advantage of *knowing* the guilty party. While he's wasting his time chasing shadows, you can be running the real criminal to earth. It would be a nasty blow to his pride if you — er — landed the bacon while he floundered in the mud."

He slapped his thigh and chuckled. "By God, I'll do it, Miss Deslines. As you say, I *know*; and if he is working on the assumption that Murray is innocent, I'll have a considerable start. Lord! how the boys would grin if I put it across that conceited know-all."

"There seems to be no actual evidence against anyone, sergeant," I said reflectively. "Even his finger-prints had vanished from the axe he used. It's going to be a big problem. If we could only get some admission from him!"

He shook his head dolefully. "Not much chance of that. He's more cunning than a fox. Still, he must have left some trace — the cleverest of 'em do — and I'm going to find it, if it takes me a year."

I felt quite elated as I walked home. The astute O'Flanagan would discover difficulties in worming details out of the sergeant. There is nothing so cogent as injured vanity to close a loquacious mouth.

That night I dreamed of Minerva for the first time for many months. She was assailed by a host of barbarians. Among them I identified O'Flanagan, Dr. Murray, the sergeant, and the coroner. It was the detective who struck her down, but the sergeant who was impaled on her spear. She pointed an accusing finger at me ere her eyes glazed in death, and a mocking smile was frozen on her lips.

CHAPTER XXIV

I RECEIVED A letter from Myrtle a few days after my visit to the sergeant. It stated that she was working hard at her studies, and missed me greatly. Following a lengthy narrative of an intimate character, she referred to the subject of Dr. Murray and the death of my father.

"The queer thing is," she wrote, "that the medical world refuses to credit his guilt. They admit the strength of the presumptive evidence against him, but dismiss it as an ironical gesture of circumstance. The students are less dogmatic, but in this case there is my own influence to consider. Knowing at first hand just what happened, my word carries weight with them. On the other hand, the graduates regard me as a prejudiced witness and steadfastly express their faith in the little monster. There even is talk of opening a special fund to assist him in rehabilitating himself in public esteem. It is common talk that Professor Batlow has had several interviews with the Inspector-General of Police, and a regular fusillade is being directed at the Chief Secretary. The medical world seems determined to force the issue with a view to clearing Murray from suspicion."

The note concluded with a lengthy array of derogatory adjectives describing Dr. Murray; and an equally extensive list of an opposite character applied to me. I kissed the

tinted paper, and sighed. It makes one miserable to be isolated when tormented by vague fears. I would have given
much to have had Myrtle with me again.

A careful review of matters served to restore my cheer-
fulness. I had little hope that the crime would be charged to
Murray officially, however he might be viewed by an undiscriminating public. It takes more than flimsy deductive evidence to bring a man to the bar of justice. Beyond the ruin
of his professional career, Murray was in no danger. He
merely had been outwitted in a grotesque contest. On the
other hand, I felt myself equally safe. Without doubt
Detective O'Flanagan was suspicious about me; but where
was he to obtain evidence? The more I pondered my position, the more I came to regard it as impregnable. The
public might suspect the unhappy doctor, and the detective might suspect me; but neither side could advance a
step beyond suspicion. Actually, both of us could afford to
sneer at our adversaries and go calmly about our business.

In this comfortable frame of mind, I was not unduly
alarmed when Jenny announced that Detective-Sergeant
O'Flanagan wished to speak to me. Certainly, I experienced a momentary palpitation, followed by a dryness of
the throat. But the disturbance was transitory; it passed
after a moment's reflection. I could be convicted only
from my own mouth, and I smiled as I contemplated the
remoteness of such a contingency. I merely had to guard
my words carefully, to remain secure. I descended to the
sitting-room, where O'Flanagan was standing with his
back to the fire, warming himself.

"Good afternoon, Mr. O'Flanagan," I said. "Have you
come to announce that you have completed the chain of
evidence against Dr. Murray?"

He leaned his shoulders against the Mantel. "I'm

afraid not, Miss Deslines. I'm beginning to think the case is beyond solution. So much time has elapsed since your father was killed, that there is little prospect of obtaining fresh evidence."

I pulled an easy chair across, so that my back was to the window and my face shadowed. "Won't you sit down?" I invited, nodding at a settee which faced the light.

"If you'll excuse me, I'd rather stand here. It's bitter outside, and I'm chilled right through."

"Please yourself. I understand from the maid that you wish to see me."

"Just a couple of unimportant questions. Headquarters have been shaking me up, and there are one or two points on which I am not too clear."

I settled my dress about my knees. "I'd be only too pleased to assist as far as lies in my power."

"Thanks, Miss Deslines. I won't worry you much." He gazed at the ceiling and fingered his chain. "Which road did you take when you and your late father drove to Wentworth Falls that night?"

"The Bathurst Road."

"Naturally. But where did you cross the railway line?"

"At the level crossing beside Katoomba Station."

"Quite so! And when returning?"

"At the level crossing again."

"H'm!" He took out his watch and commenced flicking its lid open and shut. "What time would that be?"

I affected to reflect. "It's difficult to say. Somewhere between eleven and twelve."

He dangled his watch by its chain, watching it rotate. "You're certain of that?"

"Quite."

He stirred the watch to activity with his forefinger.

"That's strange. The night watchman was in front of Goldsmith's timber-yard about 3 a.m., and is positive that your Singer car passed along Bent Street."

Again I felt that curious dryness at the back of my throat, but I gave no outward evidence of concern. Mastering the impulse to lubricate my parched throat with saliva, I leaned forward eagerly. "You mean that he saw the car there about three in the morning?"

He nodded, watching me intently, with the watch hanging inert at the end of its chain like a spent pendulum.

"Doesn't that provide you with an important link in the evidence against Dr. Murray," I asked excitedly.

He looked blank. "Against Dr. Murray?"

"Certainly. It proves that someone else used the car after we had returned from Wentworth Falls."

"Ah!"

"You remember how Dr. Murray betrayed to me that he had asked father to drive him across to the hospital?"

He said nothing, but continued to gaze with a half smile on his lips.

"Well," I proceeded, "here is corroborative evidence. Some time before midnight, daddy and I returned home. I went straight to my bedroom, leaving him to park the car. Now we find that it was seen hours later, being driven down Bent Street. Surely that is an important piece of evidence!"

"I think you're the cleverest little lady I've ever met," he said with genuine admiration, and set to spinning his watch in ever-widening circles.

I dismissed the ambiguous compliment with a wave of the hand. "I can't see anything very clever in solving that simple problem."

"Naturally."

"The trouble is," I commented didactically, "that you are handicapped by building your evidence on a false foundation. You seem to have got it firmly into your head that Dr. Murray is innocent, and you can't fit the segments into their proper places. If you would only throw your prejudices and preconceptions overboard, you might get somewhere. As it is . . ." I finished with a suggestive gesture.

He closed his watch, thoughtfully, and restored it to his pocket. "You seem almighty certain that Dr. Murray murdered your father?"

"Almighty certain," I concurred. "You see, I know so much."

"Yes," he murmured, more to himself than for my ears, "you certainly know a lot." Suddenly he grinned broadly. "You'd have made an admirable detective."

"Do you think so?"

"I do. You'd have made an excellent sleuth. As it is . . ." He paused.

"Yes?"

"As it is, you make a captivating antagonist."

I rose and faced him. "That is the second time you have said that, Mr. O'Flanagan. Would it be rude to ask what you mean?"

He waved his hand airily. "I suppose it's crudely expressed. I am an unqualified admirer of your cleverness, as I've already told you. But I can't help feeling that you resent my questions. In fact, you resent my investigating the case at all. That's why I referred to you as an antagonist. I've sort of . . . sort of got on your nerves."

"Naturally," I rejoined drily, and we both exploded in laughter.

After he had left I remained seated by the fire, thinking. I was anything but easy in mind. There was something in his cool insolence which affrighted me. I realised that more underlay his cryptic utterances than the mere words conveyed. His repeated references to my cleverness were not the spontaneous tributes of an admirer; they were ironic, fraught with sinister meaning. How much had been observed by the watchman? His intrusion at this late hour was disturbing. Had he been able to distinguish me as I drove past? I comforted myself with the thought that, at worst, it would be merely his word against mine. His testimony might be sufficient to place me in an atmosphere similar to that which enveloped Dr. Murray; but to one of my solitary disposition such an outcome would be of trivial import. The opinions of others found little place in my philosophy.

The entrance of my grandmother interrupted my meditations.

"What did the detective want?" she asked.

"He came to tell me that a night watchman saw our little Singer in Bent Street at three o'clock in the morning when daddy disappeared."

"Good gracious!" She was obviously startled.

"Grandmother," I whispered, "that proves that Dr. Murray did persuade daddy to drive him to the hospital after I went to bed."

"I hope it's enough to hang him," she exclaimed viciously.

I shook my head dismally. "I'm afraid not, grandmother. The detective won't have it that he is guilty."

"Who does he think was driving the car about at that hour, if it wasn't the man who murdered your father?"

I looked at her with mingled horror and grief in my eyes.

"I'm beginning to think that he imagines I was driving the car at the time."

She gaped. "You! What would you be doing there at that hour?"

"God knows, grandmother. He forgets that you heard me come in before twelve. Though, of course, I could have gone out again later, I suppose."

"Did I hear you come in," she inquired with surprise.

"Of course you did. Don't you remember asking me, next morning, why we went driving at such a late hour?"

She pondered, wrinkling her forehead. "I seem to remember something of the kind."

"Of course you do, grandmother. You said, 'Where were you till nearly midnight?'"

"So I did. I remember now."

She asked innumerable questions about my interview with the detective, to which I replied with apparent ingenuousness, while exercising care to withhold all information of importance. I had gained my point. In event of investigation she would be prepared to swear that she had heard me enter the house before midnight. Cross-examination or counter-suggestion would only serve to make her more grimly confident. My grandmother had her qualities.

After tea I strolled across to the police station, to acquaint my sergeant of the development about the night watchman. I was anxious to ascertain just how much the latter had observed as the car passed him.

"That's important evidence," he commented, wagging his head solemnly.

"And this detective-corporal did not inform you?"

"Detective-sergeant, miss. No, he didn't bother to tell me."

"Thinks you too much of a fool, I suppose," I sneered. "He may alter his opinion before I've finished."

"He *will* alter his opinion. I'm confident you'll solve the mystery, sergeant."

He walked back to town with me. "I'm going to interview that watchman right now," he volunteered. "I'll give him a bit of a wigging for not having told me of it before."

"I know it wouldn't do for me to come with you, sergeant; but I wish you'd do me a little favour. I'm keen on your succeeding, and know that eventually you will. Would it be a breach of the regulations if you rang me up later, to tell me if he managed to recognise Dr. Murray?"

He reflected. "I can't see much harm in it, miss, provided it goes no farther. It must be a little secret between you and me."

"Thank you, sergeant. If I learn anything from that conceited detective, I'll let you know at once. I'm on your side right through the piece."

"You're certainly staunch, Miss Deslines," he said gratefully.

It was just on ten o'clock when the telephone bell jangled in the hall. "I saw the watchman," came the sergeant's voice. "He doesn't know much. He isn't even sure it was your car; he only thinks it was. He says he did not pay it particular attention, and would have thought no more about it if O'Flanagan hadn't come nosing round him to see if he had noticed anything that night."

"Thank you, sergeant. Keep going. You'll win."

"I hope so, miss."

I went to bed with a light heart, and slept soundly.

CHAPTER XXV

NEXT EVENING I heard the bells again. I was standing by my bedroom window, striving to peer through the glass, when their musical tinkle sounded behind me. Whirling swiftly, I listened with bated breath. It was not a delusion; like an echo from Fairyland their notes trembled on the air. I felt an impulse to scream. After months of respite, during which I laboriously had remedied the consequences of my temporary mania, was I again to be plunged into the vortex of insanity—to commit God knew what follies? I clenched my hands till the knuckles grew white with the pressure, and strove to orient myself. I tried the effect of dispassionate reasoning, grimly keeping in mind the fact that the sound was due to a mental aberration. But the infernal notes persisted, swelling in cadences which echoed sweetly over my shoulder. I felt my brain reeling. Thought became chaotic. In desperation I flung a coat about me and went out into the night.

It had been snowing since nightfall. A shining mantle covered the landscape, throwing back the rays of the stars in a diffused twilight. Trees dropped under weight of their white encrustation. Roofs gleamed ghostly in the eerie light. Copings of frozen vapour surmounted the fences. My feet sank to the ankles at each step, and clouds of dry spume drove before my toes. I plunged recklessly onward, with the devilish tinkling of the bells accompanying me.

I was half-way to Medlow Bath before my wits began to function. Taking a firm grasp of my mental faculties, I sat on a snow-bound log and thought. I found it difficult to reason. In the midst of trains of logic I experienced insane impulses to shout. Once I discovered myself dancing frenziedly in the snow while I indulged in peals of laughter. Throughout the bells tinkled . . . tinkled!

I raced home like a madwoman, impelled by an unreasoning desire to outdistance that devilish music that haunted me. I cast frightened glances behind me. I dodged round bushes, sought the shadows of trees, waded in the icy waters of the gutters. It was futile. The subdued music kept pace with me, tinkling . . . tinkling!

Drenched with sweat, I ran, upstairs and sank gasping on my bed. I had left the electric radiator on, and soon trickles of water began to soak into the eider-down quilt as the loose snow on my clothes melted in the heat. The bells still rang softly in my rear. I groaned and sought the bathroom, where I lit the heater and plunged into a bath three-parts filled with hot water. It scorched my ankles until the pain grew almost unbearable. But I endured it stoically; and finally the pain subsided, to be succeeded by a generous warmth which permeated every nerve of my body. Then the bells ceased, dying slowly in the distance. Reclining in the pleasant bath, I reviewed the night's happenings. Why had The Voice not followed the overture of the bells? Would I have proved responsive had it whispered a command in my ear? What nature, would the command have assumed? I fell asleep, pondering the problem, to dream that I was lying naked on the side of a snow-clad hill. As I shivered there, Myrtle appeared over the brow and thrust at me with her foot. I began to roll, gaining impetus as I went. Over and over I sped at dizzy speed, and plunged into a creek flowing at the foot of the hill. I woke, to find myself still in the bath, whose water had cooled disturbingly. Hastily jumping out, I seized a rough towel and rubbed myself into a glow. Then I ran to my bedroom and clambered under the blankets. I was normal when Jenny wakened me next morning.

After breakfast I visited a chemist and ordered a large bottle of bromide.

"What kind of bromide?" he asked.

Dimly I recalled that bromide of some sort was used in photography. "The kind you use for developing films."

He eyed me curiously, and began to ask technical questions about photography, of which I knew nothing. I stammered and evaded, but he was implacable.

"I can't supply you with bromide," he declared. "If you really need it, the best thing to do is to get a prescription from a doctor."

Vainly I begged and pleaded. He was adamant. In desperation I pressed close to the counter and whispered a mad tale of sexual impulses. God knows what he thought; but ultimately he yielded and supplied me with a bottle of sedative, accompanied by strict instructions for its use. I caught him grinning widely as I turned to leave, clutching the precious bottle in my hand.

That night the bells jangled again. I hastily mixed a dose of bromide and swallowed it at a gulp. They ceased at once, but The Voice came a few minutes later.

"Listen, little Jean! You have outwitted O'Flanagan. You are safe. Flout him, child. Seek him out, and taunt him with your victory."

I sank back into a deep chair and shivered, covering my eyes.

"Find him, and taunt him!"

I sprang erect, boiling with rage. "I won't."

"I order you, Jean."

"I won't; I won't!"

Grandmother came running-into the room. "Whatever is the matter, Jean? What are you shouting about?"

"Was I shouting? I didn't know. I dozed off in the chair, and had a horrible dream."

"You're not looking too well," she said. "I think you need a good change. You're completely run down."

"I think I am," I concurred wearily. "I'm right out of sorts."

Thence onward The Voice and I fought steadily. It constantly urged me to approach the detective and taunt him, and I as steadfastly refused to obey. The fight was bitter, and I was given no respite. Day and night the whispers rang in my ears; but, curiously, the bells were not heard. The bromide appeared to have vanquished them. I was grimly determined to retain control of my actions; but I found that I must guard my every movement. Having failed by direct methods, The Voice initiated a campaign of subtlety. Twice I woke in the morning to discover a note on my dressing-table, addressed to Detective-Sergeant O'Flanagan, Criminal Investigation Branch, Sydney. I retained no recollection of having written them; they first were brought to my conscious mind when I saw them lying there, in readiness to post. It caused the sweat to break out on my brow in cold beads when I realised how close I had been to betraying myself. I continued to drink bromide; but, however effective it was proving to inhibit the bells, it had no effect on The Voice, which continued to tempt and torment me.

The unremitting struggle began to affect my health. My features were pinched and drawn, my cheeks sallow, and my eyes underlaid with black hollows. I was lethargic, and tired readily. Nevertheless, I always discovered the strength and courage to maintain my desperate battle against the domination of The Voice.

I believe I would have won, had daddy not intervened. I woke in the dead of night, when the struggle had been in progress about a month, to see him seated on the edge of my bed. He looked happy, and still wore the towel which I had bandaged about his head.

"You are acting foolishly, Jean," he commented, with his slow smile. "Why do you fight against the inevitable?"

"I wish to preserve my sanity."

"Is it an evidence of sanity to ignore good advice?"

"I do not consider it good advice."

He pulled at his bandage, forcing it lower. "Are you going to let this detective triumph?"

"Of course not. I have beaten him thus far, and he is helpless."

He smiled enigmatically. "Obey The Voice, Jean: it knows much that is hidden from you."

"Did it advise me for my good previously?"

He shrugged. "Did you sustain harm from obeying it?"

"No, thanks to the precautions I adopted when I realised how it had blundered."

"Possibly it anticipated those very precautions. You must realise that everything has happened for the best."

"None the less, it blundered," I persisted stubbornly.

"I don't think so. It succeeded in bringing everything

out into the daylight without casting a shred of suspicion on you."

"O'Flanagan suspects me."

"Then obey The Voice and defy his suspicions. Toss that noxious bromide down the sink. Be yourself. Recover your bloom. Restore your health. Above all, remember that forces of which you know nothing are protecting and guiding you, and cease to play the fool."

"You think I would do well to obey The Voice, daddy?"

"I *know* you would do well. I am unable to explain; I can merely give advice."

He grew tenuous before my eyes, and vanished.

I slept soundly that night for the first time for many weeks, and woke reinvigorated. Certainly black hollows still existed under my eyes, but there was a hint of colour in my cheeks, and their pinched look had gone. The extreme lassitude which had enveloped me also had fled. I felt the blood coursing in my veins, and ate a hearty breakfast. Grandmother commented on my improved appearance.

"Write to O'Flanagan," whispered The Voice as I walked down Katoomba Street in the afternoon. Without demur or resentment, I entered the post office, purchased a letter-card, and penned a brief note, stating that I wished to see him as early as possible. Having thus crossed the Rubicon, I became cheerful and contented in mind. The Voice did not worry me again; the keen wind whipped the roses back into my face; and a brisk walk impelled me to enjoy the evening meal. Another night's repose, dreamless and deep, banished the black circles from my eyes. I woke quite my old self, save for the comparative thinness of my limbs, and gave no thought to the forthcoming interview with the detective. I had resolved to await the issue of our conversation without planning a specific course.

He came next day, shortly after lunch. Although newly shaved, his jowl showed dark, and a suit of light grey tweed served to accentuate it. At his request, we retired to the little lounge-room where he had interviewed me first. A cheerful fire of coke glowed in a cast-iron basket, and the temperature of the room was deliciously warm. Idly I wondered at his suggestion that we should confer in the lounge. My wits were under complete control; but I was distressingly hazy about what I should reveal. Now that the hour had tolled, I was unable to decide how to break the ice. On his side, he appeared content to leave the initiative to me. He merely stared curiously, employing the time in his irritating habit of flicking his watch-case open and shut.

A slight noise on the veranda reached my ears. Perhaps I was abnormally acute under the stress. With the sound came realisation of his reason for having urged the lounge-room as the venue of our conference.

"Don't you think it would be more comfortable for the gentleman outside if he came in by the fire?" I asked casually.

He flushed. "What gentleman?"

"The gentleman who is making such an uproar stretching his cramped limbs."

He snapped his watch to, swung it deftly into the pocket of his waistcoat with a jerk of the chain, and laughed. "You're a particularly hard nut to crack, Miss Deslines. I'll send him about his business." Without the slightest trace of embarrassment he walked to the french window and called softly:

"Yes?" came a low voice from without.

"You need not wait, Stanton. I'll meet you at the railway station."

He returned to his chair. "Now, Miss Deslines," he said inquiringly.

I rose. "While you're putting on your coat, I'll get a set of furs. It is cold outside."

"Are we going outside?"

"Certainly. I wish to talk where there is no danger of eavesdroppers."

"The man has gone, on my word of honour."

"Quite so, but he might return. Anyhow, it's a glorious day for a walk. You'll enjoy it better than this stuffy room."

He grimaced. "Of course, it's in your hands; but I hate even to think of leaving this fire."

"Naturally," I rejoined, and he laughed.

Outside, he thrust his hands deep into the pockets of his greatcoat, and shivered theatrically. "It's a great pity," he murmured.

"What's a pity?"

"That we had to leave that comfortable room. I'm not acclimatised like you, and the cold gets me."

"You've only yourself to blame. We could have been there now, toasting our toes, only for your cleverness."

He sighed. "I'm always the mug."

"I'm inclined to agree with you."

He smiled sourly. That's consoling."

"The sergeant . . ." I hesitated.

"Is that his opinion, too?"

"Not exactly. He thinks you are conceited. I think his actual phrase was 'a conceited nincompoop.'"

"Naturally."

"I don't blame him," I commented.

"Why should you?"

"There's no reason at all."

Again he indulged that wry smile. "You're very frank, Miss Deslines."

"Naturally."

But he did not laugh. Instead, he studied me gravely. "What did you wish to see me about?" he asked, after a pause.

"About my father. Have you progressed in your investigations?"

"Yes, and no. I know who killed him, but I can't get the evidence."

"Would it be rude to ask who killed him?"

"It would not be rude, but I think it would be indiscreet."

"I own to being curious."

"That's rather surprising. I thought that you knew."

"So I do; but I'm curious to know whom you suspect. You have already indicated that you consider Dr. Murray innocent"

"You're quite right, Miss Deslines. I consider him innocent."

"I marvel that you could be so dense. Whom do you suspect?"

"To be frank, I think you are the culprit." He spoke quite casually, and adjusted a button at the top of his greatcoat. "Don't you think it's growing colder?" he inquired.

"No. It's only your imagination. It must be a dreadful thing to possess an imagination like yours."

"It frequently is dreadful for criminals. Personally, I am not affected by it."

"I can see that obtuseness has its uses."

He grinned. "It's a damned shame that I am compelled to hunt you down, Miss Deslines. I'm beginning to love you."

"Then you're in good company. Dr. Murray started the vogue."

He grew serious. "I believe you speak the truth there. Murray confessed everything to me, and admits that he permitted himself to be — er — seduced."

"How gallant of him! You must admire a medical man of nearly fifty who runs round the country bleating that he has been seduced by a child of fifteen. Did you ever consider the absurdity of it?"

"I can't say that I have. If you ask my opinion, I'll say that you are capable of seducing almost any man, except — "

He left the sentence unfinished.

"Except — ?"

"Except myself. Forewarned is forearmed. I don't know yet why you brought me here to-day; but if it was to test your arts on me, you are doomed to failure. I'm case-hardened."

"Don't worry your thick head," I said spitefully. "I'm extraordinarily particular whom I seduce. Your type does not appeal to me. Whatever Dr. Murray's disabilities, at least he has brains. I hate pudding-heads."

I saw the colour sweep over his face, and chuckled at the knowledge that I had pierced his armour.

"Why did you kill your father?" he asked.

"To mystify you."

"Then you succeeded beyond anticipation, for you mystify me completely. I can't pigeon-hole you accurately."

"Naturally," I mocked. "Such a proceeding would require at least average intelligence."

"Which I lack?"

"Naturally."

He took out his pipe and placed it, unlighted, between his teeth. Then The Voice whispered in my ear.

"Tell him, Jean," it murmured. "Tell him why you did it. There is no danger in confession to a single witness; it is merely word against word."

"Do you know what hormones are?" I inquired, when the prompting of my mentor had ceased.

He stared in amazement. "I can't say that I do."

"Or how the secretions of the endocrine glands function?"

"No."

"Or the effects of gland-grafts on the ego?"

"No."

"Then you could not understand."

"Understand what?"

"Why I killed daddy. He and Dr. Murray were conspiring to murder my identity, and I had to strike in self-defence."

"Ah," he said softly.

"I know what you are thinking; but it would be worse than futile for you to repeat my confession in a court, because I would deny it."

"Naturally."

"It would be your word against mine, and I would be given the benefit of the doubt."

"I realise that."

"So the confession is useless to you."

"Quite useless."

"Mock him!" urged The Voice.

"I broke Dr. Murray, and I've foiled you, Mr. O'Flanagan. You have both been defeated by a schoolgirl. I trust you enjoy the experience. You are a pudding-headed policeman, devoid of imagination. You have never heard bells chiming behind you at night, or The Voice murmuring in your ear. You have never seen hormones shooting

across the sky, seeking breasts to enter. You are an ignoramus. I sneer at you, I despise you. When next daddy
comes and sits on my bed, he'll roar with laughter at your
futility — roar till the bandage slips from his wound and his
brains bob in out like a jack-in-the-box. Go back to your
finger-prints and your schedules, and leave the detection
of crime to those who are better fitted to undertake it.
You! to suggest that I intended to seduce you! Why, you
poor fathead, I wouldn't insult my wits by condescending
to strive with you. I've told you everything, because I know
you lack the intelligence to utilise the knowledge."

"Good God!" he breathed, staring at me strangely.

"Go home, and pray to that same good God to give you
the gift of comprehension."

He shook his head slowly. "I think I comprehend only
too well," he said quietly, and walked away.

I danced my way homeward, grimacing at those who
turned to stare after me. "You acquitted yourself splendidly,"
whispered The Voice in my ear.

It was dark when I reached the front gate, and the
triumphant pealing of bells kept time with my footsteps as
I ran up the drive.

CHAPTER XXVI

THE BELLS CHIMED me to sleep that night; but The Voice was silent. Save for its brief word of commendation, while on my way home from the interview with O'Flanagan, it had made no comment on the way in which I had executed its command. But I knew that it was pleased, and I felt happy. Forgetful of the hour, I sang as I undressed, which made grandmother hammer on the wall beside her bed. I blew a kiss in her direction, and subdued my song to a low hum. I felt absurdly gay and irresponsible. The task completed, which I had dreaded for so many anxious weeks, I reacted from gloom to gaiety. Leaving the electric light on, when at length clad in pyjamas, I ran across the room, dived upon my bed, somersaulted across to the pillow, and snuggled under the blankets with a gleeful giggle. For a space I reviewed my recent interview with the detective, laughing aloud at his discomfiture. Then I fell asleep.

I woke, to find the light still burning brightly and daddy seated on the edge of my bed. He smiled affectionately as I caught his eye.

"You were splendid this afternoon, Jean," he remarked.

"Was I truly, daddy?"

"Splendid, child. You took all the bumptiousness out of that detective fellow. Lord! I have to chuckle when

I think of it." He suited action to the words, and fell to chuckling softly to himself.

"He can't make me out, daddy."

"Ho, ho, ho!"

"He admitted that I mystified him completely."

"Ha, ha, ha!"

"He slunk away like a whipped cur."

"Ha, ha, ha! Ho, ho, ho!"

"I wish you were home again, daddy."

"I'll come as often as I can."

"Yes, I know. But I wish you were with us permanently. I miss you terribly."

"I often wish I was, myself. It's rather cramped out there. Still, I have ample leisure to think."

"Are you quite comfy now, daddy," I inquired timidly.

"Quite, dear. It's a mighty different place from that other smelly hole, where the dirt used to clog my brain. My box is beautifully sweet and clean, and the lining is of silk. It's really fine to lie there and think."

"I'm so glad, daddy."

"I know that, child. I have nothing to worry over now; that is, if my bandage does not shift."

"Could you not adjust it, if it did?"

"Queerly enough, I couldn't. I can pull it down, or shove it upward; but if it became displaced completely, I would have to seek your aid."

I shivered. "Please be very careful of it, daddy. I doubt if I could go through . . . through . . . that again. You'll be careful of it, won't you?"

"Tush! child, don't worry yourself. I'll be careful. I never turn over without holding it in position with a hand. I'm not anxious to have my brains seeping out again, even for the brief while before you adjusted the bandage again."

"I couldn't do it again, daddy."

He gazed at me sombrely. "Of course you could," he exclaimed irritably. "Would you leave me there for all eternity, with my brains leaking from my skull and my wits addled?"

"No, no. Of course I wouldn't."

"Then don't talk nonsense."

"Still, you'll be very careful, daddy?"

"I'll be very careful, child."

Suddenly he began to chuckle again.

"What's amusing you?" I asked.

"That bumptious detective. You flouted him beautifully."

"Were you present, daddy?"

"No, dear. I sleep in the day-time; either that, or think. I only move abroad after dark."

"Then how do you know what occurred?"

He smiled slowly. "I know much that happens, Jean — so very much. I don't think you commit a single action, or indulge in a single thought, of which I am not aware."

"But how do you know, if you are asleep?"

His smile broadened. "I cannot explain, Jean; but I do know. Please don't pry!"

"Very well, daddy," I said meekly.

He was silent for some seconds, and then took to chuckling anew. "You handled him properly. Thick-head! Pudding-head ignoramus! Fathead! Oh, you sacrificed him, child. It was delicious."

"He, he, he!" I giggled.

"Ha, ha, ha!" he echoed.

Our glee burst the bounds of discretion, and we threw back our heads, to roar in concert.

"He, he, he!"

"Ho, ho, ho!"

"Ha, ha! He, he! Ho, ho!"

Suddenly my mirth ceased as though I had been douched with iced water. My horrified eyes noted that the bandage was working higher and higher as he roared his glee.

"Daddy!" I screamed. "Oh, daddy!"

He continued to roar like a Titan, ignoring my frenzied cry. I saw the towel pulsing as though driven by the thrusts of a piston, and knew that his brain was throbbing in and out the wound. With every beat the bandage lifted higher.

"Daddy!" I screamed again. Then the bandage fell from his head to the floor.

He grew sober at once, staring at it with amazed disbelief on his features. Slowly he lifted a hand, and began to feel at the base of his skull. His fingers groped higher, higher, until they entered the wound. As one in a dream; he pushed idly at the protruding brain-tissue, then gave a low cry and sank his face in his hands.

"Oh, God! Oh, God!" he muttered. And again, "Oh, God!"

I sprang from my bed and picked up the bandage. "Let me fasten it on," I gasped, crossing to him.

He smiled wanly. "You can't, child; that is, not here. You must . . ."

I stared at him with wide eyes. "Not here! Does that mean . . . ?" In my turn, I left the sentence unfinished.

He nodded, holding his brain in place with the palm of his left hand. "It means just that, Jean," he said simply. "Oh, my God!"

"You'll do it, child?" he asked, after a long pause. "You won't leave poor daddy out there with his brains slopping over? You'll fix me so that I can think. You'll take pity on the man whom you've condemned to sleep for eternity. You'll do it, Jean."

"Yes, oh, yes!" I murmured, crying softly.

"When, child?"

"To-morrow night."

"I shall expect you, Jean."

He began to fade. His substance turned to air. Suddenly he was gone. But his voice floated faintly to my ears from an immeasurable distance.

"I shall expect you, child. Do not fail daddy!"

I did not sleep again that night. The bells rang ceaselessly, and dim figures flitted about the room like wraiths. I recognised Myrtle, with her straight nose and curved lashes; Dr. Murray, with his plump body and tender limbs; O'Flanagan, with his blue jowl and florid cheeks; Minerva, with her riven back and glazing eyes. Even grandmother was there, with her jaw set defiantly and her scanty hair in disorder. Like earth-bound ghosts they drifted about the confines of the room, immaterial as ether, yet substantial and real as a haemorrhage. In this awful vortex of the imagination I longed for The Voice; but it was silent. Only the bells rang in my ears like thunder, clanging out their infernal music.

How the day passed I do not remember. I have an indistinct recollection of a meal; and twice I woke to consciousness in the cemetery, whither I must have wandered, to see a tall man in a blue serge suit idling among the gravestones. He had his hands in his pockets, and was whistling softly. He did not glance my way; he just strolled among the tombstones, peering at their inscriptions. A stranger, moved by curiosity, or perhaps seeking the resting-place of a loved one! I shivered in the keen wind, and plodded home.

As the clock struck eight I came to myself. Strive as I would, the day remained a blank, a hiatus in my memory. Only that faint remembrance of a meal, and the clearer recollection of two visits to the cemetery, could be brought to consciousness. Ultimately I shrugged my shoulders and dismissed the subject from my mind. There was a duty confronting me—a horrid, distasteful duty, yet one which must be performed in the teeth of all obstacles. Of what moment was a day's aberration? With so many memories behind me, I could afford to lose the incidents of a single day. They were a bagatelle.

I presume I looked ill, for grandmother fussed round me like a bereaved hen. To escape her attentions, I went to my room shortly after eight, declaring that my head ached. Suspecting that she might enter, on her way to bed, I climbed under the clothes as I heard her ascending the stairs, and simulated sleep. She switched on the light, gazed at me for a moment, and then crept out. I waited a full half-hour before moving. It would not do to jeopardise my venture by precipitation. I owed a sacred duty to poor daddy. He must be relieved that night.

It was after ten before I left the house. A crescent moon was low in the western sky, and a few clouds scudded before the wind, occulting the stars as they passed. I chose the overhead bridge to Bent Street, fearing that curious eyes might be abroad at the level crossing. As I turned into the main road, I fancied that I saw a figure in my rear. I halted and gazed; but only the customary lights and shadows met my eyes. It must have been a figment of the imagination.

At the cemetery I hastened to the tool-shed and procured a shovel. It was a new tool, with the handle still retaining something of its pristine polish. Evidently its predecessor had worn out since the last occasion when I had dug.

I approached daddy's grave, removed the withered flowers which lay upon it, threw a quick glance round, and began to dig.

Almost instantly my arms were gripped from behind, and the liquid note of a whistle rang on the air. In vain I struggled, my captor held me firmly. From the darkness two men came running.

"Have you got her, Stanton?" exclaimed one of the newcomers.

"I've got her, sir. She was just commencing to dig him up."

"Poor little devil! You two hold her while I get the car."

I ceased resistance and submitted meekly. Soon I was seated in the back seat of a car, between Detective O'Flanagan and another man, while their companion drove us to town. They halted at the police station, and conveyed me inside.

The sergeant gaped as we entered.

"We've got the murderer of Deslines, sergeant," said O'Flanagan quietly.

"The murderer of Deslines?" he repeated idiotically, still continuing to gape.

"Yes. Make her as comfortable as you can; but don't take the slightest risk. She's a particularly dangerous homicidal maniac. I know she fooled you, just as she fooled the coroner and everybody else. Lock her up securely. We'll put her under observation to-morrow. Now I'll have to go and break the news to her people. It's not a particularly nice job. Be very careful, sergeant."

"I'll watch her," said the sergeant shortly.

His face was so crestfallen, as he conveyed me to a cell, that I had to laugh. Sinking on the rude bed, I broke into peals of mirth. He backed out gingerly, and I heard the key grate in the lock.

Next day two doctors from Sydney interviewed me. I told them frankly all that had occurred, emphasising the manner in which I had overthrown Dr. Murray and deluded the sergeant. They were very kind and gentle, and did not pester me with silly questions.

"Do you know anything about hormones?" I asked the elder, a tall, grave man with white hair.

"A little, Miss Deslines."

"Do you know how they originate?"

He began to nod his head, but changed the movement to an emphatic shake, "I can't say that I do," he admitted.

I laughed triumphantly. "No medical man does. You are all obsessed by erroneous theories."

"That's quite possible. How do they originate?"

"From the Milky Way. Every night those which are ripe break loose from the ropes of ether on which they are strung, and flame through the sky, seeking breasts to enter. When a child is born, they penetrate its skin and determine its sex."

He nodded gravely. "I must have a long chat with you about it some day, Miss Deslines. It is evident that you have discovered a very important fact. The former theories will have to go by the board."

"It's a treat to meet an intelligent man in such a hidebound profession," I commented.

The other doctor broke into a violent fit of coughing.

CHAPTER XXVII

I WAS IMPRISONED in the criminal ward of a mental hospital. Imprisonment is the only possible term, for I was in full possession of my faculties within a week of my incarceration. The doctors sought me out and conversed on a multitude of topics; yet officially I was deemed insane. That was why I was imprisoned there, where the gum trees stood amid grassy lawns and the silver harbour sparkled in the sun. On Saturday afternoons and Sundays the boats tacked back and forth on the silvery waters, their white wings dazzlingly bright and their varnished sides shining like opal. Within easy reach a bridge spanned the harbour, and moving blurs darkened its painted struts as cars crossed to and fro. Sometimes I wondered who they were, who travelled in the cars. Were they drab people, devoid of imagination, and so accounted sane; or did they number among them persons of lofty thought, who transgressed the narrow bounds of convention and paid the inexorable penalty of isolation? Was I really mad, and my grandmother and the sergeant sane; or was it that I was the sane one of the three, and the two dolts insane? It was a perplexing problem, whose decision the law left to hide-bound physicians and pragmatical magistrates. Why were they vested with the right to deprive me of my liberty, while the human cabbages were left free to vegetate according to their own idiosyncrasies?

There were times when I considered the whole world mad, with myself the only sane person in it.

Still, I was passing happy there, amid the flowers and the trees, with the flashing harbour in the foreground and the iron causeway closing out the view in the distance. I had no desire for human companionship; I was content to eat the lotus, isolated from a crazy world. They could have condemned me to worse fates!

Nevertheless, I had not the slightest intention of remaining in my prison, for all its sunshine and shadow, and its outlook on the peaceful waters of the harbour. Within twenty-four hours of my arrival, I had begun to hatch plans of escape. I soon perceived that tremendous difficulties surrounded the breaking of my gaol. I was kept under constant surveillance. I was locked in a barred room before nightfall each day. There was always an attendant within a few yards of me. Apparently I was 'free' to amuse myself as I pleased, and wander at will about the grounds; but I penetrated the fiction, and resolved to be patient.

By the end of the first week I had developed the details of my plan, and thenceforward prosecuted it religiously. I took every opportunity of conversing with the doctors and attendants. I was frankness itself. I freely admitted my crime, and shuddered dramatically at the admission. I professed horror and contrition, explaining that the murder had been committed during a maniacal obsession. I described my mental condition: how my lapses always were preceded by acute depression extending over a week; how I experienced tremendous difficulty in recollecting what had happened during the actual fits of mania. I expressed abhorrence with the world, and satisfaction at having found a congenial haven where I would be protected against myself.

"I know, and you know;" I informed the medical superintendent, conversing with him one day, "that at this moment I am as sane as yourself. But I realise that at any moment I may feel a vast depression enveloping me, and I also realise that it will be followed by a brief period during which I shall not be accountable for my actions. Knowing this, I am content to remain in this lovable old place, where I am sheltered from the world and protected against myself."

He appraised me gravely. I suspect that I was something new in his experience, catholic though it had been.

I shivered for his benefit. "Supposing that I were free again," I commented, "God only knows what mischief I might wreak. The taint is inherited from my mother, and I know enough to appreciate that at any moment I may lose my mental balance. Thank goodness, its advent always is heralded by seven or eight days' depression. I get ample warning. Then comes the phase of actual mania, when my senses desert me and I have but the dimmest recollections of my actions. Here again, however, I have my consolation, for it only lasts a fortnight — generally less. At its conclusion I recover my sanity completely, and become normal."

He nodded. I can see that," he agreed. "As you say, at this particular moment you are as sane as I."

"Thank God for that small mercy," I whispered huskily. "I can imagine no worse fate than complete loss of one's reason."

Whether he was testing me or not, I have no means of knowing; but even now I plume myself on the manner in which I met his question.

"Being sane, you know, it is quite possible that you might regain your liberty. If you desire to write any of your friends on the subject, I shall be happy to forward the letters. Have you no desire at all to return to the world?"

Again I commissioned the shudder in which I was growing so proficient. "Please don't suggest such a terrible thing! I am quite contented here, where I can notify the nurses when I feel that awful feeling of depression coming on, so that they can restrain me if . . . if it becomes necessary." I shuddered again. "Supposing I were out there, would I do so? Would I exercise care to avoid . . . what has happened before when I lost my senses? I honestly believe that I would; but I cannot be sure."

He was watching me steadily.

"No, I cannot be sure," I whispered, as though to myself.

For three months I persisted patiently with the fable of the premonitory state of depression, and was confident that my insistent repetitions were exciting credence. I felt that the time had arrived to support my words with a practical demonstration.

Next morning I affected moodiness. I refused to converse, and resolutely avoided companionship. I spent the day on an isolated seat, staring at the ground. When the attendant came to escort me to my room, just before dusk, I lifted pleading eyes.

"I wish to speak to you," I said sulkily.

"Yes?"

"Nurse, it is coming on. Please don't let me do anything terrible. There will be a week of this, then . . . then will come . . . then will come the other. Please, nurse, please!" I caught frantically at her hand.

"Don't worry," she murmured gently. "We'll watch you carefully. You can't do any damage here. You're a brave child to let me know like this."

For six days I maintained my aloofness, though I found it difficult to moon on a seat all day, when the sun was shining and my limbs were charged with vigour. At the close of the sixth day I burst into activity. All night I sang and danced in my room. Next morning I talked arrant nonsense to the attendant when she entered, and had to fight down a smile when I noted the meticulous care which she observed to avoid turning her back on me. My conduct resulted in rigorous confinement for ten days, during which oppressive period I faithfully continued my role of maniac. On the morning of the eleventh day I felt that it would be safe to affect normality. I was still in bed when the nurse entered my room, and greeted her with a wan smile as she approached.

"I feel so tired, nurse." I passed my hand wearily across my brow. "It's peculiar, I can't recollect going to bed last night."

She stared pityingly.

"Ah," I gasped, as though understanding had come to me suddenly, "now I remember. That awful feeling of depression! I asked you to watch me. Have I done anything? Did you watch me . . . watch me carefully?" I wrinkled my forehead. "I can't recollect clearly what has happened. I just have a vague memory of dancing in this room. I haven't done anything, have I, nurse?"

"Nothing at all, my dear. We kept you locked in here. It's all over now, and you may go out into the sunshine whenever you please. I'll run and call the doctor at once."

He came almost immediately. I was fearful that he would test my heart and pulse. Being ignorant whether they should be affected or not, I dreaded that they might betray me. To my relief, he contented himself with a series of questions about my bodily and mental conditions, and advised me to try to sleep. I professed lassitude, and remained in bed until the lunch hour. During the afternoon I made the opportunity to converse with one of the assistant doctors, and discussed my lapse freely.

Thank God, there will be no recurrence for many weeks to come," I told him, "possibly for many months. You see now why I am perfectly contented to remain in this lovely old place, apart from the world. Here, I am secure; I cannot harm anyone. Just fancy" — I shuddered — "if I had been at liberty during the past fortnight! Why, I might have injured poor old grandmother or someone else whom I love dearly. Oh! thank God for this hospital and its kind-hearted doctors and nurses!"

I had won! Thenceforward my guards relaxed their vigilance. Each day witnessed greater freedom of movement conceded me. Obviously all were deluded by the belief that I was reconciled to my lot — nay, that I embraced it. I had given practical exemplification of my willingness to co-operate in the efforts to inhibit action during my periods of mania. I took to strolling along the waterfront, always exercising care to patrol in full view of such eyes as might be alert.

"I have always loved the sea," I confided to a nurse. "It is so vast and peaceful. It soothes me just to watch it."

She smiled, and bade me indulge my passion to thc full.

It was about eleven, one bright, sunny morning, when I made my escape. For days I had loitered about the waterfront; idly examining shells and pieces of weed; calling nurses to view them, when they happened to be in the vicinity; and frequently throwing myself at full length on the grass, to watch the boats and steamers passing to and fro. My gaolers seemed satisfied that a fit of depression always preceded the onset of mania, and apparently regarded me as sane in the intervals. My affection for the water occasioned neither concern nor suspicion.

On the day of my escape I patiently awaited a favourable opportunity. I fully realised that I was hazarding my future on a single throw of the die, and that undue precipitation would destroy the fabric which I had wrought with such patience and care. An abortive attempt would spell farewell to hope, as thenceforward unremitting vigilance would be exercised. When I was assured that no idle or watchful eye was on me, I slipped quietly into the water and swam to a boat which was moored a couple of hundred yards from the shore. It was some twenty-four or twenty-five feet in length, with the fore part covered by a decking as far as the mast, whence it extended completely along each side to the width of a foot. Stored under the forward decking was a quantity of sails. My heart leaped when I saw this providential litter of loose canvas.

With a piece of dry rag procured from a locker, I mopped up the water which had streamed from my clothing. I continued the process as I retreated to the bows, knowing that the hot sun would dispel the dampness in a few minutes. Within fifteen minutes I was concealed under the heap of sails, having left no betraying pools of water along my line of retreat.

As it chanced, I need not have exhibited such meticulous care about the water from my clothes, for some hours elapsed before I heard a boat approaching. Shortly after, it bumped against the side of my refuge, and I heard the voice of the young medical assistant.

"She's not here," he called. "There's only one other boat to which she might have swum. Hello! there's a pile of canvas up in the bow there. I'll just make sure she's not under it."

With my heart hammering frantically, I heard him clamber on board and walk toward me. But he contented himself-with a couple of perfunctory kicks at the outer portion of heaped sails. Whether he was too lazy to creep under the decking, or whether he considered the labour unwarranted, I could not know. I only knew the joy that swelled in my heart as I heard his retreating footsteps.

"She's not there," he said, as he climbed into the skiff again. "I'm fairly certain she did not take to the water. We're only wasting time and making damned fools of ourselves. If the artful little devil had meant to escape by water, you can bet your bottom dollar that she would not have pretended such an affection for it."

Then came the sound of sculls dipping into the water, followed by silence. My pursuers had gone, and I was free!

I had ample leisure to reflect, while waiting for the night; and it gradually was borne home to me that much remained to be done before I could consider myself at liberty. As matters stood, I merely had exchanged my prison on shore for one on the water. I had to resolve the problem of making my way to land; further, it had to be accomplished with my clothes dry. To enter a lighted street with wet garments would be to attract every eye and lead to almost instant detection. It would be difficult enough to evade capture under ordinary circumstances; to attract attention would be fatal.

By the time night had fallen, I had decided my course of action. I crept from my stifling prison, and gulped down revivifying breaths of the sweet night air. There was no moon—I had chosen the date with an eye on the calendar—but the night was cloudless and the stars shone brightly. They provided ample light for my purpose. Not a breath of air stirred, and the boat swung lazily to the tide, which was flooding. Perforce I had to possess myself in patience until it turned, which was some hours later. Then I slipped the boat's moorings, and let her drift downward with the ebb. We passed under the bridge, bumping gently against one of its iron piles, and onward down the harbour, ultimately grounding in Kerosene Bay. Fifteen minutes later the tide had receded enough to enable me to leap ashore dry-shod, and I felt that at last liberty confronted me. At no time did I consider the possibility of capture; I had extreme confidence in my ability to outwit my pursuers.

Clambering to the top of the dark headland before me, I perceived the lights of North Sydney twinkling on the next hill. I inhaled a deep breath, and sat down to think. The first essential was to alter my appearance. This task only could be effected by securing certain materials and accessories. To obtain them I needed money, so it resolved itself into acquisition of hard cash. I had not a penny with me; and where was I to obtain it?

Beg, borrow, or steal! The old saw kept running through my brain. But analysis revealed the utter futility of any course embodied in it. Certainly, I might beg; but the proceeds were not likely to be large, and the process involved bringing myself under particular notice. To borrow was manifestly impossible; it meant revealing both my identity and whereabouts to inquisitive and uncertain friends. To steal involved, first, locating an available hoard, and, second, appropriating it to my own use. I sighed as I realised that "beg, borrow, or steal" had to be excluded from the range of the practicable.

Money, money, money! how was I to get it? There was one eminently practicable method for a young and pretty girl. I shuddered from head to toe as I contemplated it. Yet . . . I must have money; and how else was it to be acquired? I pondered the problem desperately as I trudged toward civilisation. This protracted thought brought no solution, and I was driven back to the distasteful method that appeared to be my sole medium of success. I experienced no difficulty in securing a customer for my wares.

In my whole life I have not spent such a revolting night. It was my first experience of man, the brute, in brutish mood. No physical pain could parallel the exquisite agony which I endured. His touch burned me. I had to suppress an almost irresistible impulse to scream aloud. I longed to strike him in the face. It was not shame. That emotion rarely has troubled me. It was stark, hideous physical repulsion. Never have I hated anything in this world with the intensity of my hate for the man who was affording me the means of escape from my bondage. His fawning hands, his avid lips, his horrible body, united to form a whole that filled me with acute loathing and horror. I almost retched on his face, as it lay beside me on the pillow; and once I stayed my hands in mid-air, as they stretched out to strangle him.

I stole from his house at daybreak next morning, with five pounds tucked into my stocking. As soon as it opened its door, I entered a small shop on the outskirts of the settlement and purchased a coarse frock and hat for a few shillings. Returning to the bush, I removed my dress and hat, and donned those which I had bought. The discarded garments were stuffed into a log, to rot or be discovered. I was indifferent about their fate.

Then I remembered that I had an unusually small foot. My description would be broadcast through the State, and it was certain that special stress would be laid on my feet. I hastened to another obscure shop, where I bought a pair of stout shoes, four sizes too large for me. In a deserted lane I effected the change, making the new shoes as comfortable as I could by stuffing paper into their toes. I thrust the old ones deep into a garbage tin which stood outside a gate.

From a chemist I procured a bottle of peroxide of hydrogen, a similar quantity of strong liquid ammonia, and a pair of tweezers. Possibly they were common purchases, for he paid little attention to me, a mercy which caused me to sigh thankfully.

I then sought a place of retreat. I feared to engage lodging until I had completed the alteration of my appearance, so I prowled about the verge of the settlement searching for a deserted shed. My quest terminated successfully during the afternoon. In a quiet gully I found an abandoned cowshed, equipped with bails. Three crude stools were lying in a corner, and rotting leg-ropes still were attached to the posts of the bails.

At once I mixed a small amount of the peroxide and ammonia in equal quantities, and applied the compound to my hair and brows, rubbing it in thoroughly. In my excitement I had forgotten food, and now the pangs of hunger beset me. I endured them stolidly until dark, by which time they had become acute. Unable to resist the craving for food, I again ventured into town, where I bought a loaf, some butter, and a pound of cooked beef. On this Spartan fare, augmented by draughts of water from a tank beside the shed, I existed for two days. By that time, encouraged by three applications of peroxide and ammonia daily, my hair and eyebrows had changed from raven black to brown. With the aid of my pocket-mirror, which I had preserved, I plucked my somewhat heavy brows until they were transformed into a thin, arched line. I now felt that I was sufficiently changed in appearance to venture abroad.

Again waiting until it was dark, I walked to town and boldly sought the highways. A glance in a street mirror established my confidence completely. None would have recognised the *petite* and dainty Jean Deslines in the shabbily dressed slut with the brown hair, the big feet, and the moving-picture eyebrows. The sole remaining link with my former identity was my stature, and this I determined to rectify without delay. I bought some linen, a packet of needles, a roll of cotton wool, and a reel of cotton, and then booked accommodation for a week at a cheap boarding-house. I spent the night in improvising a "bust-improver." Strapped in place over my brassiere it was a huge success, completing my disguise effectively.

Although I searched the newspapers diligently, I found no reference to my escape. Perhaps it was not considered politic to acquaint the public that a homicidal maniac was at large. The knowledge abolished the last of my fears. There was small likelihood that my recent purchases would come under notice of the police. I was safe — safe, and free!

CHAPTER XXVIII

ALTHOUGH EKED OUT meticulously, my slender cash resources only lasted three weeks. All efforts to secure employment failed. I could not furnish references, and it is probable that my slatternly appearance militated against success. Once I was engaged by an Italian to serve in. a cheap café; but the work disgusted me in a single day, and next morning I stayed away. He had the benefit of my day's labour without payment.

One morning I emptied the contents of my purse on the bed, and surveyed them ruefully. There were a shilling, two sixpences, a threepenny piece, and three coppers, exactly two and six; it was all that stood between me and starvation. I realised that the scanty store must be replenished without delay. But, how? Begging and borrowing still presented insuperable difficulties. Stealing had possibilities, but where lay the money on which I could place predatory hands? There remained the obvious way which I had exploited before; but I was determined that only as a last resort would I submit to the horrors I had endured on that occasion.

Money, money! where was I to procure it?

With a heavy heart I took the ferry to the city, and wandered into the Domain. The day was dull. Masses of cloud obscured the sun and turned the leaves of the figs to a dingy brown. Even the grass had lost its customary greenness and looked as though it had been touched by a fierce frost. The waters of Woolloomooloo Bay heaved leadenly, or were churned into yellow foam by the launches which scurried to and fro. The dismal surroundings did not provide a tonic for depressed nerves; they accentuated my misery.

I returned to my lodging-house with the problem unsolved. Nor did the passage of the two succeeding days bring inspiration; they only served to deplete my shallow purse. At their close I found myself with a bare sixpence. That night I returned to the streets and earned two pounds. Thence-forward I became a professional harlot.

At the outset of my new profession I realised that I must effect radical change in my appearance. My drab attire detracted from my sex appeal, and the better-dressed men passed me contemptuously. By this time my hair had bleached to a light, almost golden, brown, and my eyebrows were in keeping. This was due to regular applications of peroxide. I had ceased adding ammonia after the second day, fearing that it would inflict irreparable damage. My cheeks had lost their colour and grown thinner; but when I removed the disfiguring hat which I wore habitually, I perceived that I still retained my good looks. I determined to commercialise them.

Next morning I visited a shop in the city and bought a complete range of clothing. It exhausted my money, but I could afford to scoff at that detail. Henceforth I intended to earn pounds, where formerly I had been forced to content myself with shillings. I felt safe in reducing my shoes from number six to number four — two sizes larger than normal — and took care that they were shapely and well made.

Dressed for business, that night, I marvelled at the transformation. My mirror revealed a slight figure (I had discarded the "improver"), fashionably clothed. With a small beret crowning my fair curls, and vivid black eyes flashing from pale cheeks, my appearance was arresting. The thin eyebrows, carefully plucked to produce a pronounced arch, accentuated the smooth sweep of my forehead, giving me a Madonna look, which, instinct told me, would prove irresistible to the prowling male. Last, but most satisfying of all, I was the antithesis of Jean Deslines. I would have defied Detective-Sergeant O'Flanagan himself to penetrate my disguise.

I earned nearly twenty pounds in the first week, and established a regular clientele. By day I reverted to my drab attire, considering it to be safer, but at night I blossomed into a peacock and prosecuted my triumphal progress. The life was hideous; but I persisted until I had $200 in the bank. I kept my head throughout, and continued to lodge in my former modest quarters. I was not anxious to excite undue attention or wilfully court danger. The most perfect disguise might be capable of penetration.

Then the bells began to haunt me again.

They rang perpetually in my ears during the waking hours of night, commencing with a discordant clash and fading in a low cadence of singular sweetness. I feared to venture abroad, lest The Voice should command me to undertake some foolish task which would unmask me. I remained secluded in my bedroom, only leaving it at mealtimes. I grew thin. My nerves were on edge. I started at shadows, and swung about, white-faced, at the slightest noise in my rear. The suspense grew so tremendous that I almost longed for that which I dreaded — the whisper of The Voice!

It came! One afternoon, as I sat on my bed reviewing my terrible destiny, its whisper sounded! I burst into hysterical tears and thrust my head under the pillow, forcing its ends across my ears. But it could not be evaded so simply. Calm and implacable as a glacier, it penetrated the kapok muffler.

"The world is leagued against you, Jean. There is a universal conspiracy to destroy you."

I flung the pillow across the room and sat erect.

"Are you going to submit passively? Are you content to be the unwilling toy of your deadly enemies without striking a blow in your own defence?"

"What blow can I strike?" I whispered huskily.

"Kill, child! kill the brutes who prey on your youth and beauty. Strike them down in the heat of their lusts. Vindicate your womanhood. Kill!"

My heart pulsed strongly, and heat invaded my cheeks. I felt the strength of a Samson permeating my processes. I would retaliate. In the bank reposed sufficient money to maintain me for months. There was no need to continue my nauseous trade. I was free to lay my plans and devastate the enemies who would destroy me.

That night the bells chimed a benediction, and I sank into a dreamless sleep to their subdued music. I woke refreshed, in that icy mood of determination and mental clarity which always accompanied desperate effort on my part.

At one shop I bought an oyster-knife. At another I procured a coarse emery-stone. A third furnished a smooth honing-stone. Such innocent purchases were not calculated to excite remark. I spent the afternoon in grinding a keen double-edge on the knife. It would not do for my strokes to be ineffective.

That night I struck my first blow against the world which had conspired to destroy me. As the beast fondled me in the darkness of an alley in Darlinghurst, I drove the keen knife through his spine, just above his collar. He slipped peacefully to the ground, and lay still. I wiped the weapon on the lapel of his coat, and strolled away.

The papers were full of it next morning, attributing the act to the Razor Gang.

Before the week was out I had sent five of the wretches to their master, the Devil, and Sydney was in a ferment. A ponderous daily newspaper castigated the Inspector-General of Police, and demanded effective protection from the assassin. The sensational weeklies advanced fantastic theories to fit the murders, one yellow print excelling itself by hinting that they were the work of an anthropoid ape. "Obviously the perpetrator possesses enormous strength," it wrote. "No ordinary man could drag his victims forcibly into the darkness of lanes and alleyways, smother their cries, and do them to death without discovery within a few yards of jostling multitudes. Are the famous 'Murders in the Rue Morgue' actually being enacted in our midst? If they are not, then a Hercules, endowed with the faculty of instant disappearance, is abroad."

The Sunday Press derided the ape theory, and inclined to the view that a demented surgeon was responsible. "The deadly accuracy of the blows, which in each instance have severed the spine at the nape of the neck," declaimed one paper, "point to anatomical knowledge. The veriest tyro in criminology would know that either a butcher or a surgeon is responsible."

I chuckled hugely over the balderdash. It was so exceedingly simple to drive a knife into a man's spine, while he was fondling you and your fingers could caress his neck without exciting suspicion. The journalistic criminologists were arrant fools, but they were imaginative and very amusing. Their place in the world was merited. They were contributing to the gaiety of nations.

So prodigious was the uproar that I feared to proceed with my labour of vengeance. I even was fearful to walk the streets by night, lest I might he suspected. There always existed the possibility that some inquisitive eye had seen me disappear into a lane with one of my victims. I changed my lodging, and reverted to the number six shoes and the bust-improver. My fashionable clothes were locked securely in a tin trunk, together with the knife which had wrought such havoc among my foes.

For ten days I lived in retirement, amusing myself by reading the daily and periodical papers. From this quiescence I was awakened by The Voice, which addressed me one Sunday night, when the church bells were summoning the faithful and the hypocritical to service.

"Again you have done excellently, Jean. You have ridded the world of five monsters who had conspired to destroy you. But their name is legion, child. Continue the work of eradication. Kill, and kill again! Remember that you are fighting for your own preservation."

Next evening I sallied forth again, taking a tram to Balmain, where I enticed a man into the park at White Horse Point, and dispatched him expeditiously. I washed my hands carefully at a neighbouring tap, to remove the blood; drove the knife into the ground thrice, for a similar purpose; and caught the ferry-boat back to the city. The body was discovered in the early morning, and that afternoon the evening papers screamed the news in black headlines. The scent was growing warmer; continuous sniffing of the breeze had brought a suspicious whiff to their nostrils. This time bizarre theories were discarded, and the Press canvassed the possibility of a woman's being the author of the slayings.

The horror engendered by the murders appears to have destroyed the faculty to reason calmly," said the *Moon*, in its leading article. "The monotonous similarity of the six crimes, the suggestive silence attending them, the ease with which the victims were hurled into eternity, all indicate that the blows came with suddenness from a companion. It is unlikely that six men, dwelling in widely separated parts of the city and its suburbs, should be acquainted with the same person. Even were such a coincidence possible, what motive would impel them to consent to visit a back lane or lonely park in his company at a time when the community was horrified by a sequence of murders committed in just such environment? The hypothesis is absurd; another solution must be sought. There is but one which is feasible: they were enticed to their doom by a woman, a female Jack the Ripper, imbued with a fanatical hatred of men. *Cherchez la femme* must become the watchword of the police, and our men must exercise caution in their amorous adventures."

I fell asleep with the paper clutched in my hand, and woke in the morning with my sanity restored. Once again my unaccountable lapses had placed me in the gravest danger. I knew that the hunt would be unrelenting; that particular attention would be paid to those who followed my nauseous calling; that a wide net would be strung, through whose meshes the smallest fish would find it difficult to escape. I also knew that the striking girl, with the black eyes burning in a white face, must have been observed by numerous officers on night duty. The fact that she was a stranger among those more or less intimately known to the police in itself would be sufficient to direct attention to her. When discovered, she would be questioned closely, and her genesis investigated. On the other hand, if she vanished the hunt for her would become specific. In either case I stood in deadly peril. I twisted and rolled on my bed in mental agony, striving to formulate some plan of escape from the toils. My fears were not lessened by an announcement in a morning paper that Detective-Sergeant O'Flanagan had been deputed to investigate the murders.

As always, I decided upon the bold course. Donning my most dowdy dress over the bust-improver, supplemented by the number six shoes, I went to a chemist and bought a bottle of henna wash. I informed my landlady that I was returning to the country, having received a letter from my parents. I paid my board and took boat to Manly, employing the journey to treat my hair in the ladies' lavatory, using hot water from a thermos flask prepared for the occasion. When I disembarked at the seaside town, it was deep auburn, and an hour's stroll sufficed to dry it. Damp hair attracts no attention at a famous bathing resort.

When my hair had dried thoroughly, I visited the police station, informing the officer in charge that I had come from Broken Hill and desired to find cheap, but respectable lodging.

"My father told me to be sure and ask the police about it," I prattled. "He is afraid that I might find myself in a bad house; and that would be awful, wouldn't it?"

He agreed gravely, suggesting a dozen accommodation houses which would suit me. I thanked him and withdrew, feeling that I had averted any suspicion that might attach to a new-comer. I called later in the day to inform him of my address, and thank him for his assistance.

Toujours l'audace! He who grasps the nettle firmly is not stung! If a systematic hunt for strangers was inaugurated, the simple girl from the far west would receive but perfunctory attention. Her bona fides had been established.

CHAPTER XXIX

TWICE IN THE succeeding week I dreamed of my Roman soldier, and on both occasions familiar faces were among her assailants. She perished with glazing eyes, her blood dyeing the dust.

I went freely about the town, confident in the combined efficacy of my disguise and the visit to the police station. It was part of my policy to be observed by the local police, thus coming to be accepted as a legitimate resident of the place. Besides, it would have been unnatural for a strange girl from the backblocks to have resisted the novelty of her new surroundings. I had to play my part.

I received a prodigious shock on the Friday following my arrival. Grandmother was standing before a shop on the Corso. She was garbed in black and wore a, ridiculous hat like a poke-bonnet, with her hair tortured into a grey fringe at its front. Her face was deeply lined, and her eyes betokened abiding grief. Determined to put my disguise to the test, I sauntered by, looking her straight in the face. She evinced no interest. Plainly she had failed to recognise me. With my heart swelling in exultation, I proceeded a few steps, and turned — to come face to face with Myrtle as she emerged from a confectionery shop. The triumph in my breast was strangled. I knew that now I was to be subjected to the supreme test. If anyone in the wide world recognised me, it would be my cousin. There was a bond between us which possessed power to overleap all artificial barriers.

Steadying my nerves by a desperate effort of will, I looked her casually in the face and passed on. The vagrant glance revealed an odd alloy of amazement and terror in her eyes. Her cheeks had grown deathly pale in the passage of a single second. She stood, like one who has been stunned, gaping at me unbelievingly.

Preserving my nonchalance, I sauntered toward the Esplanade. Then I heard hurried footsteps in my rear, and a moment later Myrtle was at my side, breathing heavily.

"Jean," she gasped.

I ignored her.

"Jean!" She caught at my arm.

I stopped, and stared at her blankly. "You're making a mistake. My name is not Jean."

She gazed at me steadily, absorbing the details of my full bosom, drab clothing, and huge shoes. Then her eyes lifted to mine, filled with grief and undying affection. "Where can I see you?" she asked.

I smiled broadly. "You're making a mistake, Miss. I'm not your friend. I've never seen you before."

She stirred an empty chocolate carton with her foot. "Don't play the fool with me, Jean. Where may I see you, and when?"

I dropped my miming. "Are you staying down here?"

"Yes, for a fortnight, with your grandmother."

"Can you get out alone at night?"

"Of course."

"Then meet me under the seventh pine tree from the Corso at eight to-night."

"The seventh tree on the Esplanade?"

"Yes."

"Walking towards North Steyne?"

"Yes."

"You'll be there, Jean?" Her voice was wistful.

"I'll be there, dear. I promise you."

I strolled on, leaving her to return to grandmother. Her wits were quite capable of devising a plausible explanation of the brief conversation with a stranger.

She was standing under the tree when I arrived, and every nerve in my body responded to the gladness which lit her face.

"Oh, Jean, Jean," she murmured, and sobbed in my arms.

"Hush, darling," I entreated. "God knows who may see us here. Calm yourself. Do you wish to betray me?"

"Oh! no, no," she breathed, clasping me to her.

I thought for a moment. "Come to my room, Myrtle; we'll be safe there. Don't walk with me; follow well in my rear. I'll take care to wait at each corner until I'm sure you've seen me." I kissed her, and walked away without further ado.

Safe in the seclusion of my room, she gazed at me lugubriously. "My God!" she murmured, half to herself, "to think you should have come to this!"

I smiled, and tossed my hat on the bed.

She broke into lamentations as she noted my red hair. "What on earth have you done to your glorious curls? And that dreadful dress! And the padding on your breasts! And the unsightly shoes on your poor feet!" She spoke in italics.

"I had to disguise myself, Myrtle."

"Disguise! you're a perfect fright. Take those horrid things off at once, and slip into something dainty. It breaks my heart to see you like that."

I obeyed in silence, stripping the uncouth clothes from

me till I was mother naked. Then I donned a silk slip and bloomers from my trunk, and stood before her with my hands on my hips.

"That's better," she commented. "You're more like yourself now, save for that disgusting dye on your hair. Come and sit beside me."

For some minutes we sat silently, side by side, with our hands twining about each other's waist and our heads laid together. It was the first truly happy moment that I had experienced since my confinement at the mental hospital. The blind was drawn, shutting out the stars; but the garish wall-paper took on fairy hues under the magic of her presence, and the slow drone of the sea beat inward to our ears like a lullaby. There was something somnolent in the warm air, charged with the sea's breath, and I felt a delicious languor stealing over me. Thus would I have been content to remain until the crack of doom; but Myrtle broke the spell.

"Jean," she said, kissing me passionately on the lips. "I have such a lot to ask you. I scarcely know where to begin."

"Then don't," I answered dreamily. "Let me just sit beside you like this. It's heavenly."

"Poor kid," she murmured sympathetically. "What have you been doing with yourself all these months?"

"Hiding from the police."

"How on earth have you lived?"

"Pretty miserably."

"I don't mean that, exactly; I mean how did you get money?"

I flushed. "Stole it, mainly," I confessed. "I worked when I could find employment, and turned highwayman when I couldn't."

"Jean! you don't mean it?"

I laughed. "Not quite as bad as that, honey. Still, I did steal when circumstances forced me."

She shivered. "Supposing you had been caught!"

"I wasn't, so why worry about that? I have enough put by to see me through the next six months, and needn't take such risks again."

She was silent for a while. "Jean," she said at length, with her eyes bent on the floor, "I want you to tell me something truly. Did you . . . did you . . . kill . . . your father?"

"I did not, Myrtle."

"Ah! then, who did?"

"That beast, Murray. I really think I must have been insane when the doctors interviewed me. The strain of the preceding few weeks had been awful. Anyway, they were his friends, and I was doomed from the outset. I was completely at their mercy."

She gazed intently. "Do you mean to imply that men of their reputation would descend to such despicable depths?"

"Perhaps not deliberately. He had poisoned their minds; they came with preconceptions." I laughed bitterly. "And I played into their hands by losing my balance under the strain."

"Poor kid," she murmured softly, and hugged me till I gasped for breath.

During her holiday, I saw Myrtle nightly. Frequently she slept with me, stealing home with the dawn. We had much to tell each other, and the fortnight passed swiftly. Her companionship was delicious after my lengthy solitude, and I missed her greatly when she had gone. But we had arranged to meet once a fortnight, and adhered to the pact.

We had spent three week-ends together, when the bells

began to worry me again. From nightfall until I fell asleep they chimed in my ears. If I woke during the night they immediately rang on the air. I was haunted ceaselessly in the hours of darkness by their mellow music. In vain I went for long walks in the day-time, returning to the evening meal in a state of physical exhaustion. As soon as the shadows of sunset expanded into an enveloping blur, my ears were tortured with their steady chiming. They drove me to frenzy. I threw myself on my bed, writhing like a woman stricken with epilepsy. I buried my head under the blankets. I stuffed cotton wool into my ears. I tried to concentrate my mind on mathematical problems. The devices were futile; the notes of the bells penetrated all obstacles and destroyed continuity of thought. I lived in dread of the inevitable Voice and its next command.

I had not long to wait. It was a Saturday night, and Myrtle was in my room. She wore a cream silk nightgown, liberally inset with lace. It revealed, rather than concealed, her noble outlines. "Kill," whispered The Voice. "The time has come for Minerva to die. Strike to-night, child!"

I clenched my hands in agony, and rocked upon my heels.

"Kill," it repeated.

I went sick in the stomach, and a great heat flushed my temples. I fought desperately to retain my sanity, knowing that a moment's weakness would mean the death of the only soul in the world whom I loved. God! how I fought! I strove to reason; argued with myself that The Voice was a delusion—that, or a trickster which had imperilled me on various occasions and would end by destroying me. "I won't," I murmured inwardly. "I won't!"

"Kill," it repeated. "Minerva's destiny must be fulfilled. Strike her in the back, as she was struck ages ago."

"No!" I whispered to myself, "No!"

"Kill!"

"I will not."

"Kill, for it is ordained." I conquered, and my beloved left me unharmed. But The Voice was inexorable. It persecuted me throughout the following week, and the next. When the time came for Myrtle to visit me again, I knew that I was yielding. Nay, in my innermost consciousness I knew that I would slay her that night. Yet, knowing, I still fought feebly.

We retired to bed early, and lay embraced tightly. So we fell asleep. The chime of bells woke me. She still slept, her mouth smiling and her dear lashes curved low on her cheeks. Through her slightly parted lips her breath came and went with the fragrance of hay.

"Kill!" came The Voice. "Minerva must die to-night." Softly, and so slowly, I crept from the bed. I fumbled blindly in a drawer for the knife which had exterminated the beasts who had conspired to destroy me. Then I stole forward, and drove it to the hilt in her breast, placing a hand across her mouth to stifle her cries.

She gave a convulsive struggle, and lay still. Her eyes were wide, but I knew that she saw nothing. Slowly the cheap quilt was touched with a crimson circle which grew wider—wider.

With an inarticulate cry I flung the knife behind me, and gently clambered into bed beside her. Taking her warm form in my arms, I held her tight, careless of the damp which spread on my nightdress. I must have fallen to sleep; for I woke in the night with a sense of cold, to realise that I was hugging the dead girl to my bosom.

Strangling a scream in my throat, I leapt frantically from the bed. My brain was perfectly cool and sane. Having slain my only friend, my madness had passed, leaving me desolate and afraid beside her stark form.

The electric light was on, as I had left it on retiring, and the watch on my wrist told me that it was two a.m. My nightdress was patched hideously with dark red, and the quilt was stained in keeping. I stared with unbelieving eyes, striving to delude myself that it was some horrible nightmare. Alas! I soon convinced myself of the terrible reality. There lay Myrtle, with her dear eyes wide and glazed, and one white arm flung along the pillow. My beloved was dead!

I almost went mad again. Indeed, for a space I was mad! I threw myself upon her. I begged her to speak to me. I covered her face with hot kisses. My lips clung frenziedly to hers. Then I sank on the floor, and sobbed my heart out.

Somewhere in the night a clock struck three. Like the funereal tones of a tolling bell the strokes sounded. One, two, three! I shivered, rose from the floor, and threw a dressing-jacket over my bloody nightgown. The deed was done. It was profitless to repine. I must consider my position, and take thought to ensure my safety. But how could I think, with those great eyes staring . . . staring? Gently I kissed her lips for the last time, and drew the blankets over her head.

Icily cool, I went to the bathroom and stripped to the skin, placing my discarded garments in a heap at the end of the bath. Then I washed myself scrupulously, taking care to remove every spot of blood. Returning to the bedroom, I extracted the best of my clothes from my trunk. I laid a stylish dress of wine-hued *crêpe de Chine* upon the dressing-table, accompanied by stockings and underwear. The rest I packed into a suitcase. Surveying myself in the mirror, when I had dressed, I was elated to perceive that nothing remained to identify me with the dowdy frump who had visited the police station and been so prominent about the town. Nor was there much resemblance to Jean Deslines. My auburn hair, my arched brows, my Madonna countenance with its dark eyes blazing from white cheeks, belonged to another type. My sole source of worry was the fact that the suspicious girl of the streets had returned. The change in the tint of the hair was negligible; it provided nothing more than a minor variant. The risk was prodigious; but what was I to do? After all, nothing more than suspicion could attach to the street girl, whereas Jean Deslines and the frump stood condemned. Unable to effect a further transformation, I could but face the issue with boldness, trusting to my wits for deliverance.

In this frame of mind, calm, alert, and coldly optimistic, I passed quietly down the hall, opened the front door, pulled it to behind me, and went out to the night. The stars shone brightly, and a waning moon sailed overhead; but I was too racked with grief to enjoy them. Myrtle was dead! The sheet-anchor of my life had been slipped. Henceforward I would tread a lonely way, with never an eye to light at my coming or shed a tear at my going.

I caught the first boat to the city, and at ten o'clock drew the balance of my savings from the bank. Before lunch I had engaged a room, in the seclusion of which I spent the remainder of the day. I had no desire for food. Something within me had died. I was a mere husk, functioning mechanically, without volition.

Poor Myrtle, so kind, and clinging, and so faithful!

CHAPTER XXX

I HAD BETRAYED myself. The hunt was in progress, and the chances of escape were slender. My finger-prints had been secured in the room, and the papers openly blazoned the fact that Jean Deslines, murderer of her father, who some months before had escaped from a mental hospital, had slain her cousin. The sergeant at Manly had given an accurate description of me, and New South Wales was being scoured for a girl with auburn hair, vivid black eyes, arched eyebrows, and thin features. The Press was careful to emphasise that I might appear stout or thin. I was described as a master of disguise, characterised by extraordinary audacity. A close watch was being kept on all trains and boats leaving Sydney, and the public was urged to inform the police of any suspicious character who accorded with the published description.

It was obvious that I must alter my appearance. I smiled sourly as I remembered that I had been described as a master of disguise. What would I have not given for proficiency in the art? However, I was in deadly peril; and necessity ever is the mother of invention. Thank heaven, I was not given to hysteria! I perched myself on the edge of my bed, lit a cigarette, and canvassed the position. It was manifest that could not alter the hue of my eyes. The alternative was to conceal them. A veil would defeat its purpose by attracting attention. I must procure glasses. A little deft manipulation with a pencil would reduce the exaggerated arch of my brows, and, if I could evade detection for a month, they would grow thicker. Severe applications of hydrogen peroxide should suffice to remove the henna from my hair, following which I could dye it an alien shade. My existing clothes, aided by such radical alterations in appearance, would serve. If only I could acquire the essentials for the transformation, and gain the requisite time to utilise them, I still might trick the hunters.

With the dark, I left the house, carrying my case, and caught a tram to Enmore. There I bought a pair of glasses with horn rims, in a cheap-jack emporium. From a chemist I procured a bottle of dark brown hair-wash. I already possessed an ample supply of peroxide, which I supplemented with a bottle of strong ammonia. Donning the glasses, I took a room at an obscure boarding-establishment. Throughout the night I bleached my hair with continuous applications of mixed peroxide and ammonia, and at daybreak I treated it with the brown dye. My safety razor served to remove the outer ends of my eyebrows, and they took the brown stain admirably. It was remarkable how different they appeared, thus truncated; they gave quite an oriental cast to my face. During the morning I went to a barber, and had a close Eton crop. Surveying myself in the mirror, I breathed freely for the first time since the death of my cousin. I had to resist the impulse to caper joyously, as I realised that indeed I was a master of disguise. I did not recognise myself!

True to my policy of boldness, I engaged a tiny shop, paying a month's rent in advance. Before night furniture was being installed, and a writer was gilding the windows to announce that Mademoiselle Lablanche, beauty specialist, had opened in business. There is nothing which disarms suspicion like an avowed place in the world. Half the art of concealment is ostentatious publicity.

I found myself accepted at face value. I even found business flowing into my parlour. With but the haziest notions of the principles of my new trade, I went confidently to work, treating pimples with hot packs, plucking brows, tampering with moles and warts, and otherwise striving to induce beauty where Nature had failed signally. As none of my patients developed blood-poisoning, I presume that I was a success. It would have taxed Jupiter or Jehovah to have wrought improvement in most of the faces which came under my treatment. At the worst, I sent them away with their skins steamed into cleanliness. It was a humorous business, and I enjoyed it.

My first male customer arrived about a fortnight after I had opened. He was a tall, fair man of indefinite age, which might have been anything between thirty and fifty. His deep blue eyes looked strangely sophisticated; and the wrinkles at their corners, supplemented by a grim mouth, an out-thrust jaw, and lined cheeks, revealed that life had not strewn his way with roses. He was abrupt to the point of discourtesy, but exuded an atmosphere of strength and efficiency which appealed to me. I had not encountered his type before.

He strode through the swing door and flung himself into a chair. "Manicure," he said curtly.

Inwardly marvelling that such a rugged specimen should indulge in the unmasculine luxury of having his nails treated, I procured my instruments and a bowl of hot water. Drawing my chair opposite his, I took his right hand in mine. It was tanned deeply, and a scar traversed its back like a mountain range. The palm was hard and calloused, but his nails bore evidence of regular attention. I reflected that all men have their idiosyncrasies, and set to work. I soon discovered that the index finger of his left hand was missing, while a glance revealed that another scar ran down the right side of his face from temple to chin.

After I had polished his nails, he scanned them critically. Then he stuffed them into the pockets of his trousers, thrust his feet out to the full length of his legs, and sank his chin on his breast. He was completely relaxed in this attitude; in fact, one might have been pardoned for deciding that he was invertebrate. I stared at him curiously.

After a brief pause, he fixed his eyes on mine. "What's your name?" he inquired.

"Mademoiselle Lablanche."

He flicked his head upward, moving as a mechanical toy would move, and sniffed derisively. "I read that much on the door. What's your real name?"

I hesitated.

"I'm not a cop," he declared. "You needn't be scared to tell."

"Oh! I'm not scared of you or any other man, cops included. I'm only wondering what my name has to do with you."

He slouched even lower in the chair. "I'm not so vastly concerned about it, sister. I'm curious, that's all. You're a pretty little piece, and I'm game to bet you'd be even prettier if you had the guts to leave those glasses off. Don't tell me, if you'd rather not."

His rudeness intrigued me. I think he was the first man who caused my pulse to alter a beat.

"If you're really curious, my name is Molly Deane."

"What do you wear those giglamps for?"

I raised my brows. "Giglamps?" I repeated uncomprehendingly.

"Yes, those dam' spectacles."

"Oh! I did not know what you meant. To protect my eyes, and assist me to see."

He sniffed again. "Protect them from what—cops?"

I smiled. "You seem to have cops on the brain. Shall I run out and get you a pair of glasses?"

He heaved himself upright. "'Fraid they wouldn't serve, sister. They've got me indexed down to the print of my missing finger. I beat them by working without leaving traces."

"How clever of you," I said innocently.

He stared suspiciously and rose to his feet. "I'll see you again on Wednesday," he declared as he strolled to the door.

After I had collected my fee, I looked up to find him studying me gravely. "I seem to interest you," I suggested.

"Like hell," he rejoined ambiguously.

"Might I ask your name, after all this inquisition!"

"Scar-faced Harry!"

"Oh!"

"I see you've heard of me," he said with a grin, and walked out.

Heard of him! Was there a soul in the State who had not? Scar-faced Harry Lees, gangster, drug-seller, thief, razor-slasher! Yes, I had heard of him.

He returned on the Wednesday, as he had promised, and again I manicured his nails. Having rinsed them in a bowl of rose-water, I dried them carefully on a soft towel, and procured a tin of powder.

"What's that in aid of?" he asked, nodding his head toward the powder.

"Just the usual thing," I replied curtly, taking his scarred left hand in mine to dust it.

He grinned. "You can cut the trimmings out, sister. I like my hails clean, but I don't fancy my pores pasted up with that muck."

"As you please," I commented, and replaced it on the table.

He rubbed his palms together vigorously, and stuck his hands in the pockets of his trousers as he rose leisurely to his feet and stretched like an animal.

I remained seated, adjusting my instruments on their tray, acutely conscious that he was scrutinising me intently. An uncomfortable silence developed; but I remained obstinately engaged with my files and knives.

"You've got me wondering," he ventured at length. I looked up languidly. "How exciting," I murmured.

"I don't know about that; but I thought I knew everyone on the cross in this State."

"Possibly you do. May I ask just what you mean by 'on the cross'?"

"Oh! don't play the innocent with me. But I suppose it's your own business."

"I suppose it is," I agreed. "I'm sorry you have to rush away so hurriedly."

He grinned sourly. "All right, sister. Keep your secret. I won't pry into it. All the same, I'd like to see you without those giglamps. Would you do me a big favour, and take them off for a minute?"

"Why?"

He scratched his head thoughtfully. "I'm damned if I can answer that. It's just a whim. Don't do it, if you'd rather not, though you have nothing to be afraid of. I'm not a snitch."

I rose and stared at him steadily. "Listen to me, Mr. Scar-faced Harry. I always please myself what I do, and don't you forget it. Why do you wish me to remove my glasses?"

He smiled frankly. "Just a whim, as I told you. I'm only asking, that's all."

Slowly I lifted the clips from behind my ears, and took the glasses off my nose. "Will that suit your Highness?" I inquired.

He nodded, and gazed at me with an intensity which somehow was devoid of rudeness. "No," he muttered, "I don't know you."

I smiled disdainfully. "I did not think that you would."

"All right, sister, my curiosity's satisfied. Now let me show you the latest puzzle." He extracted a small card from his waistcoat pocket, and held it forth.

Idly I took and examined it. It was an advertisement for shaving soap, printed execrably in small type. Unable to detect the puzzle, I turned it about; but the back was innocent of printing.

"I may be dense," I apologised, returning it to him, "but I have to confess that I can't find the puzzle. It reads to me like an advertisement, and not a particularly interesting one either."

He chuckled. "I score this time, sister. You read it mighty well without the help of your glasses. I searched half Sydney yesterday, hunting for something in specially small type."

Despite myself, I flushed, whereat he laughed immoderately. "Own up that I tricked you, sweetheart. You might as well blow the gaff now. What's the big idea of the giglamps?"

"You're abominably curious," I criticised coldly, "and

in addition, you're abominably rude. I attribute that to your upbringing. If you must know, I wear the glasses because I look so young. People don't waste cash on beauty experts who are too young to have had experience. If you think that I'm hiding from what you term 'the cops,' guess again. Now, would you mind paying for the attention you've had, and get about your business. I've no time to waste, if you have."

He gazed at me with detachment, unperturbed by my words. "I think I'm falling for you, sister. You're a snifter, little piece with your disguise off. How about running in double harness?"

I began to file my nails. "When you've finished your joking, I have some work to do."

"Oh! I'm not joking, sweetheart. I think we'd match up well. I'm making you an offer, with big money in it."

I continued to file. "I'm dense this morning. What, precisely, is the offer?"

Again he scratched his head. "To go into partnership; work together. I'm getting too well known about town. They watch me like a lynx. If we ran in double harness, I could fix things, and you could distribute the snow. It would be months before the cops got wise to you, and in the meantime we'd rake off heavy."

"In other words, you're suggesting that I should peddle drugs for you, accept all the risk, and give you half the proceeds. Is that it?"

"Something like that, sister. Don't get notions that you could take it on as a solo stunt; because you couldn't. It's a game where one has to know the ropes. That's where I come in. I do the planning and get the snow; you simply place it where I tell you. We cut the risk fifty-fifty, and we share the sugar fifty-fifty. I provide the knowledge; you provide the innocence. It would be a great combination."

I returned to my file. "A wonderful combination. I must remind you again that it's my busy day. Good morning, Mr. Scar-faced Harry."

He louted low. "Good morning, sweetheart. Think it over hard. I'll be back towards the end of the week."

Twice a week he called, during the ensuing month; and on each occasion he reverted to the proposed partnership. In the end he had his way. From the first, the alliance had commended itself to me.

"This partnership?" I asked directly, after we had settled the business details, "how far does it go?"

He made no pretence to misunderstand. "As far as you like. For my part, I'd like it to go the whole hog."

"Doubtless," I commented drily, "and that's why I've asked the question at the outset. You've been frank about your own wishes; now let me be equally frank about mine. I wish it to be purely a business alliance. Can you leave it at that? If you can't, let us break off right here and now; that would be preferable in every way to a split at a later date."

"It rests with you, sweetheart. I've fallen for you, as I told you; but you're the boss in that, and only go as far as you let me."

"Is that honest?"

"Quite honest. I won't pester you."

"A man's promise?"

"A man's promise, sister, from a man who always keeps his promises to friends, however much he may lie to his enemies."

We sealed our partnership by shaking hands solemnly.

CHAPTER XXXI

As Harry had prophesied, we made considerable money. By day I manicured the nails and treated the warts and moles of my customers; at night, I took parcels of cocaine to addresses furnished by my partner, and collected the charges which he imposed. We gave no credit; everything was strictly on a cash basis. My bank account grew amazingly. I was on the high road to affluence.

So matters progressed for nearly six months. Whether it was the arduous labour involved in my dual profession, which left me each night in a pleasant state of exhaustion, I cannot say, but it remains a fact that The Voice and the bells did not afflict me. Perhaps it takes much to disturb a brain which works strenuously some fourteen hours a day. Each night passed in unbroken slumber, from which I invariably awoke refreshed and thrilling with energy. Then the inevitable happened.

The nature of our enterprise brought Harry to my rooms nightly. He would call just after dark, to hand me the night's wares and instructions. He would call again about midnight, to collect his share of the spoil. The daylight visits had been eliminated, though he made it a practice to have his nails tended each Wednesday afternoon. There was method in this habit. His idiosyncrasy was known to the police, and we concluded that these weekly visits would not excite suspicion. Seated in my parlour, with the door wide, we were in full view of all who might chance to enter the shop. We spoke little, and he always departed immediately the operation had been completed. It was an excellent subterfuge, as none would suspect a more intimate relationship where everything was so precise and business-like. In the nature of things, had nearer ties united us, he scarcely would have attracted attention to me by patronising my establishment for attention to his nails. Thus we reasoned.

Often, when calling late at night for his money, Harry would bring supper with him — a crayfish, or some sandwiches and a bottle of wine. I suspect that it was the last which precipitated our closer union.

It was a balmy summer night. The sky was unstained by clouds, and the stars shone merrily. A bicuspid moon, its horns turned to the west, was showing in the east, throwing a pale luminance over the earth. No breath of air stirred. The temperature was warm enough to be languorous, without the intensity to create discomfort. Through the open window floated the vague noises which trouble a city even after midnight's magic hour has tolled.

Harry was seated in an armchair by the window. He loved fresh air, and even on the bitterest of nights persisted in sitting by an open window. He had removed his collar and tie, and his column of a throat rose nobly to a powerful jaw.

"It's a heavenly night, sister," he remarked. "I think I'll try another glass of that wine."

Obediently I filled his glass and handed it to him. He stretched lazily and took it. "Fill yourself one," he advised.

I grimaced. "I've already had three. I'll be blithered if I swallow a fourth." Since my association with him, I frequently discovered myself employing slang. The habit is contagious.

He raised his glass to the light and peered through it. "Bunk, kid. Another won't hurt you on a night like this. Let's drink to trade."

The mellow night, combined with the three glasses of heady port which I had drunk, had induced a pleasant feeling of lassitude. My will was torpid. I lacked the energy to protest. Silently I filled my glass and raised it aloft. "To trade!" I exclaimed.

"To trade!" he echoed.

We clinked glasses, and drank. The strong liquor thrilled my veins like ichor. I felt suddenly dizzy, and sank upon a settee. Little beads of perspiration broke out on my forehead. An ephemeral nausea gripped me, to vanish almost at once. The dizziness passed, but the torpor increased. I seemed to float inches above the couch. The pressure on my buttocks decreased. I was strangely, deliriously light, as though my specific gravity had been neutralised. The electric light danced and shimmered, expanded and contracted, as though operated by the wand of some invisible necromancer. My pulses began to beat, and my blood to riot madly. A hot flush burned my cheeks and settled in my temples.

"Are you ill, kid?" I heard Harry ask from my side.

I shook my head. His proximity added to my convulsion. For the first time in my life I felt desire.

He laid a hand gently on my shoulder. "What's the matter, sister"

For answer I snapped at his finger, biting it to the bone. "You little devil!" he cried, and took to shaking me roundly.

Suddenly I found my arms about him, and his eyes

staring into mine. Fierce fires gleamed in his, and I watched a tiny pulse trembling in and out on his temple.

"Molly," he whispered.

I held him tight.

"Molly!"

I pressed my mouth to his.

For a space we clung, mouth to mouth, and arms straining passionately. A minute passed, an hour, an age, an eternity! Then he gently disengaged himself from my grasp, walked to the wall, and pressed the electric switch. A grateful darkness filled the room. Only a thin light crept inward through the open window, born of the quavering stars. Beyond the casement I caught a momentary glimpse of a corner of the Milky Way, alive with star-clusters. Then Harry was beside me again, with his lips straying madly, and his fingers searching, searching.

So I became his mistress, and enjoyed the experience. Whether my sanity had returned, and for the first time in my life I was normally a woman, or whether his brusque masculinity had awakened my dormant hormones to life, I could not decide. I only knew that he was my man, and that the world had taken roseate hues. I loved his coarse manliness, his quaint slang, his dour self-reliance. I loved his inherent lawlessness, his disdain of convention of every description. I loved his manicured nails, the mat of hair on his lean chest, the scar on his face. I loved him, him! Nay, I even loved the missing index finger, which I had not seen, which I never could see.

What subtle change had come over me? I tried to reason it out, but failed dismally. The propositions of my logic broke in futile waves against the rock of the reality. I knew the sum of what had happened, but my most desperate efforts failed to discover the component integers.

The effect was plain; the cause was shrouded in mystery. This cheerful blackguard, devoid of culture, unversed in the amenities of the social world, devoting his life to the distribution of noxious drugs which wrecked young lives; this lawless buccaneer, whose only god was money, and whose only code was success at any cost, had won me, body and soul. For the first time in my life I loved something better than myself.

The unaccountable fact had worked a miracle. From a sexless nondescript I had, become transformed into a fully sexed woman. My homosexual soul had grown heterosexual. The neutral worker bee had drunk of a magical draught, and blossomed into a queen. Passion had supplanted calculation; heedlessness had ousted logic; the God of Love had usurped the throne of Cosmic Law. My world was topsy-turvy, and I rejoiced as I stood on my head and beat my legs aimlessly in the air. My universe had fallen in ruins, and I revelled among its pieces. The Nietzschean had turned to Eros; individualism had been drowned in sexual love. I stood blushing on the threshold of a new and unknown world, where the sun rose in the west, and the waning moon turned its horns to the east. Time had turned backward in its course, and the churning constellations of heaven grown motionless.

Nothing mattered but Harry — Harry of the scarred face, the missing finger, and the uncultured brain. He knew naught of science, of physics, of art. To him, Relativity was a huge joke, Wagner an empty name, Keats a poet bloke who had lived and died at some indefinite time in the long ago. He had not heard of Praxiteles or Botticelli. His ideals of art were photographs of boxers, and chorus girls in tights. But he was essentially masculine from the crown of his fair head to the soles of his substantial feet.

In the ultimate resolution, I think that was the decisive factor. Save for O'Flanagan, the detective with the comic-opera name and the inveterate sense of humour, he was the first real man whom I had met. The rest had been almost as nondescriptly masculine as I had been nondescriptly feminine; we had met on perverted lines of equality. In Harry I had encountered the dominant to my recessive, and the dominant had prevailed, as always. True, the recessive might be lying dormant, ready to burst forth when new conditions proved propitious; but until that indefinite date the recessive had to acknowledge defeat.

Our idyll lasted for seven weeks. Nearly two months of unalloyed happiness! The lonely days had their joy, for they were instinct with anticipation — the greatest joy in the universe. The drowsy nights had their joy, for they brought my beloved to my side to share in my transports. We sold cocaine, shared the proceeds, and dallied sensually. So the weeks came and went, untinctured by a suspicion of woe.

The end came in the eighth week, and it came with cataclysmic suddenness.

CHAPTER XXXII

IT WAS THREE o'clock in the afternoon, on the Tuesday of the eighth week, when Detective-Sergeant O'Flanagan walked into my shop. His face was more florid than ever, and his shaven jowl as dark. He had accumulated fat, for his swelling waistcoat indicated a distinct paunch. I experienced a cold shiver as he entered, and my heart raced madly; but I gave no outward sign of perturbation, and almost instantly was icy cool, with my wits taut and ready.

"Good morning, miss," he said genially.

"Good morning," I answered meekly. "Do you require a manicure?"

He laughed unaffectedly, and surveyed his hang-dog nails. "Not exactly. A cake of soap and a tap usually fix them well enough for my fancy."

"Is there anything I can do for you?"

With the old, irritating gesture, he jerked his watch from its pocket and began flicking its lid open and shut. "Yes, miss, there is something you can do for me. I'm after a little information."

"Anything I know is at your service."

He twirled the watch like a teetotum. "The truth is, I'm a detective. Do you know anything about a man called Scar-faced Harry?"

I shook my head.

"Scar-faced Harry Lees," he supplemented, watching me keenly.

Again I shook my head with deliberation. "I'm afraid not. What is he like?"

"A tall chap, with fair hair, blue eyes, a scar down the side of his face, and a finger off."

I jumped up excitedly. "There's a man answering that description who comes here to be manicured every Wednesday afternoon."

He grinned. "I know that much myself, miss."

"A man who talks a lot, and uses the most atrocious slang."

Again he grinned. "That's Harry, all right. It flows out of him like artesian water from a bore."

I peered at him through my glasses. "I think that's about all I can tell you, officer."

He flipped the watch-case open, and jerked it shut again. "Are you sure you have nothing more to tell?"

"Quite sure."

"I suppose you don't know where, or how, he spends his nights?"

"I?" My voice expressed amazement. "How should I know where he spends his nights? I see him once a week, for possibly fifteen minutes, sometimes less. Where he goes, and what he does, during the rest of the week, I have not the slightest knowledge."

He swung his watch into his vest pocket with familiar deftness. "I suppose you haven't missed any jewellery, or money, or anything else of value, in the last six weeks?" he asked.

"Why, no. What makes you ask that?"

"Only that we've been watching Mr. Scar-face pretty closely of late. It may be news to you that he enters your premises about seven-thirty every evening, and again at something after midnight. As you know nothing of this, it has struck me that he might have been adding burglary to his other accomplishments."

I stared stolidly. "You say you are a detective. I accepted your word about it; but now I would like you to give me some proof, otherwise I shall go outside and call a constable. Even if you are a detective, which I doubt, it does not give you the right to insult me by saying that a man comes to my house every night at midnight."

He grinned affably, and extracted a small leather wallet from his breast-pocket. "There's my pocket warrant. If you think I came by it dishonestly, by all means call the constable. I'll wait." He seated himself calmly on a chair, while I made pretence of examining the pocket warrant.

"It seems in order," I murmured doubtfully. "May I ask what you mean by saying that this man visits my house twice a night?"

He shrugged his shoulders. "What could I mean, beyond what I've said? We know he comes here, and I've called to learn why."

"I suppose it would be useless to tell such a highly informed officer that he is talking undiluted rot; but I can give you one very serviceable hint. Why not ask the gentleman, himself, how he spends his nights? I am not very interested either in him or you. He has a manicure once a week, for which he pays cash. Beyond that regular business dealing, I don't know the man; and, if I did, I certainly would not permit him to visit me at midnight. I have a little respect for my reputation."

O'Flanagan crossed his feet, and rammed his hands into the pockets of his trousers. "Excellently put, Miss . . . er . . . Miss . . . "

"Lablanche."

"Ah, yes, Lablanche. I suppose that is not actually your name?"

"It is not. It is my professional name, registered with the Registrar-General for trade purposes."

"Naturally. And your real name?"

"Why not turn up the registration, and find out?"

He pulled at his eyebrow. "It would save me the trouble, if you told me."

"Look here, Mr. Detective," I exclaimed in simulated anger. "I have done nothing wrong, and I don't intend to do anything wrong. I consider it a piece of impertinence for you to come here and question me. I don't know this man with the scar, and I don't know you; and I don't know that I particularly wish to know either of you. You're both rather unpleasant specimens."

He grinned again. "Several people have told me that. Even my teachers did not love me at school. I suppose that's why I'm such a success as a detective. At our game, a fellow has to be inquisitive and unpleasant."

"But why inflict yourself on me?"

"It's a fair question. Because you're consorting with one of the most brazen gangsters in this State."

I sighed. "Do you suffer with delusions habitually, or have you only one mania?"

He rose, and glanced at the xylonite clock on the mantel. "How the time flies," he commented. "I had no idea it was so late. Won't you tell me your name before I go, and save me the trouble of hunting up the records at the Registrar-General's office?"

"You certainly are persistent, Mr. Detective. However, I'm not ashamed of my name; it is Molly Deane. It is time to make my afternoon tea. I know that you'll excuse my not asking you to join me. Even if I do make a habit of entertaining notorious gangsters after midnight, as you so delicately suggest, I have to be careful with whom I drink tea in broad daylight."

"Quite right, Miss Deane. One can't be too careful, as you say. Just one little question before I go; just a tiny favour. Would you mind removing your glasses for a moment? There's something vaguely familiar about you. I've a notion that we've met before; but I just can't tab you at the moment. Still, it will come back to me. My memory is as sound as — er — your reputation. Will you take your glasses off, just to oblige me?"

"I will not."

"Naturally! Good afternoon, Miss Molly Deane. We'll meet again some day. I hope you enjoy your cup of tea."

He lounged out, leaving me in the grip of a deathly fear.

Harry looked serious when I told him of O'Flanagan's visit. "Curse that fresh bird," he exclaimed. "I wouldn't have minded any of the rest of 'em; but O'Flanagan's got brains and knows how to use 'em, too. We'll have to go steady for a bit. What beats me is, why didn't he wait and lumber you when you had the snow in the joint? Why did he put you wise, when he could have hooked you so easily?"

"Because he only could have got one of us. If he arrested you, when coming here with the stuff, I went free. If he waited, and took me, there would be no proof that I got it from you."

He rubbed his forehead, and spat viciously. "Perhaps there's something in that." He thought for a moment. "But this way he gets neither of us," he added irritably. "I don't like it at all. I wish I could get wise to his game."

"Why worry, Harry?" I asked, snuggling against him. "We know he's after us, and forewarned is forearmed. We'll just let the stuff alone for a while; then we can laugh at him."

"I suppose it's the only way," he agreed, and kissed me.

Two days later, O'Flanagan called again. He was resplendent in a cloth suit, with starched shirt, and a white flower in his lapel. His newly shaved cheeks shone darkly clean. He smiled affably as he entered.

I stared at him coldly through my glasses, but said nothing. "Don't be alarmed," he advised. "I'm here quite unofficially."

"I'm not alarmed. A shout would bring help if you allowed your natural instincts to overcome your cowardice."

He grinned wryly. "I merely wish to be manicured, Miss Deane."

"And I don't wish to undertake the job."

"I'm going to a wedding," he explained simply, and gazed ruefully at his ragged nails.

"Do I know the unfortunate lady?"

"It's not my own wedding," he said evenly.

"How fortunate for some reprieved woman."

"Isn't it? But I want to look my best, all the same."

"It would be a shocking wedding party if you looked your worst."

"Aren't you just a wee bit spiteful?" he inquired, with a shrug.

"Perhaps, but I thought that possibly you had called to ascertain what men had been visiting me since your last intrusion."

"Forget it," he advised curtly. "I'm here to get my hands made respectable. It's your business to trim nails, and I'm prepared to pay your usual fee. Are you going to turn down a cash customer?"

Without a word I waved him to the chair, and procured my implements, hot water, and a towel. Still preserving silence, I set to doctoring his nails.

A metallic sound at my feet made me glance downward. "Damn it," he said, "I've dropped my cigarette case."

It lay beside my chair, and mechanically I picked it up. The metal was strangely sticky, and I grimaced at its touch. With a mumbled word of thanks, he took it gingerly between finger and thumb. I noticed that his grasp was avoiding its sides, that he held it top and bottom. Then the significance of its stickiness became clear. He had tricked me; my finger-prints had been obtained. Next day he would know that I was Jean Deslines, the escaped murderer.

In an agony of fear I proceeded with his nails, thinking . . . thinking. Suddenly I threw my file on the table, and looked up.

"Mr. Detective," I said softly, "I have something to show you. I'm sick of this life. I'm sick of poisoning young girls and helping older people to the grave. I'm sick to death of selling drugs." I rose and walked to the inner door, beckoning him. "Come in here."

He pushed his chair back, and followed me inside. No word was spoken as we climbed the stairs to the upper storey and entered my bedroom. He stood warily by the door.

I walked to the duchesse beside the window and stood thoughtfully while he watched me. "God!" I cried, turning swiftly to him, "I'm sick to death of it all. I've a drawer full of the horrible poison here, ready to go to the poor devils who crave for it. I'm just beginning to realise what a cursed creature I am. I'm tired of it, tired of living, tired of lying and destroying human souls."

I wiped my handkerchief across my brow, and sighed

deeply twice. Then I turned slowly to the duchesse and opened a drawer. For a tense moment I leaned across it, as though wrung with remorse.

Softly he advanced into the room, still silent, and keenly alert.

"Look at the hideous stuff!" I exclaimed, gazing into the open drawer. "Look at the deadly poison I peddle to the unfortunates who tread the road of the lost!"

I heard his stealthy feet coming nearer, felt the hot wave of his breath on my neck. Then I seized the automatic pistol that lay in the drawer, and spun round with unexpected swiftness.

"Ah," he breathed, and made a futile clutch at my arm as I shot him. He staggered, and a half smile came to his lips as he lurched forward, still clutching aimlessly, and dropped to his knees. For an instant he swayed drunkenly from side to side, with his left hand pressed tightly to his breast. Through the parted fingers spurted a crimson jet, and he rolled quietly on his back. His eyes twitched horribly; then the lids closed, and he was dead.

I dropped the pistol beside him, subconsciously noticing that a thin wisp of smoke still ebbed from its muzzle, and dashed downstairs. Already a few startled passers-by had gathered in front of my shop. I joined them, asking hysterical questions. "What was it? Did someone fire a shot? What was that report I heard a moment ago?"

"Wasn't it in your shop, miss?" asked a tall man with a monstrous moustache.

"In my shop?" I repeated in amazement. "There was nothing in my shop. I was inside, when I heard a loud report. I thought it was out here in the street, and rushed out. What was it?"

"It was somewhere round here," volunteered a woman with a baby in her arms.

"Some kids with a bunger," sniffed a thin man disdainfully, and walked away. The rest soon scattered; and calm was restored. It is surprisingly difficult to identify either the nature or the source of an unexpected crack. It occurs too suddenly, and its duration is too brief, for complete comprehension by the conscious mind.

I returned inside, and sank into a chair. It was just four o'clock. It would not be prudent to close the front door for another hour. I must possess myself in patience, and maintain my customary routine. So I sat for an hour which seemed an eternity. No patron arrived to disturb my vigil; only the ceaseless beat of feet on the pavement came to my ears as the restless stream of humanity went to and fro. Upstairs a dead man stared silently at the ceiling, while a lake of blood grew on the floor. I knew that he was dead. I knew that the blood was ebbing from his shattered breast. I knew that his eyes were fixed in a motionless stare.

So I waited, clutched, in the cruel jaws of suspense. I glanced at my watch. It registered four-thirty. I sighed audibly, and took to straightening my implements. While thus engaged, for the first time in my life I heard the bells in the daylight. Faintly at first, but momentarily gaining strength, they tinkled and jangled in my rear, ultimately to clash discordantly in a devilish uproar that shrilled into a gale of sound. I feared that the din would cause an incursion of curious listeners; but through it sounded the beat of passing feet, unheeding and aloof.

A few minutes after five o'clock I closed and bolted my front door, and stole upstairs to the bedroom. O'Flanagan lay where he had fallen. His eyes had opened; otherwise there was no change, save that a rich red lake had gathered which overflowed into trickling creeks and billabongs. I went down to my kitchenette and made a cup of tea, sugaring it with care. I always like my tea with the proper amount of sweetening—one and a half spoons to a full cup.

At seven o'clock Harry's codified knock came at the front door. Tap, tap (a pause), tap, tap, tap! I drew the bolt and turned the Yale catch. He slipped inside, and stood smiling while I locked the door again.

"I did not expect you," I said, "but, oh! I'm glad you've come."

"Are you, sweetheart? I had to come. There is nothing to fear, as long as we have no snow on the premises. If they did come with a warrant, they wouldn't catch anything more serious than a cold in the head. They have nothing on us yet."

"They've got something on me," I rejoined lugubriously.

"On you! What have you been up to?"

"I've killed O'Flanagan."

"You've killed O'Flanagan?" He accented each word into a spondee.

"Yes."

He seized me by the shoulders, and shook me viciously. "Are you joking, Molly?"

I shook my head and wriggled from his clutch.

Like one stricken with paralysis, he stood and stared, believing, yet afraid to believe.

"It's true, Harry," I said at length. "I killed him this afternoon."

"Good God! Where?"

"Here."

His eyes grew round. "You killed him here, this afternoon?"

"Yes. I shot him."

"Christ Almighty! Where is he . . . now?"

I jerked my thumb at the ceiling. "Up there, in my room."

Again he grabbed me by the shoulders, and shook me. "Is that right, Molly? Are you telling the truth?"

"It's only too true, Harry."

He released his grip and stepped back, eyeing me as though I were a snake. I saw the blood recede from his cheeks, leaving them white and haggard. He shivered as if in the grip of a palsy. A vast horror, allied with something else, lurked in his eyes. Twice he commenced to speak, to break off before he became articulate. The man was overwhelmed with stark, undisguised fear.

"Harry!" I exclaimed, and crossed to him; but he shrank away fearfully, his lips shaking and blue over his strong white teeth.

"Harry!" I stretched out my hands pleadingly.

His nerve went. His terrified eyes met mine momentarily. Then he was at the front door, fumbling at the bolt.

Without a word I brushed his nerveless hand from the lock, and threw the door wide. He slunk through it, and I slammed it behind him.

Lost in amazement, I threw myself into a chair. To think that Harry — breezy, slangy, devil-may-care Harry — should be such an unmitigated cur! To think that he, who recked naught of slow-poisoning hosts of stupid girls with his noxious drugs, should be distraught when a man came to a violent end! It was inexplicable. No, it was perfectly comprehensible. He was not disturbed about O'Flanagan; he feared for himself! Yielding to an unreasoning panic, he had scampered away to save his own skin, indifferent what happened to me.

The humour of it appealed to me. I laughed till the tears flowed down my cheeks. I was still laughing when the bells began to chime again, musically soft and sweet. At least they would not desert me; I was not to be alone in my hour of peril. There was a measure of solace in the thought.

Wearily I entered my tiny kitchenette, and set the kettle to boil. I had not dined, and was beginning to feel hungry; so, to the music of the bells, I lit the griller, and procured a tender fillet of steak from my ice-chest.

My love affair had ended! Harry had failed me. He had fled like a frightened rabbit, leaving me to face my danger alone. I turned the steak; the secret of a grill is frequent turning. Well, that terminated my idyll! I shrugged my shoulders resignedly. I loved the man. I would not deny it. But never more could I respect him. I felt toward him as a mother might feel for a weakly offspring—affectionate, but superior. He was a cur, and always I detested cowards. It was queer, to love and detest a man simultaneously! Again I turned my steak, salting it lightly on both sides.

I dined heartily, and considered my position over a second cup of tea. What should I do? Of my ability to escape from the toils, I entertained no doubt; but was it worth it? Life was not so attractive that I desired to cling to it like a limpet to its rock. I had tasted almost everything but death. Should I . . . ? Why not? It was the Great Adventure, the one thing of which none could speak with certainty. Without Harry life would be a pulseless vacuum; with him, it would be a pulsing hell. Under no circumstances could I support union with a coward. I was confronted with a choice between living alone, or dying! The choice was difficult. Death held no terrors for me; but my instincts craved life. In the end I tossed a coin, and Fortune decided for death. The bells jangled merrily as I thoughtfully lifted

the fateful penny and stood ruminating with it in my hand.
The die was cast!

CHAPTER XXXIV

I have written up my diary. That, at least, I can bequeath to the world. Beyond it, my only legacy to mankind is a generous contempt. I hate society, with its purring grimalkins, its imitation men, and its ridiculous conventions. Everything is designed for the weak; the strong are anathema to vested authority.

The bells have been chiming ceaselessly for the past hour. They have run up and down the scale, broken into rhythmic dirges, rung out familiar tunes with maddening deliberation. Once they hammered out Chopin's Funeral March, painstakingly, as a child would strum the melody in the treble with one hand.

I entered my bedroom. O'Flanagan was lying on the floor, staring stupidly at the ceiling. Beside him was a congealed lake of red-brown, from which a frozen rivulet stretched past the duchesse. One eye was half closed, and its fellow wide open. It gave him such a queer appearance that I laughed. I stirred him with my toe. He was stiff. I continued to laugh; the poor fool had paid the price of his folly.

TEN-THIRTY P.M.

Ten minutes ago I dragged O'Flanagan to a couch, and managed to haul him upon it. Beneath his head I stuck a pillow. Then I procured his hat and put it on his head. There was something amiss; he looked too solemn. I cocked the hat to the side with the wide eye, and shrieked with mirth. God! he was funny. With his hat at that angle, one eye shadowed, and the other fully exposed in its static half wink, he seemed like a comedian who had been petrified in the midst of his drollery.

TEN FORTY-FIVE P.M.

I have blackened the tip of O'Flanagan's nose with a burnt cork, and jammed one of Harry's cigars into his mouth. He now looks like a comedian overcome by drink, and suddenly stricken with paralysis. The effect is excellent. I always thought that dead men's jaws dropped. His lower jaw has stiffened firmly in place. I wonder why? I shall paint his ears with cochineal.

ELEVEN P.M.

I must have fallen asleep. I have no recollection of having thrown myself on my bed; but I have just awakened, to find myself stretched at full length on it. There is a stain of blood on the pillow. It must be from O'Flanagan. Probably he splashed me when I placed him on the couch. He always was a messy, interfering brute. I dreamed of Minerva; she beckoned me as her eyes glazed. At least she had the decency to die with both eyes symmetrical, not with one open and the other suspended in the travesty of a wink. I shall see her later to-night; she will not have long to wait, for I have decided to die at midnight. Midnight is a wonderful hour to die. It is neither to-day nor to-morrow; it is zero — nothing! The details have been arranged. I shall turn on the jets in my kitchen stove, thrust my head inside, and cover myself with a blanket. They say that it is a pleasant death; simply a thickening of the blood and a delicious feeling of drowsiness. I wonder? I am coming, Minerva! Wait another hour, dear one!

Death! I have dispensed it frequently, and now the time has come to taste it in person. I suppose it is but a triviality. If a proton met an electron in collision, both would vanish in a tiny wave; they would be mutually annihilated. I shall meet the atoms of coal-gas head on and be annihilated. How will I react to the gas? That, I shall never know.

Damn the bells! they irritate me. Ding-dong, crash Fal-de-la, crash! Dum-dum-de, crash! It would upset a stoic. Now they are beating out some infernal tune. I know that it will end in that tumultuous crash as their dissonances thunder in unison. Hark! there they go: crash, crash!

Within an hour I shall be annihilated. What am I? Without carbon I could not be; yet I am more than carbonic mixtures, and other ashes, and water. Over and above it all, I am Jean Deslines; I am *Me!* The elements will be dissipated when I suck the carburetted hydrogen into my lungs; but the *Me* will remain. Yet, will the *Me* survive? I trust not, even though Minerva be waiting with her noble limbs and jutting breasts. No, there is no survival. In a universe of empty space, ridged and distorted by motionless time, there is no room for Jean Deslines. I shall dissipate like the colliding proton and electron. Thank the Fates for that mercy. There can be no bells in nothingness! Damn the bells! their ceaseless chiming is making my head ache.

Whence came I? Physically I am but a congeries of vibrations. How did they arise; and, arising, how did they amalgamate into little Jean? I bequeath the problem to biologists and physicists, it will furnish premises for polemical theorising. When they have resolved it to their satisfaction, they can attack the problem of the real *Me* — my consciousness. It surely will keep them occupied.

What age am I? Who can answer? There is hair in my armpits and groin; I have slept with men; I have been pregnant; I have matched my wits against the world, and won. Yet I am denied a vote when elections take place. I am coeval with Eve, have slain a round dozen of my fellows; yet I am accounted a child. I have toyed with a doctor of medicine and the police; yet legally I may not decide my actions without the concurrence of guardians. Thus the world estimates me on the first count.

On the second count, it declares that I am completely responsible for all that I do. It binds me in statutory gyves, which expressly deny the traditional freedom and irresponsibility of childhood.

It is queer, and amazingly ludicrous. Either I am child or woman, if we are to measure by the rod of common sense. But the law would have its cake and eat it also, it — the blundering, unjust, pathetically futile law — makes me old or young to suit its vagaries. It creates a two-sided and hypothetical *Me*, swinging aimlessly between the poles of womanhood and infancy. Caught between these millstones of responsibility and irresponsibility, I have learned much. I have learned that the big things of life are laughter, and tears, and courage to endure; tears for the weak, laughter for the wise, courage for the strong.

Nothing else matters save these three. Religion, philosophy, and learning are the veneer of life — its external physics. The fundamentals stretch inward to the realm of metaphysics and are threefold in nature — tears, laughter, and steadfastness. All else is unimportant. Beauty, health, deformity, stupidity, genius — what are they but presence or absence of syphilis or epilepsy? *Petit mal* is more potent than convolution of the brain's cortex; syphilis is stronger than heredity. A single hour with a harlot can undo the laborious work of centuries of dominant ancestors. A discharge of nervous force in the tissues of the brain, symptomatic of a disease of which nothing is known, can transform mediocrity into genius. But neither venereal complaints nor the Divine Disease can oust laughter from its throne, or quell tears, or destroy courage. They alone are impregnable. They are the pillars of being, the struts of life, behind which we crouch and gibber like so many apes. Yet, withal, they are the characteristics which distinguish us from apes. Without them we would be lost indeed.

O, mighty triumvirate! I, who am about to die, salute you! The fight has been fought, and Destiny has turned down her thumb. But I go down to defeat with laughter on my lips, triumphant, tearless, and enduring to the end. In my world, tears have found no place; I devise them to my weaker sisters. But my courage and my laughter I take with me to the grave. They are too precious to lose, even in death.

What age am I? I have asked. How old were the patriarchs? Is age to be measured by the passage of a Time which has no passage, which is static, motionless, eternally quiescent? I am just as old as the knowledge stored in my brain; just as young as the elasticity of my sinews. I have lived since the first microcosm was born in the sea. My chromosomes have persisted since the germ-plasm first was evolved. But I die to-night, for my chromosomes have not been transmitted to another generation. It is the end of all things for little Jean. Never again will she stand on a crowded quay, watching a Roman soldier done to death by barbarians.

What age am I? — The age of the world; no more, no less.

What am I? — What, indeed? A pinch of iron, some sulphur, hydrogen, oxygen, carbon, and other elements and gases, plus consciousness. Protons, electrons, and consciousness. Electricity and consciousness. Waves and consciousness. Always the consciousness, however we may simplify the rest. So, in the final resolution, it is probable that I am simply consciousness. Jean Deslines is consciousness. When I destroy that consciousness with a whiff of coal vapour what am I then? — Nothing, from which everything originally was begotten by non-existent Time! After to-night I shall be nothing, for consciousness will have been annihilated. It is ludicrous, damned ludicrous! An inhalation of electricity and electricity is destroyed, together with my most mysterious consciousness, which probably is electricity too.

I am outward bound, whither? Back to Space-time, whence I sprang! The answer is there. Motion ends, and at once matter is not. Even the Spirit is not there to brood over cosmos. There is but an empty eternity, stretching from the beginning to the end in lines which curve on themselves and form Nothing. I am just as important as cosmos, for both of us are delusions, mathematical figments, formed of Nothing, effecting Nothing, and ending in Nothing. The shadows flicker and grow still, inhibited by a mouthful or two of coal-gas. Yet how real and substantial it all appears: myself, and

Harry, and Myrtle, and Minerva, and O'Flanagan, and daddy, and that plump fool of a doctor and the rest! Just now the sky is raining hormones. They spring to life as an incandescent streak, shooting earthward to the accompaniment of the devilish music of the bells in their search for baby, breasts.

Figures are materialising in the night. Daddy and Minerva reel into view, rotating in a mad saraband. His arm encircles her generous waist, and she has laid a hand across his riven head to prevent his brains from jerking loose as they caper round the room. The roar of his laughter has a Titan quality. Ho, ho, ho! ha, ha, ha! Minerva is silent, but her corselet jangles musically, and the scarlet plume on her helm leaps in sympathy with the movements of her limbs.

Murray slinks in a corner, plump, pink, and furtive. His piggish eyes glitter impertinently. A flush stains his cheeks and ears. The little sneak pries and speculates, repulsive as always. I grimace in his direction and poke out my tongue. His flush deepens, and he wriggles.

Greyly grim, with her rebellious hair escaping from the prison of her bonnet, grandmother squats in an arm-chair. What a model for Nemesis or one of the Furies! Her mouth is a thin line. Her eyes are vindictive as those of the Jewish God. An importation from a past age, a hideous scrap of jetsam on the beach of life, a projection of yesterday, she is lost in contemplation of that which is beyond her comprehension. It is an occasion for laughter. The poor, transplanted old fool!

O'Flanagan grins sympathetically from a place by the mantel. His watch snaps open and shut, brows are lifted quizzically. His hat is cocked rakishly over one eye. His ears throw a carmine gleam on the wall. He is the most human of them all. I always had a reluctant admiration for him. Perhaps it was his mentality; he understood laughter. Besides, he was clever, this phlegmatic man with the comic-opera name and the divine gift of humour. I smile at him as our eyes engage. He waves his watch airily, flips it into his pocket, and wags a scarlet ear with grave impudence. We both laugh.

Myrtle is seated on my bed. She is nude to the waist, her virgin breasts gloriously small and horizontal. From one of them a crimson stream ebbs down her flank and stains the skirt about her swelling thighs. Never has her skin glowed so whitely. Perhaps it is a delusion, caused by the contrast with her welling blood. She bears no malice, for she smiles. I am glad that she understands.

What is that grey shape which towers by the doorway, lifting its nebulous head to the ceiling? Its features are nobly severe; its mouth set in lines of ineffable strength? Is it Death, or God, or Space-time, or the Mother of all Things? Have we all emanated from its prolific womb, and at some time drunk from its dugs? It does not seem probable, for it is sexless, detached, immaterial. Its firm outlines are mated with shrinking and expanding shadows. Its corporeal bulk melts into thinness. Its mass is gaseous. It is a perplexing compound of reality and delusion. It is there, yet absent; gross yet impalpable; tenuous, yet substantial. Devoid of emotion, it plays the recording lens and immortalises the antics of the occupants of my room. I divine that every movement is being imprinted indelibly on the retina of its terrible eyes. Perhaps it is Nature, implacable, unbending, and mathematically just.

A moment ago my room was crowded. Now it is empty, save for myself, the inanimate O'Flanagan, and the clashing of bells. I am alone, marooned in a desert of infernal musk. I shout, but cannot hear my words for the clamour of the bells. Then I laugh, and they grow silent. The echo of my mirth returns from the wall as a wave is recast from a cliff. I think of O'Flanagan's petrified wink and scarlet ears and roar with merriment. The bells are vanquished!

ELEVEN FORTY-FIVE P.M.

The hour draws on, but I am not afraid. My pulses are steady, and my heart placid. If there is a God to face, I realise that he can be only a mathematical theorem, an abstract proposition in n dimensions; perhaps none the less tangible for that, but obviously incapable of interference with me. I shall diffract through some interstice in his being, to emerge beyond him in rings of light. That way the *Me* in little Jean may survive.

ELEVEN FIFTY-FIVE P.M.

This is the last entry that will appear in my diary. I shall place the book on O'Flanagan's lap. How the finders will shake with laughter when they see his black nose, his frozen wink, his crimson ears, and his rakish hat! Excellent man, he is humorous even in death. There is quality for you! I have an affection for him.

I have procured a blanket and draped it over the stove like an Indian wigwam. Daddy is sitting on top of the dresser, swinging his legs and nodding approval. His brain thrusts like a piston against the towel which encircles his head. He smiles at me, and I smile in answer. I always did love daddy. He has survived death, so I presume that I shall do so — a beam of light diffracting through an interstitial crevice in a god's body. I must remember that, when the crucial moment comes!

Now for the head-on collision between the positive proton and the negative electron. I have laid my diary on the thighs of the comic detective. I shall enter my tent, stick my head in the oven, draw the blanket tightly about me, and turn on the gas.

Good-bye, Harry. I could wish that you had more guts . . . .

ACKNOWLEDGEMENTS

WITH THANKS TO Salt, Jim Smith, James Doig, Richy Sampson and the Estate of Frank Walford for making this book possible.

JOHNNY MAINS

Lightning Source UK Ltd.
Milton Keynes UK
UKOW03f0215100614

233139UK00002B/8/P